CHILD
OF
THE DEVIL

It was something that had to be done.

The boy wet down the knee-high grass that grew out of the crack between where the earth ended and the barn began. And when the barn had been circled, with the voices of the parents still inside and the quiet of the pastures singing night-songs in his ears, the boy plucked two wooden matches from a shirt pocket. He stepped away a foot, then another, hesitating just long enough to make certain he wasn't having second thoughts, which he wasn't. Then he slid the first match down the zipper of his pants.

The match ignited, the flicker of the flame heating something joyous inside him just before it sailed through the night air.

There was an explosive *swoosh* which forced him back then. And a flash of flames raced away in opposite directions. And before the flames would meet on the other side of the barn, Matt's ears would fill with the malevolent cracking and popping of something dying.

CHILD OF DARKNESS

DAVID B. SILVA

LEISURE BOOKS ❧ NEW YORK CITY

For My Parents:

*They said, "Well, here it is. The world.
It's big, but it's yours. As much of it as
you want. Fall on your face, and all you
have to do is get up again. Make a mistake, and all you have to remember is
there are no mistakes, there are only ex-
periences. There will always be a tomorrow, and we love you."*

What more could a son ask for?

I love you both dearly.

A LEISURE BOOK

Published by

Dorchester Publishing Co., Inc.
6 East 39th Street
New York, NY 10016

Copyright©1986 by David B. Silva

Printed in the United States of America

PROLOGUE

WINTER, 1974
THE WORK OF THE DEVIL

The curtains were pulled back, and the black night sky was peering in through the window, now and then raging with a roll of thunder, an explosion of lightning.

On the nightstand, next to the bed where Libby Reed was in labor, there was a single lamp holding back the blackness with a light bulb hardly bright enough for reading. It was the only light on in the house.

Eldon Reed was sitting in the corner of the second-story room, in shadows still untouched by the flashes of outside lightning. In his lap, opened to a dog-eared page of the Old Testament, was the Bible his father had given him half a lifetime before. His fingers were resting upon the pages as if they could feel every fiber of the paper, every up and down of the ink. But he wasn't reading.

Another strike of lightning hit in the distance, the roll of thunder eventually shaking the house and drowning out the short scream of his wife. She was panting, catching a breath, pushing, panting again.

"Eldon . . ."

"The Lord's watching over you, woman."

Another catch of breath. "Something's wrong, Eldon." Another push. "It's ripping me wide open. I can feel it tearing me apart."

Faraway, the sky lit up with another flash of lightning, and he silently counted off the seconds—*one thousand one, one thousand two*—until the thunder rolled over the fields and across the barn and the yard and the house. "Four miles away," he said quietly. "Getting closer."

His wife sucked in a lungful of air that swallowed another scream, and she fell back against the damp pillow, trying to keep the air inside her lungs long enough to stay conscious.

"Please, Eldon."

She was wearing a pink cotton nightgown, shoulder to toe in length, but it was gathered up around her protruding stomach. The bedsheets, wrinkled and damp, were pulled back. There was a sharp odor in the room, a bittersweet fragrance of perspiration, fear, and excitement.

She pushed again, not because she wanted to (she would have preferred more time to catch her breath, to build up her strength a little more) but because the baby inside her was trying to force itself through the birth canal.

"It's not supposed to feel like this," she said between breaths. "Eldon, please. Call someone, one of the neighbors. Please."

He leaned forward in the chair, crossing from shadow to light, half his face masked, half lit ablaze by another stroke of faraway lightning. "It's the Lord's work, not theirs. Let Him do it according to *His* plan."

one-thousand one, one-thousand two, one-thousand three . . . getting closer

"Oh God—ohhhh—Godddd!" A sob, a cry, almost a scream.

"It's coming, Libby." He closed the Bible in his lap, snapping it shut just as more thunder rolled across the yard outside the bedroom window. "It's almost here."

She caught a breath, pushed, caught another breath, and began panting.

Eldon felt himself being drawn out of the chair to a standing position, leaning forward toward the birth. Libby was sinking deeper into the mattress, pushing against herself, breaths held then lost, some cries swallowed, some not. Her legs were spread as wide as ever, her knees angled away from where the first dark fluids of birth were beginning to flow.

"He who hath sipped from the fountain of the Lord, shall be cleansed. He who hath followed the word of the Lord shall reap the harvest of his faith. It's our time, Libby. Not much longer and the greatest of all His blessings will be our harvest." He stood next to the bed, entranced by the sight of the baby—pale, almost colorless—as it began to emerge from its mother. "It's coming."

Her eyes were dark-rimmed, her hair damp and stringy, each hand was embedded as deep as the first knuckle into the corner of the bed's mattress.

She raised up again.

Her eyes closed, her breath held, and she pushed again.

A moan.

A groan.

Almost a scream.

"Harder, woman." Eldon kneeled at her bedside, his hands clasped in silent prayer, his elbows sinking into the mattress. It was anticipation that kept him watching as the baby's head broke free of its mother, dark fluid pouring from somewhere deep inside her, staining the bedsheets red, making life seem more like death. And it was the slow realization that the baby wasn't moving, that the colors of birth weren't as alive as they should have been, that moved him forward to look closer.

The umbilical cord appeared snugly wrapped around the baby's neck.

"Push harder, woman!" Eldon screamed. "As hard as the Lord permits!"

The baby's shoulders struggled through the opening, from the warmth of the birth canal to the coolness of the upstairs air. Then Libby groaned, and the baby slipped all the way out of its mother, plopping death-still upon the bed's mattress.

A boy.

Breathless.

Silent.

Another stroke of lightning hit, not quite as far away as some of the others. And absently, in the back of his mind, Eldon counted off the seconds between the flash of lightning and the roll of thunder.

one-thousand one, one-thousand two . . . close enough to wake the devil

Libby cried then. "My baby . . . ?"

"Something's wrong," Eldon said. He unwound the umbilical cord from where it had wrapped itself around the baby's neck, then by the ankles—the baby's skin felt as cold as a pound of meat fresh out of the refrigerator—he lifted the boy off the mattress, and gave him a sharp slap across the buttocks.

But the icy blue color of lifelessness held on.

Another slap across the buttocks.

"He won't breathe," Eldon said loud enough to be heard.

Libby started crying.

"The devil's got him, and he won't let go." Eldon gave the boy another sharp slap

across the buttocks, and when that godawful blueness wouldn't go away, he felt a
shiver pass up his fingers-hands-arms. A
shiver cold as death itself. And it was that
shiver that grabbed hold of something
frightened inside of Eldon.

"The devil's taken him," he whispered,
placing the dead child down on the mattress. "He was evil, and the Lord let the
devil take him from us."

Libby was crying softer now.

Eldon stared momentarily out the bedroom window, then looked about for his
Bible. It was lying on the floor, next to the
bed. He knelt there, taking the book up in
his hands, opening it to a random page the
way he almost always did. It read: *If my
step hath turned out of the way, and mine
heart walked after mine eyes, and if any
blot hath cleaved to mine hands; then let me
sow, and let another eat; yea, let my off-
spring be rooted out.*

But he knew he had done none of those
things. It wasn't punishment that had
taken the life of his baby, it was God's own
love, the hand of God reaching down from
the heavens to protect him from something
that had grown evil in the belly of his wife.

Eldon closed the book, glanced down at
the baby, and felt that shiver roll up him
again—as cold and frightening as the devil
himself.

Then a stroke of lightning lit up the sky

outside his bedroom window,

(one-thousand . . .)

and there was an explosion of flames and thunder and tremors that ripped through the barn, a hundred feet away, and sent debris—some charred instantly black, some still burning, all yellow and orange and red, the devil's colors—into the air and back to earth again.

The devil's anger.

That's when the baby first cried—a second, a breath, after the devil's lightning had hit the barn and set it aflame. He heard the boy's cries slicing through the roll of thunder, and when he turned to the sound, it was in time to see the color flooding back into the baby's cheeks.

(the devil's color?)

in time to see the first awkward movements of the baby's arms and legs.

(the devil's movements?)

and Eldon took a step back from the bed, because something felt terribly wrong here. There was the stench of something burning in the air. And on the other side of the bedroom window, there was the crackling flames of the fire. And right before him on the bed, where only a minute ago the baby was blue, then colorless, then dead at the hands of the Lord; there was something pink and kicking and alive at the hands of . . .

the devil?

"He's . . . alive."

Libby's tears turned to soft laughter then.

But he's not our child, Eldon couldn't help thinking. *Not this boy, once dead, now alive. That's not the way the Lord intended it.*

He was still holding the Bible in his left hand, waist-high, at just the right angle so that the cover's gold print (cracked and lined and worn, but still shiny in places) reflected back the light of the wing-like flames that were flying above the barn.

He's not our child.

He belongs to the devil.

BEGINNINGS

I am he as you are me
and
we are all together.

John Lennon and Paul McCartney

Standing before the mirror won't help.
The reflection doesn't belong to you.
Touch your fingers to it and you'll feel the
cold. Whisper to it and you'll see the lips
move. But if you look beyond the reflection,
you'll discover an unfamiliar face. It's not
the glint of your eyes that you see staring
back at you, nor the innocence of your
dimples. It's me.
If you'd like a glimpse of yourself, you'll
have to come back another time.

WINTER 1985
THE NIGHTMARE

"Who shall ascend into the hill of the
Lord? Or who shall stand in his holy
place?" the shadow-man asked. "He that

hath clean hands and a pure heart, who hath not lifted up his soul unto vanity, nor sworn deceitfully! Is that you, boy? Dare you tell me your hands are clean, your heart is pure?"

There were corner-shadows, dark as night blackberries. And narrow bands of light that slipped from outside-to-inside through cracks unseen. And a quiet that whispered of wordless death.

"Dare you tell me such things?" the shadow-man asked again.

"My hands are clean," the boy said, and he knew he had said so before.

"And your heart? Not pure at all, now is it?" Through the dusty black and whites of where they were, the boy could see where wings were slowly beating (almost gill-like) at the back of the man whose face was shadows. And as well, he could see where a pointed tail occasionally flicked out of the darkness and into the light, before disappearing again. The wings were of angels, he knew. The tail was of a demon, he knew as well. And none of it made any sense. "I know the truth, my boy. There's something evil-black where your heart should be. And it sucks up your bright red blood and spits out something gray and lifeless. I know the truth."

The boy took a cautious step back, but only a step for he knew any more than that would not be allowed.

"I know the truth," the shadow-man repeated.

"You know your truth."

"Your tongue devises mischiefs; like a sharp razor, working deceitfully. You love evil more than good, and lying rather than speaking of righteousness. You love devouring words, O you of deceitful tongue. And you must be punished."

The shadow-man grabbed hold of the boy, took his arm in a vise-like grip that was inescapable. And he took the boy—all dragging feet and voiceless screams—deeper into the corner-shadows where darkness was blinding and great gulps of air went soundless.

And the boy knew he had seen that blackness before.

"It's the tongue of the devil speaking from the lips of a boy," said the voice from nowhere and everywhere. There was that voice, and a blackness that would swallow an extended hand, and there was nothing more. Just the emptiness that dogs a dream-lost boy in a world all strange yet too familiar. *"Devouring words are the devil's words. And if you so speaketh for the devil then you shall wear his mark to separate you from the others."*

. . . *yellow—orange—red* . . .

. . . *something red-hot, white-hot, burning* . . .

Something eye-burning bright came

dancing from the cold, faceless black, dragging long flowing tails that showed themselves, disappeared, then showed themselves again, all in the wink of an eye. And the boy saw that it was an iron rod, red-hot/white-hot at one end where there was a symbol he couldn't read.

"It's the mark of the devil, my boy. So those who cross your path will know you for what you are, a child of the devil."

The boy backed blindly into something unseen and fell to the ground. And suddenly the hotter-than-fire branding iron was being pressed against his inner thigh. And he knew he had felt that pain before. And reflexively he grabbed the iron rod with his hands until the searing pain burned home and he had to pull his hands away.

When he first glanced then stared at his palms, they were red and moist and black-charred masses of flesh that seemed detached the way a mirror image seems detached. Then he noticed how the skin had peeled back, all black and worm-like, and his voice came back to him . . .

. . . and he screamed
. . . and screamed
. . . and screamed again

When he came awake, he was sitting up in bed, trying to force the screams through the clasp of his brother's fingers.

"He'll hear you," his brother said, keeping a hand tight over the boy's mouth. "He'll hear you and he'll come to see what's wrong."

The room was dark, except for where the yard lights shone hazily through the bedroom window, and for a moment, the boy wasn't sure if he had left the nightmare. Then he caught a breath and the screams stopped.

"I'm going to take my hand away," his brother whispered. "No more screams, all right? You've spit 'em all out and swallowed the rest and there's nothing left inside that needs to get out, all right?"

The boy nodded.

The hand came away.

"The same nightmare?" his brother asked.

The boy stared at his hands, held them a thumb's length from his face and stared at them. And they were pink and healthy and whole. "My hands," he said, looking to his brother. "They were burning."

"It was the nightmare. They were burning in the nightmare."

"As real as life," the boy said. *As real as life*.

And he knew he had lived that nightmare before.

AUTUMN 1985
SAYING GOODBYE

There was a string of mercury lamps that circled the area between the house and the barn, making the yard resemble the used-car lot in Jefferson, the one that used to sell old Buicks and Chevrolets before it had gone bust in '82. The night air was thick and humid, haloing the mercury lamps in faint rainbow colors that seemed to follow behind as Matt moved along the edge of shadow and light.

He could feel the farm house at his back, watching him through upstair's windows that looked all too much like eyes. And behind those window-eyes, were there other eyes watching? Was the brother still asleep? Or was he standing at the window, watching along with the house, and not caring enough to cry out? It didn't matter. The bedroom window was dark when Matt stole a glance over his shoulder. And even if it had held the curious gaze of the brother, it wouldn't have mattered.

With an audience or in secrecy, he was determined to follow through.

Still snug against the shadows, Matt pressed an ear against the northern wall of the barn, listened for the voices that he knew were on the other side, and felt their vibrations whisper back at him.

The mother coughed and said a mumbled something about " . . . the boys."

"They're fine," the Pa replied. "I need you right here. Can't have you wandering off and not coming back. The night's gonna be long enough, so just stay put. The boys can take care of themselves."

The sound of that colder-than-ice voice, deep and riding the edge just this side of anger the way it always did, reminded Matt just how much he hated the Pa, and just how badly he wanted to see the man dead. Even with the Ma inside—and the horse that was dropping a foal, and the barn owls sleeping, and the two milking cows chewing their cuds—even with the sacrifice of all those others, it was something that *had* to be done.

For the sake of the brother.

For the sake of the *pretender*.

For his own sake.

Matt stepped out of the shadows and into the light of the mercury lamps, then moved around the corner and along the eastern wall of the barn to the double-wide doors. The cool evening breeze whispered softly from the pasture just before he gently slipped the two-by-four into its cradle, securing the barn doors. For a moment, he rested his weight against the doors, his eyes closed, his breath all going out of him. And he wondered if the *pretender* was going to be sick.

It had been a long, dry summer, kicked-off in mid-April with eighty degree temperatures. And while the temperatures had grown cooler the past few weeks, the autumn rains were still absent. Matt had heard the word *drought* used more than once. And he knew if he rubbed a long-haired cat the wrong way, the static would be enough to set-off the thick, knee-high grass which lined the outside walls of the barn.

But the fire had to be hot enough, fiery enough, to burn everything crying and screaming inside without mistake. Because if the Pa somehow managed to escape the heat—with his hair singed down to his scalp and his arms and legs peeling black flesh—he'd be a monster even worse than before.

The disc harrow, shadowed on its barn side, bright and reflecting on its yard side, sculptured the night like the spine of a dinosaur. From beneath the metal skeleton of the disc, Matt one-handed a gallon can of gasoline he'd hidden in the dirt and the weeds and the shadows. It was the gutless stuff that the Pa had bought at the Rotten Robbie in Jefferson. "Good enough for making dirty things clean," the Pa had said. And Matt hoped that was somehow true.

With the exhale of pressure and the rise of fumes, he wet down the knee-high grass that grew out of the crack between where the earth ended and the barn began. And when the barn had been circled, with the voices of the parents still inside shooting sparks at each other and the quiet of the pastures singing night-songs in his ears, Matt plucked two wooden matches from a shirt pocket. He stepped away a foot, then another, hesitating just long enough to make certain he wasn't having second thoughts, which he wasn't. Then he slid the first match down the zipper of his pants.

The match ignited, the flicker of the flame heating something joyous inside him just before it sailed through the night air.

There was an explosive *swoosh* which forced him back then. And a flash of flames raced away in opposite directions. And before the flames would meet on the other side of the barn, Matt's ears would fill with the malevolent cracking and popping of something dying.

Eleven-year-old Justin Reed was lying on his bed, wearing knee-cap pajamas and wavering between sleep and non-sleep. The back of his legs still burned where his father had taken a leather strap to them earlier in the evening. But his tears were dry, and the welts had already disappeared back into the pale-redness of his flesh. He was rocking himself back and forth, trying to force the coming of a reluctant sleep, when his brother put a hand to his shoulder and held back his motion.

"Got a surprise," Kiel said, softly rubbing his brother's back. "I want you to see it."

And when Justin rolled over, he wondered for a moment if night had passed and daylight had come to take its place. The bedroom wall, where the line of sunlight so often told the time of day, was all alight with flickering shades of orange, as bright as a late-evening sunset sneaking through their western window.

"It's almost over," Kiel said, tugging at his brother's arm, pulling him off his bed and standing him at the window. They stood shoulder-to-shoulder, brother-to-brother. The flames were flapping bright wings at the sky, reaching high above the roof of the barn to kiss the stars. And the old oak tree was brilliant and alive with colors that were dancing among its leaves and branches.

"They're in there," Kiel said.

"Pa?"

"Both of them." Kiel opened the window to the outside. They could feel—almost see —the heat of the fire rush across the hundred feet of yard to warm their faces. And there was the crackling of flames, the popping of wood, the screaming of . . .

"Are you sure?" Justin asked. "Are you sure they're in the barn?"

"Both of them."

They watched till the flames had withdrawn from the sky, till the spine of the barn had collapsed in a fountain of sparks, till the crackling—popping—screaming no longer touched their ears. And when it was over, Justin went back to bed. And Kiel began to make plans for running the farm.

PART ONE
THE FIRST INKLING

1

SIX MONTHS LATER
SISTER SISTER

It was early afternoon. The kind of day that was easy to feel a touch of melancholy. A soft rain streaking the windows. The air unusually humid. An early summer day that felt more like the arrival of a late autumn.

The house was quiet in a way that sent shivers up a spine.

Faye Richardson sensed it, as if the calm were standing over her shoulder watching her work, watching her pencil absently sketching the rough layout for the cover of her fourth children's book in less than a year. *Some Things Just Happen* was the working title, and in a way it was a slice of her own life. She had never intended to make a career of writing and illustrating children's books. It had simply happened. Almost overnight. With little regard for plans made long before, she had put aside a roomful of unfinished paintings and allow-

29

ed fate to step in and change the direction
of her life. On little more than a whim. And
suddenly the children's books had become
the essence of her life, the focal point from
which everything else grew. *Some things
just happen.* Who knew why?

Faye sat back in her chair, nibbled at the
end of the pencil, and listened to the quiet
that had caught her attention.

There was the soft patter of a summer
rain against the shake roof, a sound she had
somehow managed to put out of her mind
as she was working. She found that an easy
thing to do—to shut out the world of sound
—when her concentration was at its peak,
when she became so embroiled in a drawing
that she could almost step across the magic
threshold between the reality of the pages
and the fantasy of the words and illustrations. It wasn't anything dangerous.
Nothing worse than getting caught up in a
good movie. Just a minor flight of imagination, nothing more.

And perhaps that's all she was hearing,
just a minor flight of her imagination.

Still, for a moment, she thought there had
been something behind the quiet, something that had made it not quite right. But
after taking note of the muffled hum of the
refrigerator and of the way her chills
seemed to march up her arms in rhythm
with the patter of the rain, she dismissed
the *feeling* and turned her attention back to

her work.

Probably nothing more than nerves.

The room was draped in shadows, gray near the louvered windows that looked eastward—through streaks of gray clouds—to where the pasture land blossomed into a stand of cottonwood trees lining Winter Creek, and even beyond there to where the surrounding mountains tried to keep the Valley a secret from the outside world. But in the corners of the room, the shadows were black where old paintings—unfinished relics of the past—leaned forgotten against dark-paneled walls. And between the grays of the window and the blacks of the corners, there was a single yellow-white light that hung above the drafting table where Faye was sitting.

She'd been struggling most of the morning, trying to force something usable out of the ream of pencil sketches that had flowed too easily from her imagination yet seemed more lifeless than she cared to admit. And she knew it was a lack of concentration that was softening the usual sharp edge of her work. It was the same lack of concentration that had Wade out in the garage, sorting tools, stacking old cardboard boxes, and cleaning shelves lined with four years of dust and neglect. It was his way of keeping busy until the time arrived when they would have to put everything aside and take off for the Greyhound station in

Eureka. And sitting mindlessly at the drafting table was *her* way of doing the same thing.

They were both feeling an anxiousness that was difficult to define.

Some things just happen, she thought. Then she absently tapped the butt of the mechanical pencil against the nearest sketch. "Damn it, Libby. Sisters are supposed to be forever."

Forever?

It was odd, the way she had always thought there would be enough time—*a lifetime?*—to touch bases with her sister again. And now, as sudden as a warm afternoon storm following the jet stream over the western mountains, the chance had come and gone, and her sister . . .

. . . nothing lives forever

. . . especially not the things you love the most.

That's the way it had been between her and Libby. A sister's love that had been lost to neglect. There had always been that spark of something special between them, something only sisters could understand, but something that had been lost to their childhood. And over the years since, through the distance of too many miles and too few visits, through the differences of lifestyle and belief, loves and hates, that childhood spark had gone dim, but had never gone completely out.

Until now.

And suddenly it was too late to do anything about it.

"Faye?"

Her pencil skidded across a sketch. "Damn!"

"Sorry," Wade said. "I didn't mean to scare you." He was standing in the doorway, wiping his hands on a rag, looking solemn. It was an expression she had seen more often of late—downcast eyes that were afraid to make contact, a curl of lips that walked just this side of a smile, and a sense of surrender that seemed to deepen the hollow of his cheeks.

"It's not you," she said, and for a moment she thought she was going to cry again. More tears for her sister and her nephews and the injustice of fate. *Some things just happen.*

"Are you okay?"

She nodded, her face partially buried in her hand. "When we were living in Monterey—I guess I was about eight years old, Libby was six-and-a-half going on thirty, she thought she knew everything there was to know about everything—and we were walking on the beach on a cold November day, making footprints in the sand and watching to see what washed in on the tide. Libby found a shell on the beach that day. Nothing unusual, something left behind by a hermit crab or some such thing. And I re-

member her putting it to her ear, listening
for the sound of that inner ocean. She
smiled in a way I'll never quite forget. And
I asked her what she heard. And she said it
was the sound of somewhere faraway where
dreams came true and everyone was
happy."

"Faye, don't . . ."

"And when I put my ear to that same
shell I heard it. The soft-song of the shell
whispering in my ear about places faraway
and fairytale-like. And I suddenly realized
that there were things that my little sister
saw and heard and felt that sometimes
passed me by. And I thought she was such
a wise little sister." Faye was staring
absently out the eastern window, feeling
almost as transient and meaningless as the
raindrops that were trickling like tears
down the glass panes. "What happened?"
she asked in a whisper. "How did it all get
left behind? How did we manage to grow up
so different, so black-and-white different?"

"People change . . ." Wade started to say,
but his words were soft and unconvincing,
and he let them fall away without trying to
pick them up again.

"I can't believe she's really dead, Wade.
Whatever happened to the song in that
shell? Whatever happened to that faraway
place where dreams came true?"

For a moment, the room held that same
uncomfortable silence that she had felt

breathing over her shoulder just minutes before. And she thought this time she understood it a little better. It was a held breath, a skipped heartbeat, a moment when the asker of the question first realized that the question was answerless. *Whatever happened to those yesterdays?*

They went away.

But where?

I don't know.

"It's time we were going," Wade said then.

"Already?"

"Afraid so."

Faye looked away from the gray-colored shadows, to her husband who was still leaning against the doorjamb, and they exchanged that same glance of resignation that passed between them when an argument had stalled, when neither side had won nor lost and both were willing to call it a draw. There was nothing else left to say at those times. And there was nothing left to say now.

"You look tired," she said in an awkward effort to move her thoughts away from her sister.

"I'm all right." He was two years younger than her. And those two years had somehow managed to preserve his aura of youth far better than her own. At times, she wondered if he would ever shave more than every other day, if he would ever fill

out around the waist, just enough so she
could grab hold of the *jug handles* that were
the mark of a boy grown into a man. And
yet, she realized at the same time that it
was his boyishness—his dirty-blond hair
and his light blue, almost hazel eyes—that
had attracted her to him in the first place.
Almost mother to child.

"We can't have them waiting around the
bus depot," Wade added.

"I don't know if I'm ready," she said
then, glancing out the window again, and
wondering what it would be like to see her
nephews for the first time.

It seemed ironic. Now that the time was
nearing and they were down to the last few
moments before they were supposed to
meet her sister's children, *she* was suddenly
the anxious one, the one having second
thoughts, the one hedging her last few
moments. It had always been Wade before.
Him arguing against taking the boys in, her
arguing in favor. And now that the time
had arrived, it was Wade who was doing the
prodding.

"We don't want to be late," he said.

"No," she whispered, staring at the sketch
beneath her pencil, seeing something else
entirely, seeing an errant line scratched
across her life instead of her illustration. "I
guess we don't."

And she thought of her sister again.

And she wondered if it were really true, if

some things really did just happen, without rhyme or reason or opportunity to make them different again.

It was a two hour drive into Eureka. Through breath-fogged windows and a drizzling rain, Faye watched the country-side mark the miles through Winter Creek Mills and Bridgeville and Freshwater and miles of other terrain that went facelessly by. The long drive afforded her the time she still needed to sort through her last few reservations, her few remaining uncertain-ties. And by the time they had arrived at the bus depot, she thought she was ready to put her sister's death behind her and her nephews' futures before her.

Until she first saw them.

She recognized them at first glance, seeing Libby's dark eyes staring out from behind their frightened faces. Two boys, one slightly taller than the other. Both built like young, fragile trees hidden too many years in the shadows of others. One, the taller one, with darker hair that swam in a soft wave across his head. The other, Justin, looking like an angel beneath his straight blond hair which fell in a perfect line just above his eyebrows. Both standing shoulder to shoulder, waiting, simply waiting.

They looked more like her sister than Faye could have ever imagined. And for a moment, all those morning feelings of childhood years long lost, came flooding back into her life again.

"Welcome to God's country," she said, kissing each on the forehead, trying to ignore their strong resemblance to her sister, trying to ignore the feelings that had taken control again.

They smiled lifeless smiles, empty smiles that seemed too old for their years. And for the first time, she saw the barn fire that had taken the life and breath from her sister and brother-in-law not as *her* tragedy, but as the tragedy of these children standing before her.

"This is your Uncle Wade," she said, grateful for the short opportunity to look away from the sadness on their faces and try to regain some of her composure.

Wade nodded and went wordlessly about the task of collecting their luggage and following along behind as they headed toward the car.

Justin Reed wasn't supposed to remember his aunt. She had never come to visit the farm, even when he was too young to remember such things. Kiel had told him that. But he remembered the name Aunt Faye, and when he first saw her, it was as if he had known her all his life, as if they were friends from as long ago as his memory would allow.

There was just something special about her.

She had a sad face, though. The kind of face that Pa would have called a pouting face. The corners of her mouth were turned slightly downward, her lips were trembling so softly that the movement was almost unnoticeable. And her eyes were so dark, dark and warm like a mother's eyes should be. And that was what was special about her— she looked a lot like his mother. Mostly in the way she tried to smile with her warm, dark eyes.

He liked that about her.

And he wanted to ask his brother if that was the way it was supposed to be, if there was something special about aunts, if they were supposed to smell and breathe and talk like a mother does. Because that's the way this one was. Just like their mother.

But as the scenery—mile after mile of mountains and trees and endless roads like he'd never seen before—passed by, he kept the questions to himself.

He was sitting right behind his aunt and uncle, too close for a whispered question to go unheard. And if it were the wrong question, the kind of question that Pa would have called unnecessary, he just might get the back of a hand across his face. 'Cause in the same way that Aunt Faye reminded him of his mother, there was something about Uncle Wade that seemed like a reflection of his father.

Something behind the mirrored sunglasses.

Something inside where a young boy's
eyes couldn't see what was going on
because it was darker than a night-shadow,
colder than a winter breath.

And it was smartest just to keep his
mouth clamped real tight, and stare out the
window like everyone else.

SIX MONTHS BEFORE
SECRETS

They watched, awake and wordless, until
the yellow licking flames ebbed and
dwindled and fell to gray morning ashes.
Feathered ribbons of smoke rose from the
burning, dividing the forenoon blues and
purples into opposing sides, forestalling the
customary gathering of midday oranges.
And everything seemed colored in ash.

Indistinguishable gray.

Faceless ash gray.

The torment had finally been extin-
guished.

But even as they looked away from what
had once been the barn, and let their
knowing glances find each other, there was
a sense of *what now?* which passed between
the two boys. Something had been exor-
cised from their lives, something evil and
wicked and painful. And yet, in its place, a

vacuum had been left behind. And there was an unspoken question which hung between them and asked how things had ever gotten so far out of hand.

What do we do now?

We go on.

But how?

As brothers.

"They're gone," the brother said, one hand holding the bedroom curtain away from the window, the other hand at his mouth where the fingernails were bitten one by one and torn away near their quicks.

Nicholas stared unhearing at the rubble. He wasn't sure what had happened down there where the ground was gray and black and smouldering. But he felt a strange guilt standing over him as thick and smothering as a silent shroud of snow, as if it were his fault that the ground had turned a lifeless gray.

And the feeling made him sad.

He looked to the boy standing next to him, looked to the brother, and saw the brother's lips moving, but heard no words. Then he looked again at the blackness which stained the ground where the barn had once stood.

And he knew it had happened again.

Something godawful unthinkable had happened and the *pretender* had run away to hide in the shadows, leaving him behind

to take the blame for something he'd had
nothing to do with. That's the way it
always happened. The *pretender* went off to
sleep somewhere in the shadows, and
Nicholas was left to shoulder the punishment.

And it wasn't fair.

The brother tapped him on the shoulder
and his lips were moving again. He could
feel the vibrations rattling in his ears,
trying to tell him something, trying to tell
him what the brother's lips were saying.
But he didn't understand until the brother
grabbed him by the arm and pulled him
away from the window.

They went downstairs, over floorboards
that sagged beneath the weight of their
steps, crossed sock-footed quiet through
the entryway, and ended up in the kitchen.
The morning sun was slipping through rain-
stained kitchen windows which were as tall
as he was head-to-toe, and the room was a
rainbow of washed colors. It was bright
there, squinty-eyed bright. And the brightness whitewashed the small dining table
where a laced cloth sat undisturbed, as if it
had never served a purpose beyond covering the table. The counters, all pale green
tile, were equally spotless, equally void of
anything that might imply use.

This is a house of God.

*And like His heaven, it must be kept un-
soiled and decent.*

Everything in its place.

Everything as pure as the truth of His word.

From the shelves, they brought out bowls and a box of Cheerios. Sugar from the tan canister with a painting of a wood-covered bridge. Spoons from a drawer. Milk from behind the refrigerator door where a crude drawing hung, the scribblings that the *pretender* had crayoned one day in school. Nicholas couldn't understand why the mother would hang such an ugly thing on the refrigerator door, especially since his own drawings were so much better.

They sat at the table, Nicholas with his back toward the refrigerator, the brother with his back toward the sunlit windows. And they were each careful not to spill a drop of milk on the fine-laced cloth, for there was an unwritten, often-spoken rule about spilt milk. And they were careful not to talk while they were eating, for there was another rule about wordless meals and the peace of the Lord.

And for the moment, life went on as it always had before.

After breakfast, the brother's lips moved again. There was a faint sweep of a smile, something insincere, that crossed the brother's face. And a sadness darkened his eyes. Then he pointed toward the barn and Nicholas knew the brother was going outside to visit that other place, the place that was still smouldering.

He shook his head, not wanting to follow along, afraid that a closer look might somehow be reminding of what had happened there. And he knew it must have been something terrible, something he'd be better off not knowing too much about.

The brother raised his eyebrows in question. "You sure?" Nicholas thought he saw the lips mouth. And when Nicholas shook his head again, the brother shrugged and went out the kitchen door by himself.

When the door closed, there was a vibration that sounded in his ears, then the room fell as silent and lonely as it sometimes did when he stood in the shadows, away from where the *pretender* was standing in the light, away from where things were alive and happening. Those were the loneliest times, when he was on the inside looking to get out, and the *pretender* was on the outside, looking to get in. And they couldn't seem to find each other.

The morning sun was higher above the horizon now and its colors seemed to reach out from the distance just so they could paint rainbows across the kitchen. Nicholas loved those colors, their whimsy, their laughter, the way they made things dead seem to come alive.

Just like me, he thought. *Stand me in the sunlight and I come alive, stand me in the shadows and something in me seems to die.*

And that's what wasn't fair about standing in the shadows so long.

Something seemed to die.

He swallowed up a deep breath then. And what he wanted more than anything else in the world just at that moment, was to be able to scream, to be able to shout so loud that the brother would hear him, so loud that the *pretender* would be too afraid to ever again come awake out of the shadows. Then maybe the world would sit up and open its ears and its eyes and see that he was alive inside this body.

He wanted the world to know that.

He was real, as real as the *pretender*.

And he was scared to death that someday he would be swallowed up by the shadows and no one would ever know that he had breathed life inside the *pretender.* No one would ever know that there had even been a Nicholas.

But I am Nicholas!

He tore the fine-laced cloth from the table then, ripped it away and watched it puff like a parachute before drifting in slow-motion toward the floor. And the dishes shattered soundlessly against cabinet doors. And milk splattered in wondrous patterns over the counter, down the cabinets, and across the floor.

I'm Nicholas and I didn't do that thing to the barn!

"We can't tell anyone," Kiel was saying. He was bent over the sink, ringing out the cloth he had used to clean the milk off the counters. Justin was carefully picking shards of china off the floor, placing them in the open palm of his hand as he listened to what his brother was trying to tell him. "We just have to go on as if nothing has changed, as if everything is the same as it's always been. You understand?"

"I think so," Justin said, but he shook his head at the same time, because it didn't make any sense. Things *weren't* the same anymore. They were all different. "Why can't we tell?"

"Because."

"But why?"

"Because if we tell, then they'll take us away from here. They'll put you somewhere and me somewhere else and we won't be brothers anymore." Kiel finished wiping the front of the cabinet. "They'll put us with a bunch of other kids and new parents."

"I don't want new parents."

"Then you can't tell anyone."

"Not a soul?" he asked, already knowing the answer, but asking just the same. Because he had to tell someone what was going on. Maybe not about the barn burning down, and Ma and Pa not being there to take care of them anymore, but what about how strange his brother was beginning to act? What about how Kiel had messed-up the kitchen and how he wanted everything to be a secret?

"No one," Kiel said, then he moved away from the sink and sat in one of the wicker-backed chairs by the table. He let out a lungful of air as if he were going to say something that might be better left unsaid. "Come here," he said, slapping his knee with one hand the way Pa sometimes did when he wanted to talk serious or when he wanted to . . .

"Come here."

Justin sat on that knee, feeling perfectly comfortable there, the way he almost always felt with his brother. "What's wrong?"

"Who are you going to tell?" Kiel asked.

"I don't know," he shrugged. "Just someone."

"Who?"

"I don't know."

"There's no one left," Kiel said then. "Ma and Pa, they're dead now."

And Justin looked away from his brother's eyes because they were glistening with tears, and because he knew he'd cry along with those tears even if he wished he wouldn't. "There's you. I still have you, and you have me. We have each other, don't we?"

"That's all we have."

"Then there's no one left to tell, is there?" he asked absently. And for the first time he wondered how cold the breath of a heatless night could get, how hungry an empty stomach could feel.

"No one," Kiel whispered.

I like color most of all.

Trees can be any color I choose, green or brown or black or purple. Because that's the color I want them to be. And I can paint orange leaves on the branches, with red acorns and a zebra-striped squirrel with wings that touch the sky.

When I draw, I can do all of that.

And nobody can make me change it.

Nobody can say that it's wrong.

Because when you make things up, there's no such thing as right or wrong. Things just are. I like it like that. It means that I don't have to stay in the shadow forever. It means that I really am important.

NICHOLAS
seven years old

2

Winter Creek Mills was a small town, fifty miles west of Eureka, nestled in the cradling arms of a valley. In the winter, when a December storm would butt against the mountains and hover over the small town like a well-anchored kite, folks would complain the winters were just too cold. Something was changing in the weather, they'd say. Never used to be like this, they'd say. And they'd shovel an inch or two of snow like they'd been doing it all their lives. And they had. Then come summer, they'd sit out front of the Winter Creek Market and complain about the heat, 'cause it never used to get that hot in the valley. Absolutely never. Not as far back as any of 'em could remember, it didn't. And folks would already be thinking fondly of the cool winter months ahead.

Down the street from the market, maybe

a stone's throw, maybe two, there was a
two-story brick house painted all chalk-
white like the face of a ghost. Old lady
Molly Pritchard lived there, by herself since
her husband, Ned, had died in '67 from a
boating accident on Lake Shasta. He had
been tippin' the bottle since early morn that
day, sucking on one beer after another like
a near-starved babe sucking on his mama's
full breast. By afternoon, he was feeling
king of the lake, feeling the damn boat
would fly for him if he asked it right; and he
took it full throttle, broadsiding a sailboat
he never saw, a sailboat with a young
couple and their two kids. A floating slick
of scrapwood and canvas and plastic and
oddities had been the harvest. And while the
young family had gone uninjured—though
no one understood quite how, an act of
God being the general consensus—the lake
had gobbled up old Ned Pritchard that day,
an afternoon snack, all two-hundred pounds
of him.

They never did find his body.

Since the accident, Molly Pritchard had
stayed to herself for the most part. Although she eventually took the initiative to
sign a contract with the county to operate a
small library sub-station from her home,
kind of her way of keeping busy until old
Ned's resurrection, which she felt certain
would someday come.

There were shelves of books lining her

parlor now, cluttering the spacious room
that had once served as a gathering place
for friends and relatives. It was a darker
place these days, a place where the musty
smell of time often lingered. But Molly Pritchard liked it that way. She liked the books
and the darkness and her privacy. And
some said she liked the waiting. Some said it
gave her a sense of peace that had been
strangely absent when Ned was still alive
and trying to play husband.

The Mills had its own fire department as
well, incorporated in 1973 after a fire
gutted the Garrison place on Turnbottom
Road. It was 113 degrees in the shade that
afternoon. Hotter than most anyone could
ever remember the Valley ever getting. And
the dancing flames had themselves a real
barn-burner before the Eureka Fire Department finally arrived, just as the flaming
timbers collapsed inward, taking with them
the lives and dreams of the Garrison family.
Two weeks later, the only surviving Garrison, Michael Jacob, moved away and the
folks in Mills decided it was long past the
time that something had to be done about
fire protection for their little community.

The Winter Creek Mills Volunteer Fire
Department was given birth that year,
using a mid-1930's Mack pumper and hose
car purchased from the Washoe County
Public Works Department in Nevada. It
was the best they could afford at the time,

and in fact, served them quite well on the only two occasions that a fire had since dared to raise its nasty head in the Mills. Jim Turner, who had been elected Fire Chief that first year, had since stepped down, leaving the job to his thirty-year-old son, Johnny. And for the most part, folks didn't worry about hot summer days and misplaced matches as much as they once had.

In fact, at any given time there were six firefighters on call, thirteen all together in the department. Wade Richardson was one of the *rookies,* one of the few who had never worked in an actual fire situation. And when he was being honest with himself, he would admit that he never really expected to face a real fire. He was simply donating a few hours of his time to the community; it could have just as easily been to the museum or the church or some other community function. If you lived in Winter Creek Mills, you donated your time; it was as much a part of life there as the winters that seemed colder than they really were.

Out on the edge of the Mills, less than half-a-mile from where Wade and Faye had built their home in 1981, there was the town cemetery. Like most everything in the Mills, it was a community responsibility, owned and maintained by the townsfolk on a volunteer basis. The earliest date on a gravemarker belonged to a gentleman by

the name of Elisha B. Slayden. Born on
September 8, 1803; died on September 23,
1838. Under his name were the words:

Here lies Elisha,
father of three.
He lived by the forest,
was killed by a tree.

The town historian, an elderly man by the
name of Joseph Little, had spent almost a
year, in between his duties as the museum
keeper, trying to discover exactly what the
marker was supposed to mean. He had
located a Martha Slayden living somewhere
in Tehema County, who claimed to be
Elisha's great, great granddaughter. It was
her memory—as told to her by her mother,
who was told the same tale by her mother's
mother—that her grandfather's grandfather had been cutting timber for the
winter when he had cut a huge cedar only to
have it catch within the branches of two
adjoining trees, and stand as tall and
straight as ever, as if its roots were still
solidly attached. He spent the better part
of a day trying to shake the cedar loose
from its entanglement before finally giving
up and leaving the task to nature.

He felt confident the winter winds would
bring it down in due time.

And that's exactly the way it eventually
happened.

One winter day, a number of months
later, the great cedar was swept free by a
gusty northern breeze and came crashing,
all broken branches and solid core, down.
Elisha was checking a rabbit trap at the
time, squatting in the wrong place at the
wrong time, and one of the branches caught
him across the back of the head. And that
was his undoing, Martha Slayden claimed.
And that was the meaning of the words on
his gravemarker, the very truth of them.

Joseph Little was ecstatic!

Another piece of town history had been
uncovered.

Another page added to the town's geneal-
ogy.

As the official (and sole) historian of
Winter Creek Mills, Joseph Little donated a
great deal of his time rummaging through
what he called the community's past—
poking here through old buildings, there
through crumbling family photographs,
and more often than some thought natural
—poking through the likes of the community cemetery, writing things down,
reading to midnight moons, and carrying
on about things best laid to rest beneath a
safe layer of earth. But while occasionally
the townsfolk might raise a questioning
eyebrow at his weekly jaunts to the land of
the dead, people for the most part felt they
understood what it was that made a
seventy-year-old man so fascinated with

lives long lost to the hands of death. After
all, the man was only a step or two away
from his own laying to rest, and there was
something about the past that attracted a
man with so little future.

That's what people in the Valley had to
say about it.

And in that spirit, they were willing to
forgive his occasional idiosyncracies. No
matter how distracting they sometimes
seemed to be.

Besides, Joseph Little made for good
town gossip.

He was such an odd little man, with a face
that seemed to share every tragic event of
his life. A deep furrowed forehead, left that
way by the suicide of his wife in '67. A tight
smile that dropped toward hell whenever a
spurt of laughter bubbled too near the surface, something rumors said was brought
about by a strict Baptist father who had
raged at his boy. And behind those hazel,
seventy-three-year-old eyes there always
seemed to shine a knowledge, as if there
were a single secret to life and Joseph Little
was the only soul of the world privileged
with its understanding.

It was wisdom bordering upon eccen-
tricity.

And it was generally agreed by the
townsfolk that if Joseph Little had been a
city-dweller, flatlander, he would likely
have been one of those wandering souls

with bloodshot eyes, a brown paper bag in one hand, and the other hand rummaging through garbage cans. A step away from a step off the deep-end is what he was. That's what the townsfolk had to say about it.

And that's the way it was in Winter Creek Mills. Everyone had an opinion about everyone else, and nothing ever went unreported. It was a typical small town in that sense, webbed with a word-of-mouth network that served the community as well today as it had a hundred years before.

And word was out that the Richardsons were taking in two boys to raise as their own. Nephews, the word said. Made parentless by a barn fire that had turned Faye's sister and brother-in-law to gray-black ash.

No one knew much about the boys. But the townsfolk were already wondering how the Richardson marriage would handle the additional weight of two boys. It was no secret the marriage was teetering. Wouldn't take but a single gusty argument about the kids to send it plunging to ruin.

That's the way the townsfolk saw it.

At the edge of town, after crossing over Winter Creek and following along George Bracken's pasture for a quarter of a mile, an old dirt road shot off to the right. Officially, it was an unnamed road. But folks called it Four Wheel Drive for obvious reasons. At last count, the one-and-a-half mile stretch of bedrock had more potholes than the four thousand that had plagued Blackburn Lancashire during the 60's when the Beatles wrote *A Day In The Life Of*.

The Richardson house was the first on the left, sitting comfortably amidst two well-groomed acres. Further down the road, there were six other homes, all hidden far away from the potholes, back within the cover of cottonwoods and cedars and more sparsely—scrub oaks.

In 1977, with money borrowed from Wade's father before he died, Wade and Faye had begun construction on the single-story dwelling, intending it to be their dream house, the house that would meet their needs from completion to death. Two years in the making, construction was completed on June 13, 1979 with the touch of champagne glasses and an evening bonfire fueled by two pairs of overalls, three discolored sweatshirts, a handful of gray socks which had once been white, and a pair of steel-toed work boots which stunk to high heaven. The next morning, after the smell had drifted further down the Valley, they had moved into the house. The dream had become reality.

The first thing Kiel noticed as they pulled into the driveway, was the absence of weeds growing dry and tall around the house like they always seemed to grow around the barn back home. And that meant that even though Aunt Faye liked to call this place a ranch, it wasn't really a ranch, with acres of pasture and a herd of cattle and more chores than a family could get done between sunrise and sunset. Not like the ranches back home in Hyattsville where there wasn't enough time in a day to waste an extra minute hoeing and burning weeds.

So right away, he knew this place was different than he'd expected.

"How about the grand tour?" Aunt Faye asked, herding them one after the other toward a carport door that opened into the kitchen.

Justin went in first, glancing back for just a moment to make sure that Kiel thought it would be all right. Then Kiel glanced over his shoulder, back at where Uncle Wade was leaning over the top of the green Chevy Impala. The man was wearing mirrored sunglasses that reflected Kiel's silvery glance back at himself. Only there was something dark behind that reflection, something wicked the way a flash of lightning, a clap of thunder on a lonely night could be wicked.

Something devil-eyed and hot-breathed, his Pa would have said.

Then Aunt Faye put a hand against the small of his back, as if to nudge him along a little faster; and whether it was just a chill tickling his spine or something worse, he thought he felt an anxiousness pass spark-like from her fingertips to his back. *Because of the man breathing hot air at their backs and glaring devil-eyed behind those mirrored glasses?* he wondered. *Or is it something else that makes her seem afraid to slow down long enough for him to get a good look at her, as if he might learn too much by seeing her standing still?*

What was it that made everything here feel so out-of-place wrong?

The house was an odd shape, leading off in two distinct directions, as if the kitchen and the adjoining family room served as the hub of the structure, and the rest of the house served merely as spokes. A spoke for the dining room which led to the living room which opened through taller-than-tall sliding glass doors to the backyard. A spoke for the bedrooms: a master bedroom with a water bed that brought a giggle to Justin when he tried to lie down, another bedroom which served as the studio for Aunt Faye's work—she wrote children's stories—and a third bedroom, with blue walls and a window that made the after-noon colors seem almost florescent.

"This one's yours," Aunt Faye said while she was standing in the bedroom doorway, holding the door open. "I hope you like it."

Kiel ran an absent hand along the covers

of the nearest bed, before sitting down. Across the room, there was another door, standing slightly ajar, and through the crack he saw the white, porcelain edge of a bathtub. Hanging above it from an overhead curtain rod, there was a set of brown towels and what looked to be a plastic, coffee-colored shower curtain.

"Dibs on this bed," Justin said, bouncing on the bed in the corner.

"I know it must seem like a long way from home," their aunt said then, an odd expression catching her face, making it mask-like, half-a-smile, half-a-frown. "Maybe with a little time it won't feel quite so strange. We'd both like you to feel at home here."

Kiel tried to smile back, but he couldn't hold it long enough to mean anything. And there was nothing he could think to say back to her just then. What do you say to a stranger who's supposed to be your aunt?

"Well, I bet you two are hungry." She looked away, back down the hallway, toward the kitchen. And Kiel wondered if his uncle were standing in the kitchen shadows, catching eyes with her, and shaking his head. "So maybe I better see what I can whip up for lunch." Another weak smile too quickly crossed her face. "Soup and sandwiches sound okay?"

Kiel nodded absently, because it didn't really matter one way or the other what they ate for lunch. And she was trying so hard to be pleasant that it made his stomach feel emptier than it really was.

She smiled again, still trying too hard, then disappeared into the hallway darkness, closing the door behind her.

"She looks like Ma," Justin said as soon as the door was closed. He pushed himself away from the wall and sat on the corner of the bed.

"I know."

"It's creepy."

"I know." Kiel sat on the edge of the other bed, giving the room its first close inspection. He'd seen a poster once; something called Mirror Lake. And like the mirrored glasses that had reflected Uncle Wade's folded arms as he watched Kiel escape into the house, the lake in that poster was a perfect reflection of the mountains and trees. That's the way the room was, a perfect reflection of itself. Two beds. Two dressers. Two nightstands. Two lamps. Each a perfect replica of the other. Twins. As if aunt and uncle had thought their nephews were twins, perfectly matching twins.

"Are you scared?" Justin asked.

"Are you?"

"I don't know."

He *was* scared, Kiel was. Not scared like when Pa would sometimes burst into his room with that crazy look peering out from behind his eyes. Not that kind of scared. This was something else. Like that first moment when it was time to go to bed and the room was blacker than the sludge that sometimes bubbled up from the ground at Tyler's Thistle. And your hand slid over the wall, hunting for the light switch just so whatever it was that was in the darkness couldn't get you.

It was like that.

The kind of scared that came back with every new darkness.

And even though he'd long ago quit believing in things hiding in the dark, there was still a lingering doubt that settled on his shoulder with the coming of each new night. Because how could a boy-not-yet-a-man be certain, one-hundred percent certain? And maybe . . . just maybe . . . like his Pa had told him every night for a lifetime, there really was something made of the devil waiting there in the blackness.

And here, with his aunt and uncle, he wasn't so much scared about being in the strange house as he was about the possibility that maybe . . . just maybe . . . there was something hiding behind those mirrored glasses that would scare the hell out of him if he ever saw it naked. Something as dark and evil as something made of the devil.

It was that kind of scared.

Something unknown.

"I don't know, either," Kiel confessed.

The bedroom door swung open then. Uncle Wade stepped through, still wearing those mirrored sunglasses, dropping their two suitcases to the floor. His face was expressionless, something that had never felt the slightest tug toward a smile, Kiel feared. But then a slight smile did push at the corners of his mouth, a smile more conceded than offered.

"You didn't pack much," he said.

"No sir," Justin replied, the way he used to answer Pa.

"After you put your things away, wash up for lunch."

"Yes, sir."

"Why does he always wear those sunglasses?" Justin asked as soon as the door closed and they were alone again.

"Because he doesn't want us to see."

"What? What doesn't he want us to see?"

"His eyes." Kiel handed his brother a suitcase. "Like sometimes when Pa couldn't look straight at you. He'd yell and holler without ever looking you straight in the eye. There's something magical about eyes, something that gives away too much about a person."

"He reminds me of Pa, the way you can *feel* him breathing at your back without ever turning around to take a look and see if he's really there. You just know when he's watching you."

Kiel lifted his suitcase to his bed, ran the zipper up one side, across the top, down the other side, opened the flap, and began to unpack his belongings.

"I don't think I like him," Justin added.

"Me either." He tossed a couple of tee-shirts on the bed, then added a pair of pants. Trying by his indifference—because he was the older brother and the leader and the one responsible for such things—to keep the bad thoughts (even if they were truer than he'd like to admit) at a distance.

"Kiel?"

"What?"

"Do you think we should stay?"

"I don't know." He tried to smile, but there wasn't a smile there. And false smiles weren't something a brother shared with a brother. "For the time being, I guess."

"If we don't like it, do we have to stay?"

"Just give it a chance."

"I'm not going to like it."

Looking out the Richardson kitchen, out through the long line of casement windows, one could see the land flowing over low-haired pastures until it touched against the southern mountains of the Mills. It was a beautiful sight, especially early in the morning when the long arms of the sun painted waves of yellow and orange across the kitchen counters. When they had been building, Faye had thought it was the most exciting phase of the construction, the day they installed the casement windows. What a glorious flavor the windows brought to the house.

She shivered now, as Wade first wrapped his arms around her. It seemed he was always sneaking up on her, although she knew full-well it was simply that she found it too easy to drift away to other places, too easy to lose herself to other thoughts.

"They're unpacking," he said, snatching a bite of lettuce.

"What do you think?"

"It's good."

"Not the lettuce," she sighed. "What do you think about the boys?"

"They've got your eyes."

"My sister's eyes."

He took off his sunglasses, kissed her gently on the cheek—the way he always kissed her when he thought she wouldn't understand what he was going to say—and he shrugged. "I think we've got ourselves a couple of boys who are barely old enough to wipe their own noses. And I think they're smart enough to be scared to death of the prospect of living in a strange house with two adults they don't know from Adam and Eve." He shook his head, then glanced out the window at the faraway mountains, as if he were searching for the courage and strength to finish. Then he shrugged again.

"What can I say? It's going to take time,
Faye. They aren't going to adjust overnight."

"Are you going to help?"

"I'll do what I can."

She turned to him then, holding a perry
knife playfully in one hand, taking up his
shirt in the other. "Then for God's sake,"
she said through half-a-smile, half-a-moan,
"will you quit wearing those damn sunglasses and moping around far enough
behind to go unseen, close enough to be
noticed? Give the kids a break, will you?
They're frightened enough without having
to go up against the likes of . . ."

"The Shadow?" he said, a little stiffer
than she'd expected. He was supposed to
share that gentle laugh of his, that self-
conscious way he used to have of breaking
the tension when it grew too taut between
them. He was supposed to give in to that
little smile of his and say something
wonderfully reassuring like, *the Lone
Ranger look is in this year or haven't you
heard? besides, I thought the sunglasses
added a certain aura of mystery to my
otherwise bland personality.* But he didn't
say anything quite so comfortable—he
hadn't said anything quite so comfortable
in months—and instead he seemed to
withdraw a little further into himself.

"Wade?" She touched him on the arm.
"What's the matter?"

Nothing?

Or everything?

Or secrets best kept to one's self?

There were times—too many of late—when he was depressed or worried or simply uncertain about something, and his face would draw long and smooth and childlike, and his eyes would almost beg her to step inside with him. He looked so much like a boy instead of a man at those times. And it was that little-boy Wade who was standing next to her now.

"Wade?"

"I think I'm as frightened as they are," he said, still staring out the window, away toward the southern mountains where everything must have seemed much simpler, much saner.

"Why?"

"Because . . ."

She took his hand and tried to draw his attention back from the wilderness, back into the kitchen with her.

"I guess it's because I've never been around kids before. What do you say to an eleven year old? What makes them laugh when they'd rather cry? What makes them like you when you aren't sure you like them?" He looked at her then. "Faye, I'm scared to death of those boys. What the hell do I know about being a father?"

When she hugged him, she thought perhaps she'd never let go, perhaps she'd hold on until they both cried together. And she thought she loved him more at that rare moment of vulnerability than she had ever imagined possible. "I'm scared too," she said.

And it was the special closeness of that moment that she never forgot.

3

Kiel really didn't know what to expect.
Even though they had briefly passed
through Winter Creek Mills on their way
from the bus terminal, he hadn't been
paying much attention to the look of the
town. His mind had been on other things
then, still trying to understand the current
of events that had plucked him and Justin
off their farm in Hyattsville and planted
them in this place that seemed so far away
and lonely. So he hadn't noticed the porch
of the town market all lined with old men
puffing on pipes and cigars. He hadn't
noticed the way their eyes followed every
moving thing that passed before them, or
how each face resembled all the others. He
hadn't noticed any of that before.

But he noticed it all this time, caught
every subtle detail as they walked up the
steps, past the congregation of old hollow

bodies, and into the Winter Creek Market.

"I only need a few things," Aunt Faye
told them. "Take a look around if you'd
like. I won't be long."

Back home, they used to travel into Jefferson once a month to do the family shopping. There was a Safeway in Jefferson, as
big as their barn, with slick floors and endless aisles and a thousand boxes—all cardboard and plastic-wrapped and smelling the
way a morning in heaven must smell. And
each and every box was just waiting there
to poke a finger at or steal a whiff from. It
was as good as a trip to Disneyland Pa
would tell them.

But this place was different.

The Winter Creek Market was a dark
little hollow, with three tight aisles and a
hardwood floor that was almost as wavy
and gaping as the weathered boards of the
porch. And there was a single smell that
had settled over the store, an almost musty
smell like something older than old, like
everything in the store had come here long
before Kiel had ever been born. It seemed
like a strange place to spend a hard-earned
dollar.

So while Aunt Faye went wandering off,
mumbling something about milk and eggs,
Kiel stood at the front of the store for a
moment, debating just how important it
was to venture into this place that seemed
so different from the Safeway in Jeffer-

son.

Then Justin tugged on his arm. "Come here," his brother said, dragging him along as if he never noticed Kiel's dead weight. They stopped at the head of an aisle where Justin peered around the corner, then he waved Kiel closer. "Look," he said.

He was the first kid they had seen in Winter Creek Mills, a solid big-framed boy with short-cropped brown hair. He wore tanned corduroy cut-offs, tight against his thick thighs. His butt was awkwardly misshapen, seeming as if it protruded too far. The netting of his tee-shirt ended a couple of inches above his navel, exposing a stomach neither too thin nor too flabby. He looked to be about thirteen, maybe fourteen, and he was stuffing the right front pocket of his cords with a candy bar.

"Stay clear of him," Kiel said, with barely a thought. "He's trouble."

"It's only a candy bar."

"You know what Pa would do?"

"Pa's dead."

Kiel pulled his brother away. "Just forget it, will you? You're asking for trouble. You've got enough to worry about without snatchin' every little thing that might happen to stick to your fingers."

Aunt Faye came up on them then. "I think I've got everything," she said. She handed Justin a carton of eggs to hold while she sifted through her purse. And

when the boy came walking by, the boy
with the candy bar bulging from inside one
pocket, the boy smiled the smile of the devil
at them before slithering out the door, unnoticed by the clerk.

"Who . . ." Justin started to ask.

"Trenton Maes," his aunt answered.
"You be careful around him. He's got a
mean streak."

"Trouble," Kiel said again. "He's
trouble."

Four dollars and thirty-four cents was the
total. Milk, bread, and eggs. And a thirty-
five cent Rolo candy bar for each of them.
Didn't even have to steal it.

Outside, standing on the porch next to
the bench of old men, Aunt Faye shaded her
eyes. The western sun was still above the
line of buildings across the street, bright
enough to hurt a naked eye just emerging
from the darkness of a poorly lit grocery.

It was a quarter to five.

Across the street, for the most part teetering on aged legs whose days were num-
bered, stood a line of weathered buildings.
A few of the old structures were nothing
more than three-wall boxes, time having
taken a bite out of the face where there were
once too many windows, leaving behind
nothing more than a small pile of crumbs in
the form of broken bricks. Most of the other
structures were boarded over, the window
and door patches blending eerily into the

colorless material that had been used over a
hundred years earlier to erect the buildings.
BLACKSMITH could be seen in faint lettering
above one boarded doorway. WINTER CREEK
HOTEL above another. At the very end of
the street, there was a single building still
in use, MURPHY'S FEED AND GRAIN, the last
remaining monument of a time long since
passed.

It was a lonely line of buildings, a line
that reminded Kiel of the old men sitting on
the bench next to where he was standing.
He wondered if one of them had been the
blacksmith, if one of them had been the
owner of the WINTER CREEK HOTEL. How
long ago that must have been. No wonder
their faces had grown to look so tired.

Aunt Faye was still glancing up and
down the street, still shading her eyes, still
seemingly unable to make up her mind
about what to do next.

On the other side of the road, seventy-
three-year-old Joseph Little came slowly
walking down the wood sidewalk, walking
along as if he were the only person in town,
as if it were his town and his alone. Kiel
thought he had never seen a man quite so
odd as the white-haired gentleman who
made his way along, stopping first in front
of the blacksmith shop to run a hand over
the   splintery   wood   surface—it   *was*
splintery, cracked and splintery like the old
man's face—then again to wipe something

from his eye.

Justin noticed too.

"Joseph Little," Aunt Faye said before they had a chance to ask. Then she apparently made a decision about where she wanted to drag them next, because she wandered down the steps and off to the right, assuming they would follow along behind.

"He's not very happy," Justin said.

"This town's not very happy."

"That kid looked happy, the one who stole the candy bar."

"Will you forget him," Kiel said, taking hold of his little brother's arm and pulling him down the stairs, then pushing him along big brother to little brother as they both tried to catch up with their aunt.

Henry Aikens leaned back against the wall, crossed his arms, and watched the two kids scramble down the steps like frantic ground squirrels. He was wearing a pair of Levi overalls he'd bought in Eureka in 1973, frayed around the cuffs, stained in 1977 with a splotch of tobacco where he had dribbled the dark juice after a stranger in town—just driving through—crept up behind ol' Henry and hit his horn. Henry didn't like strangers anymore, young or old, male or female. Had no use for them.

"Damn kids," Henry said, then he nodded absently at the sight of Joseph

Little walking the sidewalk on the other side of the street. For all the old man's strangeness, at least he was townfolk.

"How can they afford 'em?" Thomas Weatherbee put forth. He was a gaunt man, with gray stubble and a chalky face that looked worse than some ol' Henry had seen peering out of pine coffins. The only thing that seemed alive about the man, besides the stench of his cigars, was his eyes. But even they were just barely holding on.

"Don't know," Henry said.

"The woman must be doing it," said the third man. His name was Walter Dennison. He had yellow teeth when he smiled, but a smile was so rare no one much noticed. "Wade sure as hell ain't providin'."

The others laughed in agreement.

"Don't like it," Henry said.

"You don't like anything," Weatherbee said back at him. He ran a hand under his hat—an old baseball hat he'd picked up at Candlestick Park ten or twelve years before, the last time he'd been to a ballgame —scratched at the back of his head, and settled his arms comfortably across his chest.

"Too many people," Henry coughed up again. "Hell, a soul don't know anyone anymore. Ain't like it used to be. Things are changin' too fast. Ain't like it used to be."

And that was the cue.

They all nodded their agreement,

however slightly.

"Remember . . ." old Henry said next.

Their heads nodded before he had an opportunity to recall exactly what it was they should be remembering. But it didn't matter. They'd heard it before, not once or twice, but every day of their lives for the past five or six years. In all its oddness, it was their little way of preserving yesterdays long forgotten by most folks.

"It was different then," Henry went on.

Their heads nodded agreement.

Henry Aikens took up another huge breath.

And somewhere further down the road, beyond where their memories traveled, Faye Richardson disappeared into the afternoon glare with her two nephews trailing along behind.

The sign out front, a white hand-painted thing that was nailed to the fence, said *Library*. But Kiel thought it surely must be a mistake. It was a house, after all. A pale house in need of paint. Like eyes, two double-hung windows watched them approach. From behind the laced curtains— curtains which reminded him of the fine-laced table cloth back home—he saw a woman's face slip back into the shadows.

He tagged Justin on the shoulder then, mostly to help ease the shiver that had wiggled up his body. Because even in the brightness of an evening sun, this was a place of eerie fairy tales, a place of nightmares that came true. It had that kind of *feel* to it. The pulse of Hell, his Pa would have said. The smell of something once alive, now dead.

Justin nervously hit him back, then giggled. "She's a witch," he said.

"Shush," Kiel scolded, although it was a thought that had already crossed his own mind.

When the front door creaked open—just like it was supposed to if it belonged to the Devil—Aunt Faye put on a wide smile. "Molly," she said. "I'd like you to meet my nephews."

Molly Pritchard was her name. She was a tall woman, with a grandmotherly smile and she didn't seem at all scary up close. Her voice was soft and low; her steps short and pained. And even though her face was pale—white as the picket fence in front of her house, Justin would say later—it was a face that Kiel thought he could grow to trust, a face that seemed more honest than most of the others he'd come across in Winter Creek Mills. The hollow faces of the old men sitting like wooden Indians on the porch of the Winter Creek Market, were what came too quickly to Kiel's mind. There was something wicked in those faces, something a young boy should never turn his back to.

Ain't no place in Winter Creek Mills for young boys, he could imagine them saying behind his back.

"Guess we'll just have to do something about that, now won't we?"

Book shelves, standing back-to-back and a head or two taller than a tip-toed boy, filled the room that was Molly Pritchard's parlor, a room that only faintly resembled a real library. And the room was darker than a parlor or a library should be.

They weren't there for longer than a few minutes. Molly Pritchard conducted a short tour that seemed too long, making sure to point out that she didn't allow any Judy Blume books into her parlor, but did have at least one copy of each of Aunt Faye's books. She especially liked their aunt's *After All, We're All The Same.* And she conceded that there wasn't a huge selection available, although she could easily order anything they needed from the county and have it in their hands in less than a week.

Then she hurried Aunt Faye out of the room to share a cup of tea, telling the boys, "Take your time, browse the shelves." She promised them a library card before they left.

"Who's Judy Blume?" Justin asked when they were alone.

"Some writer, I guess."

Kiel ran a finger across the wood grain of

a shelf, checked to see if it had gathered dust, and it hadn't. Then he pulled out the nearest book, thought it looked too wordy, and stuffed it back in its place again.

There wasn't much to see there.

Molly Pritchard had a space (barely more than a shelf) for children's books, mostly picture books, three of which had Aunt Faye's name across the front of the cover. And Kiel couldn't help thinking that these were the librarian's favorites. And in a back corner, where the sunlight couldn't reach, there was a shelf of paperbacks, mostly about love and stuff. Each worn cover had a picture of a woman in the foreground, and a man in the back. Then there was a shelf of hardbacked books with brown or black covers that looked as if they had been stained with coffee, and at the front of each one there was a table of contents that was too much trouble to try to understand.

There were no Frankenstein books, no werewolves, no ghosts, no otherworld science fiction with space ships and robots.

Nothing of much interest when it came right down to it.

So Kiel was more than grateful when his aunt was ready to leave only a short time later. He'd been in Winter Creek Mills for the better part of an hour and he was already growing weary of the lazy town. He had been hoping for a town like Jefferson, with bright flashing lights and a Safeway

big enough to get him lost if he weren't
careful. But it wasn't anything like that.
Instead, it was more like Hyattsville.

Too much like Hyattsville.

Trenton Maes was sitting on the ground,
resting against the corner of the market,
munching on his newly-acquired candy bar
when he saw the two new kids go driving by
with Faye Richardson. He smiled and
tipped the candy bar in their direction. The
younger boy waved back. The older boy
looked away. So much for the amenities.

He wasn't all that interested in the new
kids in town anyway.

More important, Trenton had been
watching as that strange, skeleton-of-a-
man, Joseph Little, was scribbling a few
notes in that notebook of his. Sunrise to
sunset, winter-spring-summer, the old man
always seemed to have a pencil pressed
against a piece of paper, taking notes of
this old building, of that old road, of everything yesterday and long forgotten.

Dinner was still an hour away. And there
wasn't much to do until then, wasn't ever
much to do in a burg like Winter Creek
Mills. Not unless you kicked-up a little
excitement yourself.

Trenton swallowed the last of his hand-
picked Snickers bar, wiped his chocolate
painted fingers across the corduroy of his
pants, then stood and brushed the dust off

his backside. The sun was still above the roofline of the buildings, enough so he had to shade his eyes against the brightness. He watched the old man disappear around the corner of Murphy's Feed and Grain, walking that strange shuffle, as if he were a bit lop-sided, as if one leg were maybe an inch, maybe two, shorter than the other.

Hell, there wasn't anything else to do. The row of old geezers on the porch had grown quiet the way mindless men sometimes did, letting their pipes and cigars and chewin' tobacco do their talking for them. The main street was deserted now that old man Little had disappeared around the corner. Even Murphy's Feed and Grain had closed up, so he couldn't very well pocket any sunflower seeds for later, for when his mother would send him outside to play in the dark while she entertained Mr. Burnett from Freshwater.

So there really wasn't a hell of a lot to do . . .

Trenton Maes crossed the street and turned the corner at the feed and grain, setting his sights on the back of Joseph Little as the man trodded along the dirt road. Like always, the man was wearing a dark jacket and shiny black shoes, decked-out well enough to be attending a damn funeral, well enough to be the deceased for crissakes. And like always, he was heading toward the cemetery.

Trenton ran to catch up.

"Where you heading, old man?" he asked when they were walking side-by-side.

"Where am I always heading, boy?"

There wasn't another adult in the Mills who would talk to him like that, who would shove questions right back in his face without so much as a nervous grin. He liked that about Joseph Little. After all, in some ways they were very much alike, both being town outcasts and all. Both being pretty much loners. They were almost allies, if he thought about it long enough.

"To the cemetery," he said.

"You guessed it, boy."

The dirt path, bathing in the shadows of an endless line of tall poplars, touched pavement just on the other side of the Winter Creek Bridge, and slowly descended away from civilization to follow along the bank of the creek. It was a peaceful walk that eventually emerged at the mouth of a meadow which had first been baptized as the Mills Valley Cemetery more than one hundred and eighty years before. A cyclone fence surrounded the half-acre site, as much to keep away the outsiders as to keep away the deer and rabbits that enjoyed munching on the flowers.

"There'll be a full moon in a week," Joseph said as the two of them stood at the gate of the cemetery.

"What's that mean?" asked Trenton.

"Night work, boy. It means night work."

Then they were through the gate, standing inside the cemetery, inside the cyclone fence Trenton had always thought was there to keep the dead in as much as to keep the animals out. And for the first time, he noticed that the sun was just beginning to duck below the crest of the distant mountains; and day shadows were turning to night shadows.

He stayed close to the old man, grateful that no one was there to see his nervousness, grateful that his reputation wouldn't be tarnished by this momentary shudder.

"You come here at night?" Trenton asked.

"During a full moon."

"Why?"

It was the first time Joseph Little had ever looked Trenton Maes right in the eye. There was a glint in his stare, a flicker of something aroused, of something coming alive. "Don't you read, boy?"

"Not much."

"Why things happen when the moon's full. The air gets hot with electricity, with electrical impulses that spark a person's brain. Can make you crazy," he said, stopping before a lonely headstone with weeds growing high and untamed around its edges. "Or, it can plant ideas in your head, wild and wondrous ideas like nothing you ever thought before, like nothing you ever imagined possible to think."

"Like what?" Trenton asked.

"Like him." Joseph Little nodded toward the headstone. CARDEW JAMES MANTOOTH. NOVEMBER 3, 1913-JULY 27, 1928. "How old are you, boy?"

"Thirteen."

"Same as Cardew here." He sighed. "What is it that summons the blackness of death to come and take away a young boy of only thirteen? What is it, you suppose?"

"I don't know."

"Neither did I, least ways not until one full-mooned night, one full-mooned July twenty-seventh night when I knelt right here."

"What happened?"

"Wouldn't believe me if I told you, boy."

"Maybe not," Trenton said, knowing the old man wouldn't be able to resist telling his tale.

"But I'll tell you just the same." The man looked off to somewhere beyond the surroundings, to somewhere only his mind's eye could fathom. "It was near midnight. Cold and windless, and bright as any day under the full moon. I knelt right here." He scuffed the dirt with his shiny black shoe. "Knelt right here and waited 'cause I knew he'd somehow explain all of what had happened to him. And I wasn't disappointed, boy. I wasn't the least bit disappointed."

"Yeah?" Trenton egged. "So what happened?"

The mountaintop had half-eaten the sun. Shadows were turning darker; day sounds, like the chatter of scavenging bluejays, were fading into the background; night sounds, the sounds of crickets and owls and bat wings, were slowly taking over.

"Midnight it was," the man said. "That single second between yesterday and today, that blackness that marked the exit of July 27th and the entrance of July 28th. He rose right out of his grave at that moment. Cardew James Mantooth, age thirteen, rose out of the ground as if he had been buried alive the day before and was just digging his way out. Pale as death, he was. And he sat atop his headstone just as comfortable as those old buzzards that sit out front of the Winter Creek Market. And he smiled. And he said, 'Smallpox.' Not another damn word, just *smallpox*. And then he was gone again."

A hollowness stamped itself into the drawn lines of Joseph Little's face just then, as if it were a moment that he cherished because he knew it would never come again. Even in the light of a full moon, it had been a once-in-a-lifetime event, never to be repeated.

"The boy's face was pockmarked. That's what smallpox would do to a person, besides killing him."

For a moment, Trenton swallowed hard and almost let himself believe the old man's fantasy. For a moment, he almost thought he could see Cardew James Mantooth sitting atop the headstone. But he shuddered at the thought and suddenly realized how absurd the idea really was. A ghost was what the old man was talking about, a plain everyday ghost. And Trenton Maes knew there were no such things as ghosts.

"I checked the records," Joseph said. "And there *had* been a breakout of smallpox in the Mills during the summer of 1928."

The sun was almost an afterimage now.

"I've got to go," Trenton said.

"Mostly took the children," the old man said, absently.

"I'm sorry." He touched the man on the shoulder, not only to share the sorrow of that moment, but also to let Joseph Little understand that he was leaving then, that he couldn't stand by any longer and watch the old man drifting through fantasies of ghosts and outbreaks of smallpox. A cemetery was no place to be listening to such wild tales, especially in the dark of the evening.

Trenton Maes stumbled away into the shadows then, hurrying to get back home where his mother would be entertaining and none too pleased with his arrival. But at least in the safety of his room, in the safety of a 100 watt lightbulb, he could reason his way back to reality, back through that image of Cardew James Mantooth sitting atop his gravestone, back through the dying eyes of a crazy old man, to regain his sanity again. It frightened him that he had come so close to believing.

Joseph Little was just a crazy old dinosaur of a man.

There were no such things as ghosts.

Not even in a cemetery, beneath the eyes of a full moon.

ONE MONTH BEFORE
SECRETS UNCOVERED

When the woman first knocked at the door, the door leading from the front of the house into the kitchen, her knock startled him. Through the curtains and the misty whiteness of morning, he saw her bigger-than-life form—fat and nosey and looking as if she had nothing else in the world to do except to stand there at the other side of his kitchen door, knocking and filling up the view through the glass panes.

And for a moment, he wasn't sure if he should answer the door or not.

Then—like it used to happen every now and then and seemed to be happening more

and more often of late—his head began to
ache, stabbing at him from behind his right
eye until he began to feel that same strange
dizziness coming again to take him away.
His vision filled with the glitter of a
thousand twinkling dots, bit by bit filling in
the daylight with a blackness that he knew
was coming to keep him.

Time was going to be lost, he knew that.
Just like it always was.

Maybe a few hours, maybe the whole day.
Or maybe as long as a full week.

That's the way it happened.

And the memory of all that time would be
as black as the mud at the bottom of the
long-abandoned well at Tyler's Thistle. And
things that happened an hour ago, things
that he should know as well as his birthday,
would be swallowed up right along with all
that lost time, all of it replaced by the fog of
an empty mind.

He didn't think he'd ever know what happened to all that lost time.

And he didn't think there was anything
he could do to keep from losing it. Nothing
at all.

At last glimpse, the room buckled and
rolled into obscurity.

When Albert stepped out of the darkness
and into consciousness, he found himself
lying on the floor in the kitchen. There was
a determined woman pounding at the door

with a fist. It was the morning of the day, the sun was still in the east, still squeezing its way between two faraway clouds and streaking the kitchen air with wide bands of color and dust, interrupted by nothing more than the woman's persistent pounding.

"Well, hello," she said when he finally answered her summons. Her huge frame choked the doorway the way a half-filled water balloon presses against a holding hand, Jello-like. Her smile was pleasant but false behind the white teeth and fleshy dimples. "For a moment, I thought no one was home."

"Morning," he said, with a false smile of his own.

"I'm Mrs. Collingsworth," she said, as if he were supposed to recognize the name and invite her to fill up the kitchen the way she was already filling up the outdoors. He could see her bulk lean slightly forward in anticipation. "Thought I'd stop by and see how your mother's doing. Haven't seen her in quite sometime, you know."

"She's in Jefferson with Pa."

"They went to town on a Sunday?" She asked the question, but he could see that she didn't want an answer. Her bright bulbous eyes turned skyward like the eyes of a feeding shark as she peered above his head at the empty kitchen, as if she expected to find something there, something that would prove him a liar. "It's almost noon," she said then. "Perhaps they'll be back soon?"

"Perhaps."

"I could wait." Then, quicker than he would have thought possible, she pushed through him into the house, settling into one of the wicker-backed chairs before he could even suggest that there were things that he had to be doing and she was always welcome to call again some other time. So quickly she seemed to settle into that chair and make herself at home.

Almost out of thought, he wondered if the wicker chair would hold all of her without eventually giving way to exhaustion.

Mrs. Margaret Collingsworth was, as he shortly discovered, a talkative woman whose lungs held great bursts of air and a great collection of questions. For no less than an hour and a half her thick form remained fixed within the clutches of the wicker chair while she asked an endless stream of unimportant questions and her eyes swept back and forth over the kitchen, photographing every detail and filing it somewhere in the hollows of her mind for future reference.

For tomorrow's casual chatter, next week's vicious gossip, he rather imagined. *Why, the poor boy was left there all alone for more hours in a day than a boy his age should be left by himself. Idle minds and all that, you know. Someone should have been keeping a hand to his shoulder, the word of our good Lord to his ear, because you just can't tell with these kids these days. They just don't have the respect for things that their daddies did. What a shame. What a terrible shame.*

Then the inevitable question arose. She stopped just long enough to suck up the last of the kitchen air, then looked at him, straight and narrow, and asked, "What happened to the barn?"

"There was a fire," he said calmly, only faintly realizing that his ability to remain calm and rational and perhaps a step or two ahead of Mrs. Collingsworth and her curiosity was the reason he was standing there in the spotlight in the place of the *pretender.*

"I can see there was a fire."

"We don't know how it started," he said.

"Really?" she inquired absently, prying her release from the clutches of the wicker chair and waddling with the grace of an out-of-water duck until she was standing at the window. "No one was hurt?"

"No ma'am."

"How fortunate."

"Yes."

"I want to look, do you mind?"

"There's really nothing to see," he said, but there was a knot in his stomach that suddenly tightened, because there *was*

something to see. *You can't let her curiosity
take a casual stroll through the backyard,
Albert. She'll know then. And she'll shout it
so loud through those balloon-like lungs of
hers that the rest of the world will know
almost as soon. And then all hell's going to
break out, Albert. All hell.*

"The fresh air will be nice," she insisted.

"But it's still dangerous out there."

Keep her in the wicker chair, Albert.

"Oh?"

"Yes, ma'am," he said, with an awkward
slanting smile that wasn't comfortable on
his face. But he couldn't seem to force that
desperate smile back into the folds of his
cheeks. And he knew that in the same way
he was losing control of his smile, he was
losing his control of the situation. "We
haven't had time to clean up the mess.
There's still nails on the ground and sharp
sticks and . . ."

"I promise I won't waltz through the
rubble," she said through a twitter of
laughter, as if she found the inconceivable
thought almost tempting enough to try.

She can't see the backyard, Albert.

"Everything's still covered with black
soot," he said. "And dusty. Sometimes the
winds catch a bucketful of ash and send it
swirling black in the air like a miniature
tornado."

"I'll chance it," she said. "Besides, I need
to stretch a bit. I've been sitting far too

long. It's bad for the circulation, you know." Then she turned toward the door.

Stop her, Albert.

"You really shouldn't," he said, stepping into her path and feeling more than overwhelmed by her size leaning against his. She was truly bigger than life.

"Don't be silly."

She pushed her way past him, pushed her way right through him and through the back door into the backyard without the slightest of efforts and only a single hefty puff of breath. And he knew—without clearly understanding how—that they were both suddenly walking the fine edge of something promising trouble. Trouble bigger than Mrs. Collingsworth's enormous swaying body. Trouble bigger than the both of their masses all melted together.

And he didn't have the foggiest idea what that trouble might be.

The sun was twelve o'clock overhead, blanching the ground, washing the black ash until it seemed like the same dirty gray that was the color of the huge woman's dress. From one arm, where it had hung like an appendage since the moment he had first seen the woman, her dull black purse swung back and forth like a pendulum in rhythm with her less-than-graceful amble. Tick . . . tick . . . tick . . .

And the natural current of air that

seemed to be forever kicking up an early afternoon gust—and would, he had hoped with fingers crossed, swoop the two of them back into the kitchen before they could see whatever it was that was better left unseen —was just as calm and uncooperative as an airless day could be.

All hell, Albert. Let her see them and you'll pay all hell.

"Where's your brother?" she asked when they came to stand at the charred earth where the mass of black rubble seemed so shapeless, so meaningless. And her eyes were poring over the blackness as if searching for something unseen, as if her ears had heard the calling of something that was hiding beneath the rubble.

Albert . . .

"It's hot," he said then, taking hold of her massive arm and giving it a tug away from the gray and black ashes that had once been the barn. "You really shouldn't stay outside so long. Sun stroke, you know. Or heat exhaustion. A woman can never be too careful."

"Lose any livestock?" she asked, her body still anchored firmly to the ground. And he knew by the way she sucked up a huge breath and glanced narrow-eyed toward the fields that she had sensed something . . .

all hell, Albert

. . . not quite right.

And he didn't know if they had lost livestock to the fire.

And he didn't know where the brother of the *pretender* had gone.

And before he could find the strength to give another tug at her arm, Mrs. Margaret Collingsworth had turned away from the distant mountains, back toward the black shapeless mass that grew like weeds out of the nearby ground

. . . and a glint of sun off a tiny nail caught her attention

. . . and suddenly it was too late to keep her from seeing

. . . suddenly it was too late to keep the world from knowing

All hell, Albert.

All hell.

That afternoon would forever be with him.

The way Mrs. Collingsworth had sucked up a sudden lungful of air, then looked down upon him, her eyes already moist with tears, and asked, "How long?" He'd opened his mouth to offer an answer to her question—though it would have been something of a lie, since he didn't know how long it had been—but she hadn't waited. She pulled him into the folds of her bosom and had nearly squeezed the life out of him.

By the time the brother had returned—he'd been out in the fields—the kitchen was crowded with strange faces. Some were discussing what to do about the two graves in the backyard, talking about digging up the father and the mother and burying them someplace else; someplace proper, like they said Albert and the brother should have done in the first place.

And there was a sharp-nosed woman who wore thick glasses and a plastic smile and kept asking them questions. She wanted to know why they hadn't told anyone about the fire, why they'd tried to bury their parents by themselves. And she kept wanting to know if they had relatives anywhere.

He didn't like her.

He didn't like any of them, all chattering excitedly about this and that, all shaking their heads as if a tragedy had taken place and asking questions that they must have known had no answers.

Albert didn't like any of it.

So after a while he turned the spotlight over to Nicholas.

I guess you'd call it my birth. Although, it wasn't really like being born, not with the crying and the slap on the butt and all that. I just opened my eyes and I was.

Sounds strange, doesn't it? But that's the way it happened.

At first, I thought I was the only one. But faraway, beyond where the spotlight shined vacant, I heard other voices, sometimes laughing all alone, sometimes crying. And that's how I knew there were others.

I remember when I called to them, two hands cupped around my mouth, yelling into the blackness. For a long while, no one answered. So I followed giggles here and lonely whisperings there until we were all standing there face-to-face like strangers of the same family.

I brought them all together for the first time.

I guess that's why I tend to be the one who keeps tabs on what's going on inside here. I think I'm the only one who really cares about the others.

ALBERT
twelve years old

4

If you were an outsider, traveling a name-
less night road that spilled you out at the
Flat Rock Tavern, you'd probably find the
tired place to be nothing more than a small
country stop-off, convenient only because it
was near the half-way mark between
Eureka and Bagota.

But locals from Freshwater and Winter
Creek Mills and a handful of other faceless
towns roundabout that area, held the Flat
Rock in a little higher esteem—it was the
only tavern within thirty miles, and Agnes
Stearns, who was the proprietor and the
bartender, was a woman with a knack for
seeing right where a fellow was coming
from without him ever having to say much
more than, "Give me a beer."

The Flat Rock even had its own little
niche in California history according to the
word of mouth that had been passed down

over the years from locals long since buried
to locals almost too old to still remember to
locals—like Agnes Stearns—who never
missed an opportunity to pass the history
down another generation. That's precisely
what Agnes was doing as the last of the
evening sun was turning night-black and
star-filled outside. She was spinning a little
history lesson for Wade Richardson and he
was turning a deaf ear that just wasn't like
him.

"You've seen the old cemetery out back,"
she was saying. "Hell, that thing must
have been here long before every fool in the
country came looking for gold. Before I
even bought the place, Marcus Crabtree
was showing folks where he'd once
stumbled over a weathered plot marker
nearly as old as the earth it was stuck in.
Now what the hell was the date on that
thing?" Agnes asked herself out loud. She
paused a moment, then nodded. "Somewhere around 1813, I think it was. 1813!
Can you imagine? Right on this very spot,
it must have happened."

Wade's beer had long ago turned warm.
He hated warm beer.

And he didn't give a moose's ass about
the band of Spanish soldiers that had
massacred a family of settlers over a
hundred and fifty years before. Even if the
massacre had happened only the drop of a
nickel away from where he was sitting that

very moment.

"You okay?" Agnes asked when her tale drew no response from him.

"Sure."

"How about another beer?"

"Why not."

The Flat Rock was an odd structure, built tight against the side of a hill. And even when Wade hadn't been drinking much, if he stood back a ways to take a close look at it, he'd swear it was leaning lazily to the left. On many a night, the only thing saving a drunk from tumbling head-first down the rickety stairway was that awkward right-to-left lean of the building. Even the Budweiser neon—THIS ONE'S FOR YOU—was all cock-eyed in the window. Hell, a person felt as drunk going in as he did coming out.

That's the way Wade saw it.

He chuckled inwardly.

But once inside the old place, he'd have to grant at least a degree of credence to the tales of Agnes Stearns, 'cause there wasn't a single item hanging on the walls in that darkness, not a solitary black and white photograph or rusty railroad spike that the Smithsonian wouldn't happily grab-up.

"So, what's on your mind?" Agnes inquired, delivering Wade his fourth beer, and trying to talk above the break of billiard balls in the back room where Ben Williams was having himself the loneliest kind of night. "How come you're so quiet tonight?"

"Too busy drinking," he said.

"It probably won't help." Her hair was frizzy, something she claimed she couldn't do much about unless she shaved her head. And she had a front tooth missing, knocked out one hot August night by her first husband. She never seemed to miss it, talked on just as if it were still there, still filling the gap that made her appear dumber than she really was. The apron she wore was homemade, fashioned from a slicker given her by Charles Mallory Hatfield, better known as the *Rainmaker*. She had met him in 1922 after his celebrated Sand Canyon success. The slicker was his own little publicity gimmick, something he gave out freely to anyone who requested one. But ask her today and Agnes couldn't even tell you what the *Rainmaker* looked like.

"A drink always helps," Wade said through his glass.

"Still looking for work?"

A slight nod. "Isn't everyone?"

He had donated—that's the word he liked to use, because looking back on it now, the time wasted seemed every bit gratuitous— seven years of his life to the city of Eureka as a building inspector. Seven goddamned years! All wiped away with the single swoop of a red pen. Here a recession, there a balanced budget and poof! the department was cut fifty percent, the union's knees started knocking, Wade Richardson was handed directions to the unemployment office

. . . and life became a pisser.

"Something'll turn up."

"Nothing'll turn up." He glared over the rim of the mug, glared at her as if it were her fault. "It's already been six months. Nothing'll turn up. An honest man doesn't have a fighting chance any . . ." The rest of the sentence went down with a swallow of beer that didn't stop until his mug was empty again. "But *she's* doing great," he said. "Things couldn't be better for her." He shoved the empty mug at Agnes-the-proprietor, Agnes-the-psychologist.

"Last one," she said.

"It's all I need."

As she poured him another draft, he could tell she was watching him, thinking things inside her head about him, the way Faye was always doing. He could see her sitting back and making judgments about him, then keeping them to herself like they were special secrets. Little somethings to keep around until they might be useful the way a low blow could be useful. Just like Faye was always doing. *You've been tipping the bottle again, haven't you Wade? Gonna pickle your brain if you aren't careful. And for God's sake, it's been forever in a day since you had a job, when are you gonna start earning your way around here?*

Huh? Tell me that, Mr. Richardson. When are you gonna start earning your own way?

"Last one," Agnes repeated.

"Sure."

A solid swig.

"You know, she's got a contract for three more books. Hell, it's raining dollars. She don't know how to spend it all, it's coming in so damn fast. Can you imagine? She could walk out on me tomorrow and I'd be the one requesting alimony." Wade laughed into his mug. But there was a sadness to the laughter. "Hell, I'd have to hire that Mitchell lawyer."

"Faye's not going to walk out on you."

"Naw, I know that," he said. "I know that."

Then Agnes wiped the counter, a gesture of habit and a way of keeping a little closer to Wade Richardson since he wasn't far from sliding off his chair to the floor. And in the back room, there was the crack of billiard balls as Ben Williams broke a rack.

It wasn't that late, a little after midnight, when he finally stumbled into the kitchen, bouncing the door off its stop with surprising force. He fell back, hit his head against the doorjamb and slid to the floor. Then he laughed and quieted himself with a finger on his lips. "You'll wake up the house," he said above a whisper.

But the house was already coming awake.

And when the kitchen light went on, Faye was standing with crossed arms, like an enormous scolding shadow, next to the oven. She was wearing cotton denim jeans with a rose-colored oxford shirt that looked blood-red through the haze of too many beers. Her eyes appeared tired, her face rouged.

She hasn't even been to bed yet, Wade thought. *Probably been up working on her next book, locked away in that sacred studio of hers, tossing out a thousand ways to make her next hundred thousand.*

"Hi," he said, none too clear.

"Guess I don't have to ask where you've been."

"Shhh," he touched a finger to his lips. "You'll wake up the boys."

"I'm sure they're both wide awake by now," she said, suddenly at his side, helping him back to his feet.

"Shhh." He chuckled.

"Why tonight, Wade? Why did you have to make it tonight?" She was supporting a good portion of his weight, guiding him helter-skelter down the hallway toward their bedroom.

"Because . . ." he said. And there was a thought behind it, a thought that had somehow become sidetracked during the long journey between his brain and his mouth, because he couldn't remember the rest of

what he was going to say. It was right there
one moment, suddenly somewhere else the
next, and his mind couldn't seem to find it
anymore.

Twice he slipped from her grasp and his
body spilled over the thick, pile carpet like a
spineless rubber band, like a glob of Silly
Putty waiting passively to be gathered
together again.

"Are you going to leave me?" he asked
when she had at last managed to unload
him onto the bed. He was staring at the
ceiling, at the thousands of snowy little
hills and gullies formed by the white texture.

"Not tonight," he heard her say through
a tired breath.

"Thank you," he answered, not quite able
to prevent the rest of the words from
stumbling over his tongue. "Because the
alimony . . . you'd have to wait until I found
a job, you know."

Then there was a warmness that
gathered in his eyes.

And he thought he was going to cry.

"You awake, Kiel?"

"Yeah."

"He was drunk, wasn't he?" Justin's
arms were folded behind his head. Through
the bedroom window, he could see where
the clouds were breaking up and the stars
were peeking through. And there were

white streaks of moonlight painting the
tips of the cotton-puff clouds. "He was
drunk like Pa used to get."

"Yeah," Kiel answered. "Like Pa."

And Justin wondered why people got
drunk, why they were so determined to
force down that burning taste of liquid until
they became limp-muscled staggering and
mumble-mouthed the way some people with
only half a mind were. 'Cause even though
it had been a long time ago, he still remembered—rather painfully—that first
scorching sip of beer he'd stolen from his
father. How could people drink that pee?
"Do you think they're alike?"

"In some ways, maybe."

"Yeah? Like how?"

"I don't know," Kiel said. His voice was
hoarse, nudging softly against a whisper.
"I was just talking, that's all."

"He doesn't like us." Justin still held the
sight of that first moment at the bus depot
when his uncle had been standing behind
his aunt, army-still and mannequin-like, a
mouth so straight it looked as if someone
had penciled it across his empty face. He
was an eerie sort of man, standing there
cold as an icicle, staring sharp-eyed and
silent out those sunglasses of his. "I know
he doesn't like us."

Kiel rolled away from him, rolled onto his
side as if to end the conversation right
there before it got out of hand. Sometimes

he did things like that. He was funny that way. Sometimes right in the middle of their gabbing back and forth he'd just all of a sudden turn away and he wouldn't say another blessed word. Just like somebody'd come along and cut out his tongue.

"You know it too," Justin said.

From the next room, a cry softly rose, then he heard what sounded like his uncle's voice, a deep resonance with a so-drunk-his-mind's-turned-to-mush slur to the words. It said, "I'm sorry."

"Like Pa used to be," Justin whispered soft enough to keep to himself. "Sorry, like Pa used to be."

Nothing ever seemed to change.

Like father.

Like uncle.

Here a sponge, there a sponge.

"Won't ever happen again, woman," his Pa used to say on those Saturday nights when he couldn't get himself up from his chair and she had to shoulder his dead weight one step at a time up the stairway to bed. Then he'd say, "I'm sorry." As if it made a difference.

Just like Pa used to say.

"Kiel, you still awake?"

A partial moon slipped pale blue through the bedroom curtains, and Justin could see his brother's form, a dark unmoving form except for the slow rhythm of his breathing. He wished Kiel wouldn't wander off to sleep and leave him awake that way, especially his first night in the strange house with the strange smells and sounds.

He hated feeling alone.

PART TWO
THE NIGHTMARE

There were corner-shadows, dark as night blackberries. And narrow bands of light that slipped from outside—to—inside through cracks unseen. And a quiet that whispered of wordless death.

"My hands are clean," the boy said, and he knew he had said so before.

"And your heart? Tell me how pure is your heart?" Through the dusty black and whites of where they were, the boy could see where wings were slowly beating (almost gill-like) at the back of the man whose face was shadows. And as well, he could see where a pointed tail occasionally flicked out of the darkness and into the light, before disappearing again. The wings were of angels, he knew. The tail was of a demon, he knew as well. And none of it made any sense. "There's something evil-black where your heart should be, boy."

The boy took a cautious step back, but only a step, for he knew any more than that would not be allowed.

"*Your tongue devises mischiefs; like a sharp razor, working deceitfully. You love evil more than good, and lying rather than speaking of righteousness. You love devouring words, O you of deceitful tongue. And you must be punished.*"

The shadow-man grabbed hold of him, took his arm in a viselike grip that was inescapable. And he took the boy—all dragging feet and voiceless screams—deeper into the corner-shadows where darkness was blinding and great gulps of air went soundless.

And the boy knew he had seen that blackness before.

"*It's the tongue of the devil speaking from the lips of a boy,*" said the voice from nowhere and everywhere. There was that voice, and a blackness that would swallow an extended hand, and there was nothing more. Just the emptiness that dogs a dream-lost boy in a world all strange yet too familiar. "*Devouring words are the devil's words. And if you so speaketh for the devil then you shall wear his mark to separate you from the others.*"

. . . yellow—orange—red . . .

. . . something red-hot, white-hot, burning . . .

And the boy saw that it was an iron rod, red-hot/white-hot at one end where there was a symbol he couldn't read.

"It's the mark of the devil, my boy. So

those who cross your path will know you for what you are, a child of the devil.''

The boy backed blindly into something unseen, and fell hands-and-elbows to the ground. And suddenly the hotter-than-fire branding iron was being pressed against his inner thigh. And he knew he had felt that pain before. And reflexively he grabbed the iron rod with his hands until the searing pain burned home and he had to pull his hands away.

When he first glanced then stared at his palms, they were red and moist and black-charred masses of flesh that seemed detached the way a mirror image seems detached. Then he noticed how the skin had peeled back, all black and worm-like, and he looked from his hands to the face of the shadow-man, wanting to ask why? *but having no voice.*

And the face of the shadow-man, all darkness and light and magnified, was his father's face . . .

. . . when the boy first woke from the nightmare, he fought to catch a fleeting breath, lost it, then caught it again. *It was Pa.* His cheeks felt warm, his arms were damp and perspiring, his heart was beating piston-like in his chest, faster than he thought he might be able to stand.

It was Pa.

He sat up, taking some of the pressure off

his lungs and heart. In the bed next to him, his brother was asleep, his back turned away, his breathing slow and rhythmic and untouched by the godawful nightmare that had been the feature attraction only one bed away.

The shadow-man and Pa, they're—

With one eye closed, one eye half-opened, the boy slowly peeled back his bedsheets, expecting—fearing—dreading what he might find hiding there beneath them. But he had to know, didn't he? Because the nightmare was too real to be nothing more than just a dream gone sour. It played almost real enough to be a . . . bad memory.

He slid the blue-and-white cotton pj's down his legs, feeling a shiver of goose pimples follow his fingers from thigh to knee, from knee to ankle. Then he pressed back the fleshy part of the inside of his left thigh, and the nightmare came true.

There was a scar there, the size of a dime. And it read: 666.

ONE WEEK LATER
THE GREAT RACE

Faye Richardson was sitting alone in her studio, pencil in hand, leaning over a sketch and thinking about yesterday and the day before and every other day that had come and gone since a week ago when her nephews had first arrived. It had been a week made long by the awkwardness of strangers getting to know one another. But everyone had apparently survived, which made the week sound a little more melodramatic than it really had been.

In fact, after that first hectic day, things had fairly well settled down again. Wade had spent the better part of his morning-after sleeping off his "sponging" (as Justin liked to call it), while Justin and Kiel had taken their first adventuring steps outdoors to touch and smell and kick a foot at their new surroundings—which, after the farm, must surely have felt a little confining to them. And from there things had gradually begun to slip into a daily routine that had grown more and more comfortable as the week had moved along.

Although Faye suspected the everydayness had still not quite found its way back into all of their lives.

She paused for a moment, eraser-to-cheek, and thought she had caught herself feeling suddenly unsettled, the way she sometimes felt when there was something gnawing at her and she refused to acknowledge the irritation. It was the first time she had realized that not quite everything was feeling comfortably familiar.

Wade was different.

And that's what had made the week feel longer than a week should.

Faye sat back in her chair, letting her hand drop lifeless to the drafting table, all dead-weighted and tingling the way she felt her marriage was at times beginning to feel.

Wade was somewhere in Eureka again, knocking knuckles against the door of one employment opportunity after another, forever in search of his self-respect. And Faye momentarily hoped that maybe he'd find it hiding behind one of those doors. But she didn't think it was likely, because she didn't believe self-respect was something you found in a job any more than it was something you found in a bottle.

By special request—or more straightforward, by special threat—he had promised to discontinue his nightly stops at the Flat Rock Tavern. And perhaps that was part of the problem, now that she thought back on it. Because Wade hadn't been himself all week. He had been quiet the way a windless spring day could sometimes pass without the falling of a pine needle, the flapping of a wing. Unnaturally invisible, as if he were silently pulling back within himself and finding it safe enough and comfortable enough in that solitude to consider staying there indefinitely.

He was slowly pulling away from her, that's what he was doing.

And she was failing to understand the why of it.

Faye glanced absently at the cover sketch she had been tinkering with for *Sometimes I Can't Help It.* Just beginning to come alive out of the penciled lines, there was a young girl sitting head-in-hands on the front steps of an apartment building. Her eyes were made wide by the tears she was trying to hold back, and there was a sense of bleakness reflected between those glistening eyes and the sterile buildings nearby.

"That's me," Faye thought. "All childlike and pouting and feeling as small and helpless as I used to feel when I was still ten years old."

And just as confused.

How do you hold a crumbling marriage together?

You super-glue it.

Faye smiled and shook her head, feeling a little embarrassed by the errant thought. Although, in a strange way, it wasn't really that wild of an idea. Add a few drops of the sticky stuff to Wade's fragile male ego and maybe he could hold it together long enough to find himself another job and feel whole again. Because that's what it was really all about, wasn't it? The fact that her success was just beginning to blossom at the same time his was just beginning to wilt?

That sounded hauntingly simplistic.

A sprinkle of wishful thinking.

She leaned further away from the illustration she had long ago stopped sketching, the same one that seemed destined never to be completed. The morning was growing late. Somewhere out of sight, the sun was just beginning to push and pull and stretch the mid-day shadows like stiff taffy, making them longer and thinner. Morning purples had long ago slipped beneath the early orange sky, eventually giving way to that lake-blue color that could seem so peaceful on a late spring day. Almost stealthily, the studio had seemed to slip from morning to afternoon.

Faye slipped a sheet of wax paper over her drawing.

Through the studio walls, she could hear a soft, spontaneous laughter coming from the next bedroom. Justin and Kiel, laughing the way only children can laugh, lighthearted and natural and sung on a breath lasting longer than long.

And she thought how sweet that song of laughter sounded.

And for a moment, it was the only song to touch her ears.

Trenton Maes was skipping rocks across the calm waters of Millhouse Pool when Justin and his brother came out from behind a line of cottonwood trees that kept the creek in shade during most of the day. For a moment, it was a standoff—him postured there with rocks in hand, staring down the outsiders, them trying to stare back without giving away their uneasiness.

He tossed another rock, watched it skip-hop-jump its way to the middle of the pond before sinking out of sight. Then, without catching the eye of either one of them, he shrugged and said, "There's not much else to do in Winter Creek Mills. Skip a few rocks. Five finger a few candy bars. And hope that tomorrow comes and goes faster than today."

"Kiel says you're trouble," Justin declared just half-a-second before his brother tagged him with a fist to the shoulder.

"Who's Kiel?"

"He is," Justin said with an accusing nod of his head. His brother whispered something that sounded like a warning, but he never looked up to see Trenton's reaction first hand.

"You believe him?"

"Sometimes I do, sometimes I don't."

"And this time?"

"I don't know," Justin said, catching a quick glance at his brother standing stiff as a wooden Indian, mute as a muzzled dog, nearly shoulder-to-shoulder with him. "Should I?"

Trenton shined a set of perfect teeth, then shrugged, then tossed another rock at the water. "He's probably right," he said with a sigh that seemed sad enough to be the truth. "It's what everyone else thinks. 'Watch out for that Trenton Maes, the little hellion. He's one big wind of trouble, that kid!' I've heard it all before."

There was a moment of quiet, an awkward time of waiting while each of them gathered up his thoughts and tried to guess what should come next. Then Kiel suddenly spoke up in a way that none of them had quite expected. "Pa used to say things like that about us."

"Oh yeah?" Trenton knelt to grab up another flat rock, but he was still listening, because suddenly it was sounding as if there were something the three of them had in common, and he wanted to be careful not to let it slip too easily away.

"More often than not," Justin nodded.

"Little hellions?"

"On the good days," Kiel said with a friendly grin. "Children of the devil on the days when he was sponged out of his gourd."

Trenton Maes laughed, and it was the easiest laugh that had come to him in longer than he could remember. And he liked the way it seemed to set things free inside him, as if being known as a troublemaker wasn't as bad as he'd always been given to think it was.

"I skipped a rock nine times across the bass pond back home," Justin said then. He had dark wide eyes and deep dimples, and a look of innocence that Trenton thought might be deceiving, the face of a tiger cub. But he wanted to be friends—even his brother seemed willing, although

he was a bit more tentative—and friendship
was a scarcity in Winter Creek Mills.

"Twelve times," Trenton said, tossing
each of them a flat rock good enough for
skipping the best of ponds. "The record
here is twelve."

The three of them kicked around most of
the afternoon, talking about odd people
known and odder people heard about, tossing
skippers across the pool, not doing much
more than killing time and getting to know
one another. There seemed to be an abun-
dance of time to kill in Winter Creek Mills,
time enough for doing nothing and everything.

The sun had moved and the afternoon
shadows had lengthened when Trenton
tossed his last skipper and smiled that
devilish little smile of his for the first time.
And at the very first inkling of that smile,
Justin knew it wasn't going to be an
ordinary afternoon, that this mischievous
new friend had suddenly stumbled head
first over an idea that was going to make
tomorrow seem a lifetime away.

"The race of a lifetime," Trenton called it,
leading a path through the cottonwoods
and scrub oaks away from Winter Creek,
through a barbwire fence in need of repair,
and into a grazing pasture with memories
of home.

Toward the south, where the grazing

lands all seemed to hub, Justin could see
the dark outline of a small house, its front
porch sagging at one corner, its windows
snow-white cold as if no one lived behind
them. There were patches on the roof, dark
squares that gave the appearance of something missing, something added. And
without knowing why, the sight of that
place, all alone in the pastured land, seeming more familiar than it should, sent a
shiver up his body.

"Old Henry Aikens' place," Trenton said
through that devil's smile. "That makes it a
little more fun. He's a grouch of a man, mad
enough at the world for ten men."

"Won't he care?" Justin asked.

"He'll care, that's half the fun of it."

And Kiel never said a *yes* or *no*. He just
went along.

Ten minutes later, Trenton was holding
his hand in the air, ready to drop his arm
and start the race—from the lonely oak to
the barbwire fence and back again. Three
aspiring jockeys, three black and white
thoroughbred milkers. All in a line. All
eager at the bit. At least until the imaginary gates went exploding open.

With barely the kick of a heel, Trenton's
cow took off, donkey-trotting, as straight
and determined as any uninterested milker
could be. Justin's thoroughbred, even less
interested, took its first inspired steps only

after several solid whaps on its backside. But at least their cows were moving. Kiel's staged a sit-in or more appropriately a stand-in, refusing to budge even as little as an inch while he was sitting on her back. Kiel slid off and tried pushing from behind, but it was all for naught.

At the barbwire fence, Justin leaned too far to the left and went sliding off, feet-butt-arms-face. He laughed then, and he couldn't stop laughing. His butt was sore from bouncing off the hard, bony hips of the cow; a hole had been ripped in the knee of his jeans; he was spitting dirt; and he couldn't stop laughing.

Because Winter Creek Mills just wasn't supposed to be this much fun.

From his front porch, one hand draped around a four-by-four support, the other hand nervously rubbing finger and thumb, Henry Aikens watched Trenton Maes cross the imaginary line of the lonely oak and win the race.

And he didn't like it. He didn't like it one bit.

Justin and Kiel were in their bedroom that night, sitting cross-legged on the floor, over a game of Payday. They were each dressed in identical blue pj's with white cuffs at the ankles and wrists. That twin mentality again.

Dinner had been a faceless casserole,

something Aunt Faye had mysteriously cooked up from ingredients gathered witch-like from the back of dark kitchen shelves. She had teased them with her raised, un-witting eyebrows when asked what it was they were eating. "Trust me," she had said, in a manner that seemed contradictory. It was a good casserole just the same.

Uncle Wade had missed dinner. He had come in an hour or so later, after they had bathed and wandered off to the privacy of their room like they did almost every night.

They were playing a six month game of Payday. Justin rolled the die, moved his yellow marker, landed on INHERITANCE, and held out an open palm, waiting for his pay-off. Absently, he scratched at his left thigh where the pj's were itching.

Through the thin bedroom walls, they heard the telephone ring softly in the kitchen. For a moment, they each held a breath, then just as quickly, they turned their attention back to the game.

"Kiel?"

"What?" His brother-the-banker handed him five hundred dollars. No matter what game they played, if there was money involved, his brother was granted banker-ship. It was something that had simply taken form over the years, something never questioned because it had always seemed so right.

"How come you don't like him?"

"Uncle Wade?"

"No." Justin watched his brother roll a four and count his steps to SWEET SUNDAY. "Trenton—how come you don't like Trenton?"

Kiel sighed.

"How come?"

"Because I don't trust him."

"You hardly know him," Justin said, scratching again at his pajamas.

"It's just a feeling, that's all."

"I think he's great."

"I know you do."

Justin started to giggle, the way he'd been giggling all afternoon, with the memory of Kiel pushing at the backside of his milker, trying to get it to move off the starting line. *An elephant,* Trenton had called the lazy beast. *A pregnant elephant.*

Another giggle.

Then there was a heavy knock at their bedroom door, and Justin knew—without knowing how he knew—that his uncle was about to burst into their room and ruin their game of Payday. Some days were just too perfect to be left alone by adults, and this was one of them.

"Quiet," Kiel said, as if the knocking might go away. But he didn't have to say a word, because Justin was already swallowing whatever had been coming up his throat in defense of his cow-riding. Both of them moved away from the game board, to their beds, with their backs up against the wall.

Uncle Wade opened the door without waiting for permission, and he stepped into their room, fogging up the air with a chill. "I just talked to Henry Aikens," he said, too controlled and calm under the circumstances.

Trouble, Justin thought, feeling the gloom begin to shadow him like the dark outline of an eagle over a frightened rabbit just before its razored talons reach to snatch the poor creature from the face of the earth. Trouble like Kiel warned me. And the giggles were slowly swallowed back, replaced by something heavy and gray and guilt-like.

He caught a glance from Kiel, a warning not to say anything.

"Did Faye introduce the two of you to Mr. Aikens?" their uncle asked. Behind him, standing to his left, in just enough light so that the curiosity of her expression could be seen, was Aunt Faye.

"No," she answered for them, shaking her head. "They haven't met him."

"Well," he said with a sudden down-home inflection that smoothed over something not quite so friendly, and sounded a bit too much like their dead and buried Pa. "Henry's a grumpy old coot. He doesn't much care for anything, complains about most everything. So we're kind of used to hearing him gripe."

"But he's a nice man," Aunt Faye added, moving out of the shadows, further into the room where she stood next to her husband. She was saying one thing, he was saying another, and Justin guessed both of them were having trouble describing Henry Aikens. "All the people of Winter Creek Mills are nice."

"He's a neighbor, we have to live next to him. We have to try to get along with him."

"In a small town like this, everyone has to try to get along."

"It makes life easier," their uncle said; then he sighed. "Anyway, Mr. Aikens says you were down at his place this afternoon. He says you and that Maes kid were riding three of his dairy cows. Running 'em ragged is what he says. And he isn't very happy about it. Says the cows are okay, but they probably won't give milk for a week after what you put 'em through; which is a lot of bullsh—"

"Wade." Aunt Faye elbowed him.

"The man likes to exaggerate," Uncle Wade said reluctantly.

And Justin kept waiting for the sudden explosion of anger to erupt from his uncle. And he wondered how long it would take, how many minutes of monologue would pass before the man would work himself in to an emotional frenzy the way his Pa used to do, and then suddenly go mad with a belt in hand. He winced at the image-flash of a belt coming down on him.

"You boys did it, didn't you?"

There was a thick, too obvious silence, a teetering toward-then-away from confession, neither boy looking at the other, neither boy raising a head in answer. Justin knew that if a confession became necessary it would be expressed in unison with his brother. All for one, and one for all. The pain never seemed as bad when the both of them shared in a punishment.

But Kiel was deaf-and-dumb silent.

"Well?" A soft flush slowly washed over their uncle's face. His hazel eyes sipped from a darker pool of blue, seeming deeper, more alive. That quickly, he seemed affected by a change of emotion, as if he were always standing at the edge of his anger, leaning forward over livid flames, bridled only by a wavering self-restraint.

Justin could feel the man's burning temper filling up the room.

Aunt Faye wrapped a hand around his forearm, as if to hold him back.

"Answer me." He slapped a fist at the door, which bounced against the wall and back into his open hand again.

It's coming, Justin thought through eyes too frightened to watch. *Any moment now, the man's rage is going to break its restraints and out of nowhere a strap will suddenly appear and then . . .*

"That's enough, Wade," his aunt said

then. Her grip on him tensed and she tugged him backwards a step, out of the room and back toward the hallway. "You're scaring them. Can't you see that?"

"They should be scared!"

"Wade—"

"They're damn near an old fashioned whipping!"

"That's enough," she said again.

And suddenly there was a thoughtful pause, as if he'd actually heard what she was saying and was trying to understand it. And that didn't make any sense, not from where Justin was sitting. What was happening here? What was it that made his aunt's voice so coldly stop his uncle, as if she were he, and he were her? Because it was the father that did what he damn well pleased, and the mother that tried—and failed—to put out the flashfire rages with paper words. That's the way it had always been. So what was it that made things different here?

"Just calm down," Aunt Faye was saying, both hands squeezing his forearm now. "My God, Wade, they're children, little children."

"They shouldn't have been riding Henry's cows."

"They know that now."

"Well, damn it, why won't they say anything!"

"Because they're scared, Wade." She

gently but firmly pulled him further in the
direction of the door. "This isn't getting us
anywhere; it's really not that big of a deal.
You know Henry complains about the way
the sun comes up in the morning. No harm
was done." They were slowly slipping back
out of the room as her voice became softer,
more consoling. "Knowing you, Wade
Richardson, racing dairy cows was
probably a daily event in your childhood."

"I'm sorry," Justin thought he heard his
uncle say. Then the door was quickly closed
again, and oddly, the room felt as if it had
taken a great breath before exhaling.

Kiel moved away from the wall, back to
the game board.

"Are you okay?" Justin asked. His
brother had been closest to the door, only a
hot breath away from where their uncle had
stood.

"Yeah."

Justin sat cross-legged on the floor, next
to his brother. "He didn't beat us. That's
something."

"He wanted to."

"But he didn't."

"Maybe not this time," Kiel said. In his
hand, he held a die which he shook noiselessly before tossing it at the board. It came
up one. Before he moved, he stopped and
glanced at Justin and said, almost as a
promise, "But he will."

* * *

An hour later, after the house—settling back on its foundation, like the calm after the storm—had grown quiet again, and after Justin had won the game of Payday by almost three thousand dollars, there was a soft knock at their bedroom door. Aunt Faye peeked in before they could answer it.

"Still awake?" she asked.

They were both in bed, covers pulled neck-high, the room dark. And the conversation that had been fresh in the air suddenly turned stale.

"We're awake," Justin said.

"Can I come in for a few minutes?"

"Sure."

She slipped through the door like a wisp of Christmas ribbon on the breath of a breeze. Sometimes she seemed almost like an angel, and Justin almost expected to see thin, finely-veined wings flapping at her back. She was wearing a heavy robe, pink with a pattern of flowers sprinkled evenly over the fabric.

She sat on the edge of Kiel's bed.

"I guess I just wanted to talk to you, to let you know that we both love you." Absently, she twisted the cord of her robe around one finger. When she caught a glimpse of eye contact, she had trouble holding it. "This is all so new for your uncle and me. We aren't really sure of ourselves as parents yet. We want you to be happy here, both of us do. But we also want to do what's right; we want to make sure that the two of you understand the difference between right and wrong."

Outside, a slight breeze had kicked-up. The spindly arms of a shrub scratched at their window, momentarily taking attention away from here—where their aunt was stumbling awkwardly with her words—to there, where crickets chirped and winds whistled and words went unheard.

"He's a good man, your Uncle Wade. He's just having a difficult time right now." She looked absently at the coil she had molded with the sash of her robe. Just as absently, Kiel sketched a picture in his bedspread with one finger.

And for Justin, it felt as if the tension that had followed their aunt and uncle out of the room only an hour before had suddently returned. Though it was different now—not quite as emotional, not quite as intense—it was there just the same. And Justin wanted to wish it away.

"Kiel lost," he finally said.

"What?"

"The cow race." Remembering again, he smiled. "His cow wouldn't move. He had to push it to get it off the starting line."

Aunt Faye laughed, a hand to her mouth, as if she felt a bit guilty for allowing the laughter to come out of her.

"And Justin fell off," his brother added.

"Just before I got to the fence."

"That's how he ripped his pants."

They each tripped over the telling, Justin complaining how sore he still was from the ride, Kiel trying to explain why pushing a cow from behind wasn't a good idea. And for the moment, everything else was put aside, because thoughts of Uncle Wade suddently didn't matter anymore.

And the telling of the tale became almost as much fun as the running of the race. Even when they took a moment to catch their breaths and Aunt Faye said, "But no more cow races, right?" and they answered, "Right!"—even then, there was only enough room in the *now* to remember the fun.

It was eleven-thirty by the time they had all settled down again. Justin and his brother were buried a little deeper beneath their bedsheets. The breeze outside had gone whispering elsewhere. Aunt Faye was still with them, still sitting on the edge of Kiel's bed, still full of the funnies.

Justin liked that.

She had told them about her first children's books, and about the one called, *Sometimes I Can't Help It,* which she was still working on, finishing up the cover illustrations. And she was already toying with an idea for her next book.

The Joke's On You, she was going to call it.

"What's it about?" Justin asked.

His brother was fighting to stay awake, eyes at half-mast, one wavering hand propping up his head, holding onto the last few moments of his wakefulness with a dying determination.

"It's about a boy a little younger than yourself, maybe nine years old. He's new in town. He's scared. And he's always been shy, so it isn't easy for him to make friends."

Justin yawned. "Why's it called *The Joke's On You?*"

"Well . . . his name is Rodney, and more than anything in the world, Rodney just wants to be accepted by the other kids. But he doesn't know how to get them to like him. Then one day, he meets a clown and he knows right away that he wants to learn how to make people laugh. And after a while he learns a few tricks of the trade and the other children begin to enjoy being around him when . . ."

Her voice was slowly fading, slowly pulling away from him, growing softer and softer in his ears until he didn't think he could hear it anymore. And for an instant, the world turned upside-down again as he fell off the cow in slow-motion. He smiled.

The great cow race.

His aunt's voice whispered from faraway.

All because of Trenton.

Then sleep came and took him away, took

him away from his aunt's whisperings,
from the still strange bedroom, and delivered him back to the lonely oak sitting in
the middle of Henry Aikens' pasture with
three black and white milkers all standing
in a line.

*What's green and red and frothing at the
mouth? Give up?*
A frog in a blender!
*That's great, isn't it? Albert and the rest
of them, they never laugh. I think it scares
them. I think they're afraid of having fun.
Stupid, huh?*

SCOTT
twelve years old

5

Morning brought another sunny day. Yellow-white rays of sunlight slipped between the branches and leaves of the oak trees and fell spectrum-like across the dirt the way the afternoon sun used to paint rainbow oranges on the eastern wall of their bedroom at the farm. But it was different here. The colors were brighter, more alive. Back home, back at the farm, the afternoon colors were thick and heavy; tinted a gloomy, almost-dirty orange that seemed to never leave, even with the warm autumn rains.

It was different here.

Justin shaded his eyes with one hand and watched his brother toss another dirt clod at the trunk of a tree. It was already ten-thirty, half a morning come and gone, quicker than a morning should. And it felt like all the other mornings come and gone in

Winter Creek Mills, as if they had never been at all.

"We could walk into town," Justin said, still shading his eyes.

Kiel let go another toss, then straightened up—his legs robotic and stiff under Levi jeans that had never been washed. The sun was at his back, masking his face in shadow, but Justin thought he saw his brother start to say something, then change his mind. Kiel snatched another dirt clod from the ground, shook his head—not into town—and splattered it against a tree trunk that would have been hard to miss.

And that's the way it was in Winter Creek Mills. One empty morning chasing after another, all in a hurry going nowhere.

"Wanna hike to the creek?" Justin asked. "Catch a frog or two and jump one against the other?" He was wearing a pair of blue and white shorts, a tee-shirt with a picture of Christopher Reeve as Superman on the front, and a pair of Nikes that his feet had been trying to grow into all week. "What do you say?"

Kiel held up another throw, as if giving the suggestion at least a cursory consideration, then shook his head again. And Justin decided that was the way the rest of the day was heading—him asking this and that, his brother turning up a wrinkled nose, and the both of them doing nothing much of anything.

So he quit asking.

And he found himself a little patch of shade and curled up there, safe from the sun, exposed to the boredom, just waiting for something like a strike of lightning to come along and liven things up.

By eleven o'clock, that lightning bolt came riding by on two wheels.

With that ever-present smile, Trenton Maes skidded to a stop just in front of Justin. His hands twisted on the grips of the bike, a *scrapper* he'd built around a Mongoose frame and apehanger handlebars. He'd been looking for his new young friend, partially because his mother had told him to get lost, and partially because he wanted to share an overnight inspiration that had come to him, another *time-of-your-life* adventure.

"Hey," he said, still twisting the grips. "What's happening?"

Justin looked back at his brother who was still busy tossing dirt clods at an old tree stump, and who seemed totally disinterested in Trenton's arrival. "Killing time," he answered.

"Looks like it."

"How about you?"

"Nothing much." He shrugged, and watched his friend's brother absently scrounging around for more dirt clods, as if he weren't even there. And he knew Kiel still didn't trust him. *Bastard, and that starts with "B" and that rhymes with "T" and that means trouble.* Just like everyone else.

"Just checking things out," Trenton said.

Kiel called to his brother then. Justin looked away, then back again, still shading his eyes from the glare of the sun. "I'll be right back."

"Sure," Trenton said, watching the eleven year old rush off at his brother's call. He knew what they were talking about. The same old crap that everyone in Winter Creek Mills talked about. *Stay clear of Trenton Maes. That bastard's trouble.* And even though there was a part of him that hurt everytime he saw that contemptuous look in another person's eyes, there was another part of him that thrived on being the outsider. So they could talk until they turned blue in the face for all he cared. Kiel could tell his kid brother whatever he wanted. It wouldn't matter anyway.

They chatted for a couple of minutes while Trenton practiced wheelies in the street. Then big-brother Kiel tossed an angry dirty clod as far as he could—which wasn't all that impressive—and went pouting-stomping-mad off into the house. The next best thing to a flying leap.

"What's he so pissed about?"

"Nothing," Justin said, kicking at the road gravel.

"Still mad 'cause his milker wouldn't budge?"

"Naw, he just worries too much."

"He does, huh?" And Trenton knew he'd been right, knew he'd been pegged as trouble before he'd even had a chance to stir up a little homemade mischief. "How about you, are you a worrier? You afraid that if you hang around me too long that I'll get you in trouble?"

"How'd you know?"

"Everyone around here thinks I'm trouble."

"Are you?"

"Naw." He lifted the front wheel off the ground and looked away, briefly considering the honesty of his answer. "I just like to have fun, that's all."

"Me too, I like to have fun," Justin said, a little more eagerly than Trenton had expected. The kid was a follower, a purebred follower. Jesus, just lend an ear to his gung-ho, high-pitched voice, catch a glimpse of that hunger in his eyes. He's looking for something bigger-than-life to come along and nip him on the ass, just so he can feel more alive than dead.

"Wanna go for a ride?"

"Where to?"

"Just around," Trenton said with a shrug

of his shoulders. "I've got a proposition I'd like you to hear. Come on, get on."

Half an hour later, they were back in front of the house, Justin climbing off the bike, Trenton nervously twisting his handlegrips again. "Tonight," he said. "Meet me there tonight, before midnight."

"Before midnight." Justin pointed an imaginary pistol at his new friend, and fired it with the snap of his thumb. I'll be there."

"The time of your life—guaranteed."

Justin grinned—a curl of lips, a dig of dimples, that were almost slavish to Trenton's smile—then he slapped the back of the bicycle as Trenton turned and began to zig-zag his way through the rocks and potholes of Four Wheel Drive.

"Midnight!" Trenton yelled over his shoulder.

"Midnight!" Justin yelled back at him, only vaguely wondering what kind of devilment he was spinning for himself. And did it matter? Did it really matter if it were good or bad, right or wrong, as long as it was something more than sitting in the shade of the eaves, watching his brother toss dirt clods at trees big enough to hide an elephant?

He kicked at an acorn cup, missed it, then turned around to see if Trenton had been looking. Bike and rider were already out of sight. And he thought again, as he had a

thousand times since, about the day before
and his bucking milker—because *bucking*
was what it had become—and the hole in his
pants and the wind-swept laughter.

The time of your life.

And why couldn't there be more than one
'time of your life?' Why not?

Justin smiled at no one there, then
wondered when evening had turned dark and
the darkness had turned to midnight, if he
would still have enough guts to go through
with it. Why not?

Around the edges, it was dark, the kind of
dark that would swallow up a curious hand,
a careless foot, and maybe never give it
back. In the center, there was the *spotlight,*
stand on it and the world was yours, but
stand beyond it, in the breathless shadows
at its edge, and suddenly you were nothing.
Light or dark, alive or dead, that's the way
it was.

Scott was there now, standing alone in
the spotlight and feeling like king of the
mountain. The *pretender* had gone away to
sleep, because he was bored or frightened or
sad or maybe just indifferent. It didn't
really matter why, there were a thousand
reasons for his coming and going, and who
was Scott to care which one it was? All that
mattered, that really mattered, was that he
was standing alone in the spotlight.

He was alive.

And his time was his.

Scott was sorting through old boxes in the carport, dumping a little of this, a little of that, mostly junk of one kind or another, into a shopping bag he'd confiscated from beneath the kitchen sink. That's when a hand touched him on his shoulder and he thought he felt his heart stop beating.

The way it sometimes stopped when he was standing in the shadows.

It was the brother of the *pretender*.

"What are you doing?"

"Building a nuclear reactor," Scott said with a twisted grin that must have seemed a bit unnatural to the *brother*. But it was his grin, his alone. Not a curl of it, not a dimple of it, belonged to the *pretender*.

"Better not let Uncle Wade catch you fooling around with his tools," the brother said.

"I'm only borrowing his wire cutters."

"What for?"

Scott opened his eyes wide, wide enough for the white around the edges to become as prominent as the dark pupils. "When was the last time you had a haircut?" he asked, snipping the air with the cutters, then laughing.

"You're gonna get in trouble," the brother said with a shake of his head and not even the remotest hint of a smile.

"Cutting hair?"

"You know what I mean."

"I know what you mean, *he* knows what you mean, we all know what you mean. But do *you* know what you mean?" He dropped a ball of string into the bag, tucked the bag under one arm, and held out the palm of his free hand. "Give me five, bro. I'm going where no man has gone before."

"Where's that?"

"You can come."

"No thanks."

"Catch you later, then," Scott said.

"But where are you going?"

"Follow the yellow brick road."

It was bright out, as bright as standing at the edge of the spotlight, eyes shaded, gazing at that life-light. And the afternoon breeze was blowing softly out of the south, whispering against his back the way the other voices sometimes whispered in his ears. Faraway and vaporous.

He followed a dirt path that serpentined away from the house, one world—a rather humorless world—disappearing behind him, and another world coming alive before him. Down one side of a small reed-infested ditch, up the other. Beneath a short span of trees, their shadows ink-blotting the ground in strange and wondrous patterns. He saw a naked woman in those shadows, riding a camel. And he giggled and laughed, and looked a little closer. And here he saw a

smiling pumpkin head, there he saw a cross-
eyed dragon. All hiding there, just beneath
the surface of shadows. He saw each one
and shared his laughter equally.

And then he was there, standing next to
the lonely oak in the middle of Henry
Aikens' pasture. He dropped the bulky
grocery bag to the ground with a giggle,
and began to measure out two-foot lengths
of string.

There were some afternoons, not many
mind you, when Henry Aikens just wasn't
up to wandering down to the Winter Creek
Market to whittle away the hours. Mostly
they were afternoons when he wasn't feeling as good as he knew he should, a little
too stiff in the joints, a stomach that felt
sour and rumbled like a volcano near erup-
tion, or maybe just a lack of energy.

It was one of those afternoons.

He sat on his front porch, much the same
way he would be sitting on the porch at the
market, watching, just watching, trying to
sip up every little movement of note with
his eyes. Sometimes the minutes became
hours, the hours became days, without so
much as a gardner snake slithering lazily
through the front yard shrubs. Other days,
he'd see a mother and her fawn feeding in
the pasture or maybe a porcupine or even a
bobcat. On those days, sitting by himself
on the porch wasn't such a godforsaken

thing to be doing.

He'd been sitting for longer than he could remember, his arms folded across his chest, frozen in place. And he'd been considering taking a stroll into town after all, even though it was one of those days when just getting out of bed seemed to be asking too much of his body. So he was sitting there, still debating with himself, when he first noticed the boy out in his pasture.

He stood for the first time in hours, and leaned against one of the porch supports while he watched the boy rounding up his dairy cows.

It was one of them Richardson kids, he was certain of that.

And he yelled at the kid to leave his poor cows alone. But his voice wasn't a young man's voice and it died on the breeze long before it was able to find its way to the boy's ears. So he simply watched. The porch post held him up, and he watched as the boy gathered together the dairy cows.

He felt helpless then. And it was the first time in Henry Aikens' life that he realized just how much he hated being old.

No one ever laughs in here. They cuss, and they try to sound smart, and sometimes they even cry. But they never laugh.

SCOTT
twelve years old

6

It was eight-thirty. Faye was working in her studio, sitting absently at the drafting table—producing anything had seemed more and more of a chore lately—trying to bury herself as deep in her illustration as possible, but resisting her own determination. She was more concerned about Wade, who had never made it home for dinner.

Outside, evening had turned to night, deep purples to black. Inside, the studio was a dark hall, sopping up the empty night except for where a single light hung as always over the illustration.

Morning, noon, and evening gone.

Just like Wade.

Coming home tonight, dear?

Maybe.

Maybe not.

There was the chance—once slim, now maybe not—that he had simply decided he'd had enough, that he had already walked, closed-mouthed, right out of her life without even feeling a need to let her know. It sounded insane, but it was something she was sure he was capable of doing. And she had let the possibility quietly gnaw at her all evening.

Damn you, Wade Richardson.

The pencil slipped from her fingers, and she pushed away from the drawing board. After dinner, she had treated herself to a leisurely soak in the bathtub. Now, she was wearing her heavy robe and a pair of fur-lined slippers, and she thought how much like a housewife she must look. The perfect wife for the perfect husband, Wade would be quick to say.

From the next room, she heard a rise of laughter that sang to her as it did almost every night. There was something so care-free about those two, even after all the hell they'd been through. She marveled at the way they had survived, at the way they seemed to carry on without ever letting things overtake them.

Then she smiled, unable to keep down the grin that poked at her cheeks.

Henry Aikens had called that afternoon, in one of his usual fits of anger, tossing out a barrage of four-letter expletives. And he didn't know which one was responsible—*they both look like goddamn siamese twins,* he had said—but he was certain it was one of her kids. One of them little hellions—as he so distinctly put it—had tied tin cans to the tails of his dairy cows. *Probably won't ever give milk again; and if they do the damn stuff'll be so sour it'll turn a goat's stomach, for crissakes.* She'd never heard him quite so upset.

But she let a laugh slip out of her, not meaning to be rude or insensitive, and honestly trying her best to keep it to herself. It's just that it was so funny, thinking about all those milkers with cans tied to their tails. They couldn't get lost that way, could they? He'd always know where they were.

Maybe that's what her husband needed, a can or two tied around his neck? Or better yet, a cowbell. She might at least be able to keep track of him then.

Damn you, Wade Richardson.

The momentary humor went quickly out of her, and she paced the floor for a few minutes, losing all track of the laughter that was still bubbling from the next room. And she wondered if it ever came down to it, if she would be able to find the courage to leave her husband.

Damn you, Wade Richardson.

Joseph Little had been looking forward to this night for weeks.

It was a full moon, his favorite time of the month.

The time was eleven-fifteen. He was walking along the bank of Winter Creek, a flashlight in one hand and a leather tote bag in the other. The tote bag contained a portable cassette recorder, several pens and pencils, a notebook, and a copy of *A Discourse of Spirits* by Sebastian Michaelis which he had obtained through the friend of a friend who knew someone who owned a small occult bookstore in the middle of New York City. There was a night chill which reached for the marrow, and Joseph was wearing a heavy overcoat.

As he emerged from the creek bank to stand at the front of the cemetery, he looked skyward to the moon, marveled at the beauty of something so distant, and slipped the flashlight into the tote bag. He was winded, spent a moment letting his breath return, coughing up a throatful of phelgm—from a minor cold—then went about his way. The hillside was a wash of gray and black shadows, distinctly outlining long, dreary aisles of the dead. Like gray-shadowed dominoes, lines of gravestones reached higher in the night than they had ever reached during the day, reaching toward the life of the moon.

There was something magical about a full moon.

Joseph Little had known that ever since that long ago night when he had first stood before the grave of CARDEW JAMES

MANTOOTH and listened to the whisperings of a boy who had been dead for more
than the seventy-three years Joseph Little
had been alive.

Justin's eyes had never closed long
enough for sleep.

It was eleven-thirty.

Kiel was asleep in the next bed.

The full moon, the moon that Trenton
had told him was so special, was casting a
thick arm of light through the bedroom
curtains. Enough brightness so Justin
could change from his pajamas to his jeans
and a tee-shirt without disturbing his
brother. He tied the last knot in his shoe
lace, a double knot.

The house was quiet, too quiet, he
thought as he slipped out of the bedroom.
Quiet like a held breath. And too dark. Dark
like an endless tunnel.

He felt the nervousness of his heart
pounding at his chest.

The hallway appeared different in the
shadows of the night, longer and less
definite in its cast, as if it were a living,
breathing nocturnal thing that came alive
in the darkness. He could hear the hum of
the refrigerator, the soft purr of the heater.

He questioned for the first time, as he
stood there just outside his bedroom, if it
were really such a good idea, if perhaps it
would be wiser and much smarter to do an

about-face and go back to bed where it was
warmer and safer and not quite as dark.
But he knew Trenton would be waiting for
him. And if he didn't show up, if he chick-
ened out, well then . . .

. . . he just couldn't let that happen.

His first steps down the hallway stirred a
moan from the floorboards, a much-too-loud
moan, and he froze in place, listening. But
there was nothing to hear, no movement
from his aunt's bedroom, no sudden
clearing of his uncle's throat. No one had
heard; no one had cared. And he quickly
soft-stepped down the hallway, through the
kitchen, and slipped out the door into the
cool night air.

Trenton had been hiding in the brush,
watching the creek where he knew the old
man would eventually appear. Under the
full moon, the night was much brighter
than he had anticipated; he hoped the light
wouldn't create a problem, even hoped that
it might somehow add a special eeriness to
the prank, as if it weren't eerie enough in its
conception.

He checked his watch, a Timex quartz he
had lifted from the Payless store in Eureka.
It was eleven-thirty.

Someone coughed.

He smiled.

The old man had just emerged from the
creek path; he paused there, looking off at

the moon like some mindless wolf-creature. The beam of his flashlight went flutter-crazy for a moment, then went off altogether. In the moon's light, Trenton could easily follow the shadow-form of the old man as he slowly made his way through the cemetery gates. And he knew exactly where the man was heading.

He checked his watch again.

Eleven-thirty-one.

Impatiently, he wondered where his young friend was, wondered how much longer it would be until he arrived, and prayed that the kid wouldn't chicken out at the last second.

This was going to be one to remember.

Faye Richardson couldn't sleep.

She had thought she heard Wade come in a few minutes before, had thought he had come in through the kitchen door, but the house had grown disturbingly quiet again. She glanced at the clock on her nightstand. It was eleven-forty.

Damn that man.

She wondered if perhaps he'd made it home safely, had even made it into the house safely, then, all sponged-out, had passed out on the kitchen floor for the boys to discover in the morning. The thought wouldn't let her alone, wouldn't let her drift off to sleep. So she rolled back the covers and slipped into her robe.

The house had grown chilly, too chilly for a spring night. *Never used to be like this,* she thought. Then she smiled, realizing that somewhere over the years she had picked that one up from the men on the market porch. *Never used to be like this.* It was the first time she had ever realized how well-integrated she had become to the town of Winter Creek Mills. In some ways, that comfortableness frightened her, and she wondered if perhaps she had been in one place for too long.

Then that image of Wade lying limp on the kitchen floor worked its way back into her mind, and she slowly dragged herself off the bed and down the hallway to put her imagination at rest.

A block away from the house, Justin suddenly realized he had forgotten to bring a flashlight. For a moment, the thought stopped him in his tracks and he looked back at the house, debating if he could afford the time to return. But the house was so clear in the moonlight, so clearly vivid, as had been the journey to this point, that he decided not to worry about it. He'd have to stay out of the creek; he'd have to follow along the bank, staying above the line of trees that might otherwise drop black shadows on him; but he'd be all right.

Everything seemed different under the moonlight, grayer, softer, like the makings of a dream. And the night was so quiet, so still, that he imagined he was the first person to ever venture out at this strange hour, the first person to ever experience the passing of a full-mooned midnight. It should have frightened him, but it didn't. He felt somehow safe under the grayness of the moon-night.

He crossed through Henry Aikens' pasture, wondering for a moment where the milkers had gone, before realizing they were sleeping in the barn. At night, the distance from the lonely oak to the barbwire fence seemed no further than the hallway that led from Aunt Faye's bedroom to the kitchen. Even distance was distorted under the moon, he thought. Even distance. He slipped under the fence, scraping his belly on an unseen slab of rock.

Then he picked up his pace, hoping he wouldn't be late.

Trenton might not like him anymore if he were late.

The shadow fell forward across the face of the gravestone, in such a manner that Joseph Little wasn't able to read the CARDEW JAMES MANTOOTH that was imprinted there. It was of little conse-quence. For nearly fifteen years he had been returning to this site in hopes that the boy-ghost would make a reappearance. Every moonlit night. And on every July

27th, the day of the boy's death, whether
the moon was full or not. Blindfold Joseph
Little at the gate of the cemetery and he
could smell his way to the gravesite.

"Evening, Cardew," he said, standing
before the grave. "Full moon tonight."

He slipped the tote bag off his shoulder,
resting it in the lap of the surrounding
weeds. Then he knelt in the dirt, knelt and
cupped his hands as if in prayer.

"Fifteen years," he said. "Such a long
time between reunions. But I'll wait longer.
If you insist that I must, I'll wait longer.
Only, please, realize that I'm an old man
these days. There are not many more full-
mooned nights left in my life, even fewer
July 27ths."

His voice was a quiet whisper that
bobbed on the mountain air like a helium
balloon, softly, with a fragile tenderness.
Tiny, cotton-ball clouds fogged the air as he
spoke. Silently, he prayed that the boy-
ghost was listening, that tonight would be
the night he had waited so long to come
again into his life.

"Smallpox," he muttered with a shake of
his head.

Then he sat in the tall grass.

"So many children taken."

He pulled the tote bag to him and
searched through its contents for the flashlight and the book. It was a matter of waiting now, a matter of sitting back, doing a

little reading, and waiting.

It was in the hands of Cardew James Mantooth now.

Justin stopped long before the cemetery entrance. He was winded and breathing heavy, his arms propped against his thighs for support as he tried to catch his bearings.

In the distance, within the cemetery boundaries, he could see a light, fixed, moving only on occasion. Its beam cut a short path through the moon-shrouded night, like the beam of a flashlight. And he realized that Joseph Little was already there, already waiting.

He wondered what time it was.

Then a hand fell over the crest of his right shoulder.

"Shhh," Trenton said, putting a finger over his lips.

Justin swallowed back the scream that had erupted from somewhere deep inside, deep enough to have been a piece of his soul.

"He just got here," Trenton whispered.

With the moon-gray light falling across his face, Trenton had a look of death about him, as if his flesh had turned cold and lost its resilience. When he smiled, his teeth shined yellow. When he looked away, the whites of his eyes glowed.

And Justin shivered.

"Calm down, will you?"

"It's cold."

"Not that cold." Trenton took him by the arm and escorted him away from the front gate. "We haven't got much time."

They circled the cemetery, silently working their way around the outside of the cyclone fence, keeping a safe distance from the beam of light that was the old man. Justin had lost his bearings in the strangeness of the night, nothing seemed familiar, so he kept close to his friend. At the other side, across from where the flashlight fluttered, Trenton showed him where he had dug under the fence. He motioned for Justin to slip under; then he followed behind. Once inside the cemetery, they uncovered a bag of flour that Trenton had planted there that afternoon.

He checked his watch.

It was eleven-fifty-three.

"What time is it?" Justin asked.

"We'll make it if we hurry." Trenton looked away to the flashlight, then back again. "Take off your shirt."

It was cold, but not cold enough for the goose bumps that were marching over him like an army of ants. Or cold enough for the uncontrollable chill that shook his body the way a playful puppy shakes a rag. But he shivered just the same. He shivered, and felt embarrassed because he knew it was fear that was shaking his body. What if

Joseph Little didn't think it was such a funny prank? What if the old man recognized him and told his aunt and his uncle what he had done? Uncle Wade would beat him; he knew Uncle Wade would beat him.

His shirt was off.

Trenton was smearing him with the white flour, rubbing it deep into the roots of his hair until he was gray like the color of the moon-shadows, rubbing powder into every pore, every crevice of his skin until he was ghost-pale. It felt good. And he began to warm up a little, began to lose some of the fear that had sat at the pit of his stomach.

"How does it look?" he whispered.

Trenton backed away a step. "Great."

Justin giggled. *The time of your life.*

"Now, take off your shoes and socks and your pants."

"My pants? Why do I have to take off my pants?"

"You wanna be a ghost, don't you?"

"Yeah."

They were both whispering now, careful not to let the excitement rise above the sounds of the evening. Trenton glanced nervously over his shoulder at the flashlight, which was still there, still waiting.

"Ever hear of a hundred-year-old ghost dressed in new Levis?"

"No, but . . ."

"He'll know it isn't real if you've got your pants on."

"You never said anything about—"

"Shhh." Trenton clamped a hand over the boy's mouth, and searched the area as if he had heard something sounding in the bushes, something of the night. Then he seemed to relax. His hand slipped away. He checked his watch once again.

"What time is it?" Justin asked.

"We've got three minutes."

"Then it'll be midnight?"

"Yeah." Trenton reached out and unsnapped the boy's pants. "We've got to hurry."

"Okay." Justin pushed the unwanted hand away. If it had to be done, he'd do it himself. And he wondered what he was doing there. And he wished he had the courage to turn around, to head back home, back to his warm room, back to the bed next to Kiel where he would feel a hundred times safer. But like an accidental spark touched to dry, hungry grass, the midnight prank was too-quickly getting out of hand. And he felt himself being swept along in the haste. The spark was sailing on the wind, touching earth all around him, and suddenly it was too late to even think of scampering back home where this was faraway and that was safe and warm.

He slipped off his jeans, left on his shorts.

"Those too," Trenton insisted.

"They're white. He won't even notice them."

His friend—was he a friend? Justin began to wonder if Kiel had been right all along, if Trenton was someone to avoid—let out an exasperated sigh, then tugged at the cotton briefs without trying to debate the issue.

"Okay—okay."

The shorts came off. Justin shivered again, hugged himself with both arms, and knew he wasn't nearly as cold as he was frightened and embarrassed. And he thought he was beginning to feel the heat of the grass fire licking the cold air around him.

"Hurry up," his friend said.

"I am."

Flour was hastily splashed and flung and painted over him, sending fine, white puffs of powdered wheat ballooning into the air, whitewashing the gray moonlight. He coughed twice, into his hand. Quiet coughs. Ghostly coughs.

When they were finished, and he stood for a breath beneath the grayness of the moonlight, Trenton backed away, looked him over, and smiled that twisted, never-satiated smile.

"Well?"

"Fucking fantastic!"

Justin gazed down at himself, down at his paleness, tinted slight by the moon's gray. Bloodless flesh, touched and turned by time, by death. He wiggled his toes, just to convince himself that they belonged to no one else. With the slightest effort, he could imagine himself transparent, vaporous. It *was* fantastic, wasn't it? Fucking fantastic!

"No time for flashing," Trenton said.

He grinned, still admiring the white-flesh of himself. "I'm a ghost, Trent. Like the chalky-white whispers that haunt the stairwells of old houses. Like the headless horseman under moonlight." He giggled softly, his fear having taken a back seat to his wonderment, his embarrassment having been pushed out of his mind.

"It looks good."

"It does, doesn't it? It looks good."

A puff of wind escaped from somewhere else, slipping over the crest of the hill and whistling cool against their faces. Whiffs of flour blew aura-like around him. And he realized he no longer felt chilled.

"Let's do it."

Trenton led the way. Softly, along the outer edges of the cemetery, sliding tender hands over the raspy metal of the cyclone fence. Noiselessly. Breathlessly. Until they had worked their way to the top of the hill and were looking down a gentle slope at the beam of light which was Joseph Little waiting in vigil.

"I almost believed," his friend said as they paused before the final descent. "In the shadows of dusk, when the old man told me about his boy-ghost, I almost believed."

"You don't think it's true, do you?"

"Naw."

"But maybe?"

Trenton smiled with yellow teeth. "If you had been there, sitting on the cut of stone, all white and grinning, I would have believed every word the old man spat."

"But it's not really true?"

"Ghosts? No way."

Two minutes past midnight, past the witching hour. And Joseph Little was still there, still waiting for the ghost of Cardew James Mantooth to perch itself upon the gravestone and smile a century-old smile.

"This is it," Trenton said.

Justin nodded.

"You remember everything?"

"What's to remember?"

With soft, stealthy cat paws they edged their way down the cemetery hillside, over and around hundred-year-old grave-markers, some groomed as recently as a week before, some haggard with weeds of timeless neglect. Carefully. Patiently. Without a single breath of speech, for they were beyond words now.

The beam that was Joseph Little never shifted, never stuttered before casting its curious light in their direction.

The old man never sensed their presence.

They crouched against the back of the gravestone.

Cold, gray stone.

White-gray like Justin's powdered flesh.

Trenton flashed a yellow smile and nodded.

And the moment had arrived. The moment when it would all come to pass, when he would either back away to swallow the fear that quivered and stuck in his throat, or . . .

. . . he would become the ghost of Cardew James Mantooth.

The moment of truth.

Joseph Little cleared his throat on the other side of the stone. His flashlight wavered in the night air, then returned its attention to the book held in the old man's lap.

Justin looked to Trenton, looked for something in his eyes, something offered up like honey and lemon to make it go down easier. But there was nothing there, nothing beyond the hungry glimmer of anticipation.

Do it!

Now or never!

With a prayerful crossing of fingers, he hopped, soft-landing atop the cold slab, crossing one leg over the other the way Trenton had told him he should. Then he smiled, the widest, most conceited smile he could muster, the way Trenton had told him he should.

From the old man's lap, a book slipped.

From the old man's face, astonishment.

The flashlight fell and arched away,

strewing its beam like ice shards among the weeds, against the corners of nearby grave-markers.

"Cardew?" Joseph Little slowly came to his feet. "Cardew James Mantooth?"

Justin cocked his head.

"You've come back?" Deliverance touched his face; like the tender hand of an angel, it eased the old man's furrowed features, softened the lifetime of sadness that had cut deep into his flesh. "I knew you would. I knew a full-mooned night would bring you back again."

Justin remembered. "Smallpox," he said, the way Trenton had told him.

"Smallpox," the old man repeated, his face sliding into a distant serenity. His eyes sparkled, then suddenly fell empty. He grabbed for his left arm. "All the children . . ."

He stiffened,

and swallowed a breath,

and the blood fell away from his cheeks.

Wade hadn't been lying flaccid and inco-herent on the kitchen floor as she had expected. He hadn't been lying on the kitchen floor or in the living room or anywhere else in the house for that matter. So Faye Richardson dismissed the noise she had heard as nothing more than nerves, nothing more than anticipation; and she sat at the kitchen table, sipping a cup of coffee.

It was five minutes after midnight.

There were fantasies floating in her head, swimming in the caffeine she had consumed, sipping freely from the stimulant, spiriting forth the annoyance which was building from within. It was a simple matter to imagine her husband spread-eagled over the rack, slowly sweating the beer from his pores as each socket inched a breath closer to that godawful *popping* sound. She didn't smile at the vision, but it was there just the same, hiding behind her eyes as she wondered if this time would be the final straw.

She sipped the last of her coffee.

The cup trembled lightly against its saucer.

In a few more years, she'd be doing this same thing for the boys—sitting up late, waiting and wondering, ready to ring their necks as soon as they wandered in giggling from a late-night double date. Long lonely nights. Too many cups of coffee. Too much time to worry and wonder. Just like tonight. Like father, like sons.

In a few more years.

But for now, the boys were more blessing than burden.

Then suddenly, the way a memory of something forgotten sometimes appears out of nowhere, a mild chill wound its way up her spine. She shivered and clasped the

collar of her robe tighter around her neck.
But it hadn't been a cold shiver. It was
something more than that, something like
the breath of an ill wind which brushes
against the nape of a naked neck and
stands the hair on end. An uneasy feeling.
A whispered warning, vague and teasing.
Something more than just the eerie hush of
the house.

Check the boys, is what she thought it
meant, though she felt it was an odd
thought. And just like that, she supposed,
almost subconsciously in fact, she was em-
bracing motherhood and one of its little
intuitions. *Check the boys.* She had often
wondered if there was something instinctual inside her that would automatically
take over and give some direction to her
mothering instincts, and now she knew.

She slid her coffee cup away from her.

The hallway light was dim, a single bulb,
sixty watt.

Her steps were fur-soft, hesitant,
debating. And she promised herself just a
quick look, then she'd wander back to bed
and try to sleep without granting Wade the
pleasure of any further worry. He'd come
stumbling home when he came stumbling
home.

Noiselessly, she turned the doorknob.

A shaft of light cut through the darkness.

She heard a great breath slurped from the
bedroom air, a single breath swallowed then

held . . . held . . . held . . . and released again.
Soft. Slowly rhythmic. A single breath.
And a strange, impossible thought
scampered through her mind before she
reached for the light switch.

A spurt of something wondrous had
rushed through his veins when Joseph
Little had first laid eyes on the resurrected
boy-ghost. The book had slipped from his
hands with little notice. The flashlight had
rolled away. And he had slowly risen to his
feet.

Something wondrous.

But as the ghost of Cardew James Mantooth smiled and whispered that magic
word—*smallpox*—everything suddenly
changed. A tingling numbness wormed its
way up his left arm, then a sharp pain cut
through the musculature, and he clutched
at the pain, trying to choke it off before it
made its way further up his arm. He could
only think of the children then, of the
children who had died over a hundred years
before from the fever and vomiting and
pustular eruptions that were the curse of
smallpox.

He wanted to cry.

He wanted to laugh.

Cardew James Mantooth had returned,
white and fragile and grinning.

He knew the boy-ghost would return. He
had always known.

But before he could reach to touch the boy, before he could lay his hands on something from the other side of death, every muscle of his body embraced him and slowly began to constrict. His breath was taken from him. His strength was suddenly made weak. And he couldn't help wondering if someday, a hundred years from then, if he would be sitting atop his own gravestone, grinning yellow-white teeth, and whispering his own words . . .

heart attack

The old man had looked at him, caught his eyes with the pleading sigh of his own, and Justin had turned cold, cold and fixed and already regretful.

"All the children," the man said, clutching at his own arm. Then his mouth had opened wider, his eyes wider still; and his body grew rigid. Joseph Little was going to reach out to him; Justin could sense the will of the old man's hands, they wanted to touch him. But before the effort could be made, the old man turned white—flour white like Justin—and collapsed to his knees before tumbling over in a cloud of moon-gray dust.

"Trent," Justin heard himself whisper then.

Every midnight imagining—the voice of *The Shadow* which he had heard once on a radio replay, the persisting discolored

bodies of the dead that a friend had once
described after sneaking into *Night of The
Living Dead*, and maybe worst of all, the
chicken blood tainted by the light of
mercury lamps late at night when his father
had once gone on a stupored rage and
chopped the heads off thirty-two of their
egg-laying hens—every wicked image came
back to play in his mind at that moment.

"Trent . . ."

"Shhh."

"There's something wrong." Never
letting his eyes stray from the old man's
resting body, he reached thoughtlessly to
where Trenton was hiding behind the stone
and touched the boy on the shoulder. "He's
not moving," he said. "Joseph Little's not
moving."

And his friend came out of hiding.

And they stood over the dead man,
Justin wondering why the man's eyes were
still staring off into the moon-lit heavens,
wondering—no, praying—that this man he
had hardly known, this Joseph Little, had a
bit of wickedness in his soul, that he was
only playing along, that he had known all
along of the prank and was simply repaying
the impishness.

Trenton nudged the man's arm with one
foot.

"Is he?"

"Dead."

"But . . ."

"You killed him," Trenton said with a voice that acquitted himself.

Justin denied it, his head slowly swaying from side to side in disbelief even as Trenton's words echoed endlessly inside him. *Dead. You killed him.* "I didn't mean it," he heard himself say.

"Doesn't matter, you killed him."

"But it was your idea."

"It was your deed."

"I didn't mean it."

It was your deed
  your deed
    your deed.

They caught eyes, one last time, Trenton's face shadowed only partially from the moon. His yellow smile was buried beneath thick, silent lips. His eyes quickly looked away.

"What do we do?" Justin asked.

"There isn't anything to do."

"Are you sure? Are you really sure he's dead?"

"Touch him," Trenton said with a narrow crack of a smile. "See if he's turned cold. They turn cold when they're dead, all the heat goes out of 'em, like the soul was the only thing keeping 'em warm in the first place. I touched a dead jack rabbit once, not more than a minute or two after old lady Pritchard ran over the damn thing. Touched its naked belly. It felt shivery, like thick melting ice cream gurgling on the other side of a sandwich bag."

Justin's stomach rolled.

"He's dead," Trenton said again.

"Then what do we do?"

"Nothing."

"Just leave him? You mean we should just leave him here, dead and cold and all alone until someone stumbles over his bones some week?"

"If we're lucky, no one will find him."

"But we'll know he's here."

"You'll know," Trenton said, shaking his head and backing away from Joseph Little, sprawled dead at their feet. "But not me. I've already forgotten."

"But we can't—"

"You're on your own, Justin. Do whatever you gotta do, but I'm scooting. Stay and bury the old fool if you'd like."

"Trent?"

"You killed him."

killed him
  killed him.

Before the words quit echoing in his mind, Justin found himself standing alone under the gray moonlight. Trenton's shadowy form having been swallowed by the inky sketches of tree surrounding the creek. And if it weren't for his nakedness, he would have followed close behind.

Under a moon which seemed dull and depressing, he fumbled and stumbled his way around the outer edge of the cemetery, back to where he thought he had left his clothes to the ground. The night chill had returned, its cold breath stinging his flesh as he knelt in the dirt, tickling low-lying weeds in search of something warm to slip over his flour-dusted nakedness. He found his pants and one sock and both shoes, had to sit in the dirt while he dressed, and when finished, wasted not an "alligator one" before scampering homeward again.

The ghost of Joseph Little hitched a ride on his shoulder.

You killed me.

7

The bedroom light went on.

And it was true, just the way she had imagined it.

One bed alive with slow, rhythmic breathing, the other empty and lifeless.

"Kiel." He was sleeping on his side, with his back to her. The blankets were gathered at his waist, a formless mass. She touched his shoulder, jiggled it. "Wake up, Kiel."

He shifted. His eyes were crusted and heavy, his face soft with the innocence of sleep. Like Wade's when his sleep was deep and restful.

"Kiel."

"What?" A one-eyed response.

"Where's your brother?"

He glanced wordlessly at the vacant bed next to his, gazing with an empty expression as if the connection between his eyes and his brain had been severed. But it was only sleep trying to keep him a little longer.

"Where's Justin?" she asked again.

"I don't know," he moaned, wiping the crust from his face.

And as she sat on the bed next to him, she felt a rise of uneasiness within her. There were whispers in her mind, quick flashes of dread which arrived uninvited. "He's only eleven," she said. Her throat was dry, her words parched. "It's past midnight, and your brother's only eleven years old. The town's still a strange place for him."

Her nephew glanced again at the empty bed beside them. And she felt him tense; she saw his shoulders rounding as he pulled himself tighter into the fetal position.

"Kiel, please . . ."

"I don't know where he is."

Then the back door slammed.

They each held a short breath.

"Faye?" Wade's voice came rambling down the hallway—clownish, nearly operatic. "You here, Faye?"

She thought—for just an instant, because it was a fairy-tale thought—not to answer him, then thought better of it. She tapped the bedsheets at Kiel's legs, hoping her eyes wouldn't say too much, wouldn't tattle on the disappointment she was feeling. Wade was home safe, but where was her nephew? Then she practiced a smile. "It's your uncle," she said. "I'll be right back."

He was drunk and he knew he was drunk.
And he didn't give a damn as he latched
onto the refrigerator door with both arms.
He was wearing a red plaid flannel shirt
rolled up above the elbows. And he was
sweating.

"Wade, you promised."

She was a shadow standing at the edge of
the kitchen light, vague and changing. But
he recognized her voice. He'd know that
sound even in the thickest buzz.

"Promises, promises," he said through a
throat that was dying. He felt his grin
slowly sinking back into his cheeks then.
There was more, there was something more
to what he was going to say, but it had
stepped-out on him and he had to take a
minute to find it again. And when he did, he
laughed. "My fingers were crossed," he
said.

"Oh, that's wonderful."

"I thought so."

"Cross your fingers and anything goes, is
that it?"

"You're just angry."

The shadow-voice sighed and said,
"Justin's missing."

"Justin?"

"Your nephew."

"But I did," he answered, unconscious to
what she was saying. "I had them crossed

—my fingers." He tried to make them cross again so he could show her, so she could see that it hadn't really been a promise at all. But they wouldn't do it.

"Wade, he's outside somewhere." She started to cry.

"No, don't do that." He touched a finger to his lips. "No more, I won't drink no more. Just don't start bawling on me."

But her sobbing didn't stop; and when he reached for her, his legs wobbled and gave out from beneath him. He slid off the refrigerator door, slid like something wet and spineless and out of water, and splattered against the floor with a slap.

Then the kitchen door flew open to the moon-lit night.

And something small stumbled, white-faced and two-legged, into the room. It stood in the open doorway, unbreathing and silent for a moment.

And Faye's crying stopped.

"Where have you been?"

"Outside."

"Do you have any idea how worried I've been?"

It wasn't supposed to be there—this shadowy-white thing standing in their kitchen. Wade sat up on his haunches, an almost acrobatic manuever. And he was trying through his drunkenness to understand what it was that had so suddenly burst through the kitchen door. But he couldn't understand, and he felt an uneasy fear settle over him, and he slid clumsily across the no-wax linoleum until he was propped against the side of the dining room hutch. Over the years, the cabinet had become a catch-all for miscellaneous odds and ends. But there was something in particular he was looking for as he opened the door.

"Never again," Faye was saying.

The shadowy-white thing had turned silent.

Wade's hand touched cold metal. It was a .22 pistol his father had given him on his fifteenth birthday. A Baretta that he used mostly for target practice, occasionally for blowing the tail off a too-trusting squirrel. It was the only gun left in the house, the only gun Faye would allow him to keep after they had married. He'd given away a *Remington* 12 gauge shotgun, and sold another pistol, a colt *Python* 357 Magnum. But the .22 stayed or it would be the shortest marriage in history.

He grabbed the gun by its barrel.

"For God's sake, you're only eleven years old."

The white thing remained in the doorway, swaying nervously from side-to-side, like a caged animal. Waiting. That's what it was doing—just waiting, like an animal looking for the crack of an opening before attacking.

Faye's voice had softened. "It's getting late," she said. "We're both tired, and I know you're cold. I can see your goose bumps from here. We'll finish this discussion in the morning."

His trembling hands managed to get the gun turned around.

"You better go to bed."

The whiteness took a step away from the doorway.

Wade cocked the pistol.

"Watch out," he screamed, trying to take aim at the moving form before it could pounce.

Someone yelled, "No!"

A hollow shot echoed.

A splinter of molding from above the door drifted to the floor.

He had tried to go back to sleep, as if his brother's absence was something that could be easier dealt with in his dreams. But sleep wouldn't come. And when he heard the rise of voices in the kitchen, Kiel finally dragged himself out from under the blankets and made his way down the hall.

"You better go to bed," his aunt was saying.

His brother was standing in the doorway, head hanging low. His shirt was missing. His chest and face and hair were all bleached a powder-white.

Then he heard a click.

When he turned to the sound, he saw his uncle leaning against the china cabinet, pointing a gun at Justin. His uncle's hands were trembling as he tried to take aim. Then the man shouted, "Watch out!"

And Kiel screamed, "No!"

And the gun fired.

And when Kiel looked back to his brother, Justin was lying motionless on the floor.

"My God, Wade!"

A sliver of wood fluttered toward the floor, splintered from where the slug had hit above the door. Then Justin began to cry.

"It was going to attack," his uncle mumbled.

"That's your nephew for God's sake!"

The gun slipped from hand-to-floor.

"Your nephew!"

"I didn't know." Then his uncle began to cry, and it was the first time Kiel had ever seen a man cry. He had always believed a man was dry, that a man's tears were lost to boyhood. Pass from boyhood to manhood and certain things were automatically lost in transit. That's why his father had never laughed, nor ever cried. A boy left behind his laughter when he became a man, left behind that reflexive giggle that erupted at a Don Martin strip in *Mad Magazine*. And he left behind his tears. He passed beyond boyhood and left it all behind.

"I'm sorry," his uncle said, burying face in hands.

Aunt Faye fell silent. Then she went to Justin and swooped him into her arms, cradling him like a baby for the longest time, until he finally began to settle down and his tears were dry again.

It was another ten minutes before they were herded like cattle back down the hall to their rooms to try and recapture a sleep that would be nearly impossible in coming. Uncle Wade was still jelly-spined and sobbing in the corner, only a foot away from the china cabinet, where Kiel watched his aunt replace the gun.

"He cried," Kiel said.

The bedroom light was off. But there was the glow of the full moon seeping through the curtains, coloring the room in shadowy-gray, a chalkboard gray. Justin had never bothered to wash the whiteness from his face, had simply slipped off his pants instead, and climbed into bed. And all of him had been powdered white, from head to toe, white as a bloodless ghost.

"I've never seen a man cry before." Through the darkness, under the gray tint of moonlight, Kiel could see his brother's white hair peeking above the blankets. He felt uncomfortably distant from his brother then, farther apart than this bed to that bed, as far apart as stranger to stranger.

"Where did you go?"

"Outside," he answered, a pouting answer.

"But where?"

A long, thoughtful silence.

"Justin?" *Go easy.* There were no secrets in brotherhood, but the truth, like a kitten caught in branches too high, caught a notch above where its trust ran out, sometimes resisted. *Go easy.*

"The cemetery." His brother rolled over to face him. His eyes were dark, hollow places—empty sockets—surrounded by streaks of skull-white. "Trenton and me."

"I told you he was trouble."

"It was only supposed to be a prank, that's all. Just a midnight scare."

"You're white, all painted white."

"I was supposed to be the ghost," Justin whispered with soft, moist words—clear as a hoot owl on a soundless, star-littered night. "Cardew James Mantooth, the ghost of a dead boy."

"And?"

"And Joseph Little believed."

He went back to explain, back to retell how Trenton had floured him all white like pie crust dough, and how he hopped up on the gravestone like Trenton had said he should, and how he smiled like Trenton said he should, and then . . . how old Joseph Little had swallowed his gums or some other godawful thing and had fallen over dead, looking whiter than the white flour smeared all over Justin's body.

"Really? He was really dead?"

"Trent gave him a kick."

"A good one?"

"Good enough."

"And?"

"He was dead." Justin's voice trailed off.

"A mishap," Kiel said. "That's all, just a mishap. It could have happened to anyone."

"I scared him to death."

"You can't scare a man to death. No more than you can bring the dead back to life. That's just comic book stuff."

"I don't think so."

"Believe me," Kiel insisted, as much of a pleading as not. Because his brother was wavering, he was standing hip-deep in the middle of Tyler's Creek suddenly uncertain if he could make it all the way across. "It wasn't your fault."

"We left him there," Justin said then. "Left him on the ground, cold and dead and all alone like a jack rabbit at the side of the road for the buzzards to pick apart." His voice was cold and dead and all alone as he spoke. "You think the buzzards will pick him apart?"

"Someone will find him."

"It's a lonely place."

"Someone will visit. Someone will make a special trip there to leave flowers at the grave of a friend or a relative or maybe just a memory. And they'll find him."

"There's weeds."

"They'll find him!" Kiel's teeth clenched. *And then, maybe they wouldn't.* Maybe instead, the old man's body would do something unholy. A little after-death tap dancing, a little midnight jaunt to look in on the inspiration for his last glorious vision. "They'll find him and the buzzards won't bother him. Human flesh stinks. Animals hate it, they won't touch it. Honest."

"I should tell someone."

"You already told me."

"An adult."

"You can't do that." Kiel was sitting up now, sitting with his back against the wall, glancing on occasion through the crack in the curtains and wondering what it was really like to be lying dead in a faraway cemetery where no one knew you were. Would dead Joseph Little care? Would it matter to him that he was all alone in his death? Would he be watching them now, waiting to damn them if they didn't tell someone about his death? "We can't tell. They'll send us away."

"Together? It wouldn't be so bad if they sent us away together."

"Maybe, maybe not."

Justin sighed. "Trenton knows."

"He won't tell."

"He said he'd blame it on me if I told anyone."

"Jeeze, he won't say anything, I tell ya."

"And Aunt Faye," Justin added. "I'm supposed to explain."

"We'll make up a story."

"Something believable. Something she won't question. She's got to believe."

"We'll say it was Trenton's idea."

"But—"

"Quiet for a minute. It's a good tale. She'll believe, and I'm telling you, Trenton won't say a word." Kiel thought a moment, thought long enough to straighten it all out in his mind. "We'll tell her you were digging in a chalk mound, down by the creek. That you and Trenton were searching for something hidden, some lost treasure from years and years ago. Before the town ever existed."

"That's dumb."

"Think about it, Justin. It's not so dumb if she believes you're an ignorant little kid who wouldn't know any better. If she thinks you really believed what Trenton told you and met him there because eleven year old kids only have half-a-brain anyway, well . . . what can she say?"

"But at night?"

"Sure. You wouldn't want to go digging up treasure under the eye of the sun, with the world looking over your shoulder."

A thoughtful quiet came.

Justin wrestled uncomfortably under the blankets, covering himself with their feeble sense of security; and though it would surely be a sleepless night, his white form settled deeper into the bed.

In the next bed, Kiel remained leaning against the wall, absently wrapping and un-wrapping his fingers in the coolness of his bedsheets, glancing with a casual sense of wonder at the lumpy blankets which were his brother. A single year younger, he was. Four seasons. A naked fall. A cold winter. And a few short months separated them, kept their births from being a singular event, kept them from being twinned.

There was nothing really special about being twins, nothing that they didn't already have. Whisper a word in his brother's ear and Kiel would feel the breath against his own, would feel the splashing cochlea fluid—something he'd learned about in school—alert his nerve endings, and he would hear the whisper as if it were his own. Thinly nick his brother's palm with the slip of a pocket knife and . . .

and . . .

Kiel sighed.

He would gladly accept his brother's pain.

He would gladly hear his brother's words, gladly feel his brother's pain, but he wasn't his brother. And they *weren't* twins. And he felt his brother so faintly slipping away from him. And the feeling left him lonely.

Nicholas sat up in bed, gazing open-mouthed at the streaks of shadowy-gray unevenly dividing the strange room. And as he often did at the beginning of a painting, he spent a moment or two trying to puzzle together some sort of sense from the empti-ness of the room's canvas.

He was sitting in a bed . . .

. . . *standing in the spotlight* . . .

. . . awakening to a place unfamiliar, eyes met with sights fresh from the future, nose tweaked with *somewhere-new* fragrances. As if he'd just been hatched, passed from the womb of an eggshell into a world too big, too full of lights and darks, softs and hards, sweets and sours.

He rubbed his eyes with hands still young and fragile.

A thin sheen of sweat waxed his forehead, bubbled at his upper lip.

In the bed next to him, he could see the outline of the brother growing larger with each new breath, smaller with each exhala-tion. A column of gray window light fell across the boy's face, holding his eyes shut, keeping them from watching as Nicholas climbed out from under the blankets.

nightmare-like

Because that's what had brought him out of his sleep—out of the darkness, into the spotlight—a nightmare. A laughing vision of a boy sitting ghost-pale upon the slab of a gravestone. A wicked little smile twisting the boy's face. Chiseled shallow in the stone the name: CARDEW JAMES MANTOOTH. In the dirt, at the base of the gravemarker, a man with bulging eyes, his mouth held open wide, one hand grasping his left arm.

portrait of a nightmare

And behind his eyes, Nicholas felt the searing pain of the vision still taking form: a flashlight, a book, a moon-flooded night. Rising and ebbing inside his head. Nightmare clear, stick-figure vague. Rising and ebbing.

And he had to let it out.

Sometimes there's things that he doesn't want to have to look at. You know, just scary things. And well, I guess, it's just easier if I look for him. Things don't scare me like they scare him. Especially if I can draw them, that takes away all their power.

The scariest thing I ever drew was a picture of the barn.

Once I drew a portrait of Matt. But the pretender tore it up. I think it was because it scared him the way the barn scares me. He was looking at himself, thinking it was someone else, but all the time knowing better. That's why he *tore it up.*

I don't think he *even knew that I drew it. I think* he *thought that he was the one.*

NICHOLAS
seven years old

8

It was ten o'clock going on noon by the time Kiel first opened his eyes the next day. Back home it would have been first recess. There would have been a chorus of slamming books. Caroline Bartley would giggle —she giggled at everything. And in a matter of seconds a baseball game would rise ghost-like out of the sandlot where it had been put to rest two hours before and would be put aside again in another fifteen minutes. But in Winter Creek Mills, it was more simply a time to be rolling out of bed. The mornings came later here. And life seemed much lazier.

The room was still a stranger. Like the cold hand of someone brought in from winter, it chilled and felt lonely and joyless. Even after a week of waking to its symmetry—its identical beds, identical nightstands, identical lamps—Kiel had to scrub the dreams from his eyes and remember where he was before he could fall back against his bedsheets again and breathe his first morning breath.

Justin was still asleep in the bed next to him, still powdered white, still wrapped protectively within his blankets. Something had softened the usual morning glare. A dark sun was shining outside, blocked now and then by a slow-moving cloud, a non-threatening puff of gray casually drifting through. And oddly enough, a brush of sunlight had stained the bedroom wall, had charcoaled a dull, hideous portrait of . . .

Kiel sat up again.

On the wall, next to the door which led to the bathroom, in a space that had been a lifetime blue the night before, there was a mural, penciled, crayoned, scratched into the sheetrock. Exactly the way Kiel had imagined it to be. Tall wisps of grass growing untamed at the base of the headstone, cold and gray. CARDEW JAMES MANTOOTH, crudely lettered across the rectangular block. And sitting atop it all, with a twisted, self-confident grin, white and naked, was his brother. Bigger than life itself. Etched in permanance like a quickly scrawled name in setting cement, for everyone to see, for everyone to know.

Was it me? he wondered. Sleep painting in the dead of night? Squeezing the colors and shapes out of my head because they hurt too much?

Then his brother yawned, wide-mouthed and groaning.

"Justin?"

Another groan.

"Wake up, Justin. You've got to see this."

His brother, still drugged with sleep, rolled over for a one-eyed, can't-it-wait glance. Some of the white had been left to his pillow and there were dark, unrestful circles under his eyes.

With the nod of his head, Kiel pointed toward the wall. "Look." Then he watched as his brother's eyes came suddenly awake.

"Wasn't me," Justin said.

"Me, either."

His brother sat up and pushed himself back against the wall, absently shaking his head. He was near tears. His eyes had turned glistening, watery, polished; puddles were collecting, threatening to spill. "Not me," he said again.

"It was like that, wasn't it?" Kiel said. He had imagined it just that way, but seeing it come alive on the bedroom wall, seeing the shadowy-gray color of his brother's face and that wicked, enjoying smile that belonged to someone he didn't know . . .

"Wasn't it?"

Justin nodded.

"You don't suppose—"

"The ghost of Joseph Little?"

"Like the ghost of Cardew James Mantooth," Kiel said. "Come to say why he died."

"Scared beyond death."

They paused to think on that, shivers and goose bumps skittering up their bodies. The hand of a ghost had sketched, shaped, splashed the color across their bedroom wall, had brought the dead scene back to life again. Right there, right in their room, in the dark of night as they slept within the reach of a see-through arm.

"We've got to hide it," Kiel said.

One room away, Faye was brushing her hair, forcing herself to face her own reflection in the mirror, wondering how many years had been taken from her the night before at the exact second of the gunshot. More than enough for one lifetime, she imagined.

"You tried to kill him," she said.

Wade was still coming awake. He yawned and whiped the stubborn sleepiness from his eyes. The room was oven hot. His sheets were heavy and damp with perspiration. His answer was something of a moan.

"You don't remember, do you?" She put aside her hair brush and watched him struggle to sit up in bed, as if it were a nearly unsurmountable chore. And she imagined it probably was a chore, as taxing on him the morning after as supporting himself had been the night before. There was something pathetically helpless about the sight, but she had already promised herself no compromises.

"Do you?" she repeated.

He shook his hanging head.

"I don't know what's got into you, Wade, but something's got to change. This marriage is hanging together by the barest of threads."

"What time is it?" His first words of the day, sandpapered and deep.

"And I don't think Kiel and Justin should have to be living here in fear. This is their home, Wade. This is the one place in the world where they should always feel safe." She tightened the sash of her bathrobe. "You nearly killed him last night."

"For crissakes, Faye." He fell back into his pillow, his hands dragging down his face over a muffled moan, his head shaking slowly from one side to the other. Then all the air went blowing out of him, whalelike. "Quit playing us off against each other and just make a choice, Faye."

"Huh?"

"Them against me, me against them. You can't have it all. You can't bring two strange kids home, give 'em the name Richardson and then expect everything to go merrily on its way. I want things to be the way they were, Faye. Just you and me."

"You can't be serious." She sat next to him on the bed, and he pulled away from her, turned his back and pulled his legs into his chest. His eyes had been tired and bloodshot, not full-awake yet. But she wondered now if something crimson were growing just beneath the pupils, something she'd never seen in him before.

"Just make a choice, them or me. Because if you don't, I'll make it for you and you won't like it, Faye. You won't like *my* decision, I promise you that."

"You won't like mine either." It just slipped out. Sad, whispered words that were supposed to remain thoughts. True as they might be—for she knew full well what her choice would be if she were cornered and forced to make one—the words were still supposed to be a secret.

There was the longest moment of silence then, when he seemed to quit breathing and the room seemed to close a little tighter on them. Then he rolled half way over, running a quick hand through his damp stringy hair, and catching eyes with her for the first time that morning. She thought she saw a wash of crimson disappearing from behind those eyes of his.

"Sorry," he said, whispering fatigue, both emotional and physical. "But I'm just not ready for parenthood, Faye. Being around those kids makes me nervous. I don't know what to say. I don't know how to act. And I hate feeling responsible for them. Christ, I can't even take care of you, how in the hell am I supposed to take care of them?"

"What are you so afraid of?"

"Nothing, I just want things the way they were."

"They're children, Wade."

"I know that." He fell back into his pillow again, in silent faraway thought. In that pose, he was a child himself, poking and probing, trying to stir a reaction in her, any reaction. Because after the small talk and the surface feelings, he was never really able to share anything more of himself. "Maybe if I moved out for a while . . ."

Faye pulled her hand away from his back, where she had been massaging and soothing him. "What is it, Wade? What's really bothering you?"

"Agnes has a spare room she's willing to rent."

"You know I can't send the boys away. You know that, don't you?" But he didn't. When she asked, he glanced over his shoulder at her and she could see he didn't understand. She could see the questioning in his eyes. *Why not? That's the way it was before, just you and me. It can be that way again, can't it? They'd be okay. A foster home doesn't have to be such a terrible place. They might even be happier? Isn't that possible?* He had it all rationalized there inside his head.

"Not forever," he said. "I won't be gone forever."

"They need a father."

"I know, but not me. I can't do it."

"Maybe if you gave it some time?"

"It won't work."

"And what about us?"

Us? His feet slipped from beneath the bedsheets. He rested—elbows on knees, head in hands—and sighed as if he were close to crying. But he didn't cry. His lips trembled, but he never cried, and never answered her, and he couldn't (or wouldn't) look at her.

"Wade?"

"I don't know," he said.

And suddenly she could no longer look at him. When she turned away, she suddenly found herself staring at the rows of shoes that lined the floor of her closet. Shoes for work and play, for dress and casual, for every imaginable occasion, except this one. What do you wear to a separation?

"You want a divorce?" she asked.

"I don't know."

"But you're sure about leaving for a while?"

"I think so."

"You *think* so?"

"Okay, I'm sure," he said, a quick rise of irritation entering his voice. "At least for a time. I don't know what else to do."

She thought to offer a few suggestions, a chosen obscenity or two that normally would have never entered her mind, but before she could share her sarcasm the conversation was interrupted by a disturbance rising out of the boys' bedroom. There was a high-pitched splintering squeal, followed by a breath of silence, then a dull thud which shook the floor and walls.

Faye was slow to react, as if she were waiting for an inevitable aftershock—a cry of pain, a scream for help. But as quickly as wall and floor between the bedrooms had thundered, they fell silent again.

"The kids," Faye said absently, and she was off the bed and hurrying down the hall.

Justin was still undressed, naked except for the powdery white that hadn't rubbed off on his bedsheets during the night. He was kneeling at one end of an overturned dresser, fingers hooked beneath the simulated wood grain. Next to him, dressed in pajamas, Kiel was trying to help lift the dresser back to its upright position.

She stopped and wondered for a moment what it was they were doing.

Wade crowded in behind her, peering over her shoulder.

Then the mural stepped out from the wall, grotesque and intruding. A boy with a twisted grin sitting atop a gravestone. A boy with Justin's straight blond hair and dark brown eyes. CARDEW JAMES MANTOOTH chiseled not only into the stone, but into the wall as well.

"What in God's name?" she said without thinking.

And the boys realized for the first time that they had been joined by their aunt and uncle. Justin released his grip and backed away from the dresser, an expression of surprise catching his face. Kiel tried to practice a smile, but it was a faltering attempt.

"It fell over," Justin said.

Wade's hot breath blew against the nape of Faye's neck. She knew what he was thinking and looked back to read his eyes. *They're yours, your nephews. I told you it wasn't going to work. Now do you believe me?*

"What's with the painting on the wall?" Wade asked.

The boys exchanged glances, as if passing a silent message from one to the other. But neither one said a word. Kiel finally stepped away from the dresser and went to stand next to his brother, half a room away from where their uncle was growing larger.

Wade squeezed by Faye.

She grabbed him by the arm. "What are you going to do?"

He was already slipping off his belt. "They're old enough to know better than that," he said.

"No, you can't, Wade."

"Are you making your choice now? They stay, I go?"

"They didn't do it, Wade."

"The hell they didn't."

"Just look at it. That's not their work. Look at it! *I* can't draw that well. Look at the boy's twisted face, the haunting weeds growing up the side of the gravestone. It's professional. They didn't do it." Then she felt a shiver run up her body, for at that very second she realized what the alternative must be, the possibility that a stranger had entered their house.

"I don't believe you just said that."

"Just look at it."

"I don't give a damn what it looks like. *You* look at it. There were only two kids in this room last night. No one else. No one slipping in through the window with a pen in each hand, just so he could brighten up our gloomy walls with a little homemade graffiti. What the hell's the matter with you, Faye?"

She wouldn't let go of his arm. "They didn't do it."

"Fine." He buckled his belt. "At least you've made your choice. I can live with that." Then he pulled away from her. "I hope you can."

"Wade, don't be ridiculous . . ."

But he was already out of the room,

storming heavy-footed down the hall, and slamming their bedroom door with a vengeance.

Momentarily Faye felt held in place—uncertain if she should chase after her husband or stay behind and try to explain things to the boys. Finally, she smiled uneasily, almost apologetically, then hurried down the hall after her husband's footsteps. "Wade?"

Kiel looked at his brother, standing white and naked next to him, then glanced back at the painting on the wall. "The ghost of Joseph Little."

Justin nodded, and mouthed in silent agreement. *The ghost of Joseph Little.*

In the summer of 1968, one year after her husband had been swallowed by Lake Shasta, Molly Pritchard made arrangements for a cemetery plot for her missing husband. She had saved her money for a full year, hoping she would never have to use it, hoping that somehow God would surprise her one day and her husband would come walking through the front door, all flesh and blood and just as jolly as ever. But as the days mounted, her hope slowly faded and at the end of the year she conceded her loss.

It was then that she collected those things she knew her husband valued most —an old bowling trophy; his collection of

antique tools, all wood-handled and steel;
an old Winchester rifle that he had
mounted over the fireplace mantle; and his
favorite fishing pole—and added his only
suit, a blue pin-striped double-breasted
outfit which he hadn't worn in a quarter of
a century, and she had the whole collection
of memories buried in a casket at the town
cemetery. Headstone and all. NATHAN-
IEL "NED" PRITCHARD. A LOVING
HUSBAND WHO LEFT MUCH TOO
SOON.

And ever since that hot summer day so
long ago, when she had first watched that
$800, satin-lined casket lowered into the
earth, Molly Pritchard had faithfully
returned once a week to pay her respects
and leave a small bouquet of flowers at the
foot of her husband's grave.

So it was on this Friday.

Even though she rarely received a library
patron on a Friday afternoon, Molly
Pritchard waited responsibly for five
o'clock when the library hours ended,
before locking up and making her way
through town toward the cemetery. It was
a cool day, slightly overcast, though rain-
less. The townspeople usually sitting out
front of the market gabbing about life and
death and taxes, had already gone home for
the day. The street was quiet enough to
hear the soft, peaceful creeksong rising
from around the bend.

At the end of the path, where the creek turned away and waved a last goodbye, Molly Pritchard stopped to pick wild flowers. She always managed to find color here—purples and yellows, reds and oranges, greens, always greens. And as she picked the fragile flowers, her imagination placed them together in a free-flowing design for her next quilt.

By the time she had arrived at the cemetery, one hand full of flowers, the other shading her eyes from a sun that had dipped below the line of thin clouds, it was near six o'clock. She had long ago forgotten that her husband's casket was bodiless, had long ago pushed that sadness out of her mind. So when she stood before the gravestone, she still saw her husband's face smiling up from the ground, wishing her a good day and expressing appreciation for her visit.

"It's been cool, Ned. Not like the old spring days when summer was always in a rush to arrive early."

She placed the bouquet in the grass.

"The library's growing," she said. "Just received two more Louis L'Amour novels. You always liked his westerns."

Her dress, a thin flowery polyester knit with ruffled jabot (her own special touch) ballooned in a sudden breezy gust. And she turned against the wind, holding a hand protectively over her eyes until the puff had died away. And when her eyes opened again, she caught sight of a form—something man-sized and motionless—lying in the dirt only a few feet from her husband's resting place.

"Ned?" She called his name absently, not even realizing it was on her lips. But in her mind, there was a strange glimmer of hope. Had he come back after all these years? Was this the day that God was going to surprise her?

She took a wobbly step forward, hand held to mouth as if holding back a grand welcoming that could hardly be contained.

"Ned?"

But as she drew closer, near enough to see the form was as still as death itself, she recognized the thin, graying hair and the face lined with a lifetime of tragedy. And she cried to think it wasn't the resurrection of her husband. And she cried to think that the lovely town of Winter Creek Mills had lost another from its dwindling populace.

She had tried to work away the day. Locking herself in her studio, Faye had busied herself putting the final touches to her current illustration and doing a couple of rough sketches for the next layout. But the effort had been a mindless run-through-the-motions with little enthusiasm and even less attention to detail. It was an effort meant simply to derail her concerns about Wade and the boys and how her life was suddenly turning itself upside-down.

Hours before, Wade had packed a suitcase and left.

The boys had dressed, then tried unsuccessfully to remove the mural from their wall, still unable to explain its overnight appearance.

Faye had locked herself in the studio.

And the day had begun to drag endlessly by.

It was half-past seven. The sun which had been in strange absence for most of the day, had stretched its golden muscles and yawned and opened its eyes for the first time only an hour or so before. And almost in harmony, Justin and Kiel had knocked on her studio door, cooing in tiny distant voices that their hunger had at last become more than they felt able to contend with. And she had felt another swell of guilt, even greater than the guilt which shook its finger at her for letting Wade escape so easily.

Now she was back in the studio.

Justin was taking a bath.

Kiel was again trying to exorcise the mural from the wall.

And the phone was ringing.

When she answered it, her heart held its breath for a beat . . . for two beats . . . while she listened for Wade's voice at the other end. But it wasn't Wade at all, and as Molly

Pritchard began to chat, Faye felt her
hopes sink unenthusiastically back into
place.

"It was dreadful," Molly was saying. "He
was lying in the dirt. All sprayed with dust,
his face smudged. And his eyes—they were
still open, still staring empty as if he were
daydreaming. Dreadful."

"Who? Who was lying in the dirt?"

"Why, Joseph Little," she said. "At the
cemetery. All sprawled out in front of a
gravestone like he was waiting to be
taken."

"Dead?"

"Heart attack, Doc Townsend said. The
man was still clutching his left arm. You
know, that's where the pain is when there's
a heart attack. Not in your chest like most
people think, but in your left arm. It
cripples your left arm."

"When . . ." Faye stuttered, tripping over
her own thoughts as she flashed back to the
mural that was still etched on the wall of
the boy's bedroom. "When did he die?"

"Last night sometime, I suppose."

"In the cemetery?"

"Just a stone or two from where Ned is
buried, rest his soul."

"By a gravemarker?"

"Of course."

"And the name on the stone? Do you remember the name on the stone?"

There was a thoughtful silence. "It was

an odd name," Molly Pritchard said. "From the early days of the cemetery. The names then—they were always as unusual as not. Never two alike it seems. Let me see, something like Carter, I believe."

"Cardew?"

"Yes, I believe that's it."

"Cardew James Mantooth?"

"Yes, that's the one. An odd one, isn't it?"

"Yes, odd," Faye answered, only partially aware of the comment. Her thoughts had already ventured away, had already turned to a vision of her nephew standing shirtless and white in the kitchen doorway at an hour well past midnight. And there was another vision, a vision someone had etched in the wall of the boys' bedroom, a vision with the gravestone of CARDEW JAMES MANTOOTH at its heart.

Molly Pritchard had talked excitedly for another ten or fifteen minutes before she had sensed Faye's wandering disinterest and had quickly signed off, eagerly moving on to Winter Creek Mills' next waiting ear. And Faye had sat back in her chair, questioning her own imagination before finally making her way down the hall to the boys' room. She lured Kiel away with the promise of a bowl of chocolate-chocolate chip ice cream. And then she sat at the end of his bed, waiting for his brother to finish up with his bath.

Justin came out of the bathroom, his hair damp and messed, his shirtless back still sprinkled with water, and his pajama bottoms sticking to his legs where he hadn't bothered to towel himself dry. And he stopped cold when he saw her waiting.

"Feeling better?" she asked with a mustered smile.

He nodded. It was the first time in two days that he hadn't been painted white with that thin layer of powder. *Ghost white.*

"You look better."

He sat at the foot of his own bed, half-heartedly drying his hair.

"I believe you still owe me an explanation."

"I don't know how it got there," he said.

"About last night."

"It was just supposed to be fun."

"Like tying tin cans to Mr. Aikens' cows?"

He appeared genuinely unknowing, his eyebrows quickly raised and lowered in question, and she wondered if Henry Aikens had mistaken someone else for one of her nephews. Trenton Maes came sprinting to mind.

"He said it was you—either you or your brother."

"Not me."

"He seemed fairly certain."

Justin lowered his head, finished drying his hair, then placed the towel across his lap. His fingers began nervously tying and untying, twisting and untwisting the damp cloth. And she knew he had pulled protectively away from her.

"Well, it's not that important. I expect Henry's cows will survive," she said, making an effort to sound free and easy and unconcerned. "But I'd still like to hear about last night. Where were you?"

An uneasy silence.

"Justin?"

"Just outside."

"After midnight?"

He shrugged—almost a surrendering of his shoulders—then fiddled again with the towel. "It was supposed to be a secret," he said.

Of course, she thought, quick enough to calm the anxiety that had settled over her after her conversation with Molly Pritchard. *Something boyishly clandestined. A dare to meet under the full moon and be whispered to about ghosts and rats and things that go bump in the night. An innocent, boyish flight of fancy. Of course!*

"Trenton said there was a treasure buried there, buried beneath a layer of chalk by the bank of the creek. He said there were gold coins and knives made of silver and shiny stones like diamonds—all buried there and waiting."

An innocent, boyish flight of fancy.

"But there wasn't anything there. Not like he said there was. No diamond treasure or coins made of gold, nothing of the sort."

"And you became white from digging in the chalk?"

He nodded, ashamed.

"And your shirt?"

"Lost," he said. "We didn't want our clothes to get covered with chalk, so we took them off. I couldn't find my shirt, or my socks."

Of course, she told herself again. Then the sight of the mural—the twisted smile, the headstone of Cardew James Mantooth, the body of Joseph Little—caught her eye again, and that moment when everything suddenly made sense, quickly disappeared back into the folds of a dying smile.

"The cemetery," she said. "You never went near the cemetery?"

"Never."

"But the mural on your bedroom wall?"

He shook his head and shrugged.

"There was an . . . accident there last night," she said. "At the cemetery. Joseph Little had a heart attack. Do you remember him? He was the elderly gentleman I pointed out to your brother that first day, the day I showed the two of you around Winter Creek Mills. Remember?"

"Yeah," he said quietly.

A tightness had taken her throat in its

hands. CARDEW JAMES MANTOOTH came too quickly back to mind. She wanted to believe her nephew, wanted to believe that he had simply been digging in a chalk mound down by the creek. But the mural? How could she explain away the mural?

"The name on the gravestone painted on your wall . . ."

"Mantooth?"

"He died next to the grave of Cardew James Mantooth," she said, searching for a reaction that never arrived. Her nephew's face remained fixed and cold, an emotionless sculptured mask. But she sensed it just the same, sensed the slightest tremble of discomfort. And it made her wonder all the more.

There was the longest, waiting silence.

"Well," she said finally, patting him on the knee. "Perhaps it's something we'll never really understand."

He relaxed, let his muscles visibly ease, took a heavy breath.

She stood to leave, knowing she'd probably never have the real truth, but wanting just the same to believe what he had told her. Even with the phantom mural on his bedroom wall, she couldn't imagine how Justin, eleven-year-old Justin, could have known anything about Joseph Little's passing.

"How about some ice cream?" she asked

"No thanks."

"It's chocolate-chocolate chip."

"I don't think so."

At the door, Faye stopped for a moment, turned back to her nephew, and said, "You know, I just thought of something. Maybe it was sleepwalking? Are you a sleepwalker —you or your brother? People can sometimes do bizarre things while they're walking in their sleep. Maybe that would explain the painting on the wall."

"Does a person know when he's sleep-walking?"

"I don't think so."

"Then I guess . . . maybe that's what happened."

She smiled. "Maybe."

They sat in the spotlight, in a circle:
    Albert, the one to keep the peace
    Matt, the angry one to keep them safe
    Scott, the careless one to make them
        laugh
      and Nicholas, the silent one, who drew
        and cried and felt alone
        . . . all called together by Albert,
        who knew each of them.

"He's slipping," Albert said. He was pacing the room, wall-to-wall, back and forth, nervously twisting a stub of chalk in his fingers. And as he spoke, he looked to each of the others to see if they understood what he was trying to say. "The pressure's

too much; it's getting too much for him.
He's going to crack."

"Crack a book . . . crack a smile . . . crack a
back . . . crackerjack," Scott chuckled. His
legs were crossed as he sat at the outskirts,
back against the darkness, eyes following
Albert back and forth. He was wearing a
pair of tan cut-offs and a tee-shirt with a
picture of a mouth with its tongue sticking
out.

Albert stopped next to him, sucked up a
lungful of air, and delivered a warning
glance. They were the same age, but as
different as hot and cold, black and white.
Scott, forever dimpled and laughing, at
times a joy, at other times a pain in the ass.
Albert, thoughtful and plodding, always
well under control, never careless about
anything he did. As different as night and
day.

"Crack down," Albert said.

Scott giggled.

"This isn't what I'd consider a humorous
matter. If *he* slips too far, and if *his* aunt or
his brother or someone else begins to notice
something *different* about him, then we're
in trouble. Big trouble. There's always the
chance that *he'll* say something wrong, or
worse yet, someone might notice one of us
talking out of his mouth. And if that
happens, we could all be exposed."

"Naked as jaybirds?" Scott asked
through a grin. "Flour white and naked and

sitting on gravestones under a full-mooned night?"

"That's not the kind of exposed I had in mind."

Matt had been lying near the center of the spotlight, propped up on one elbow, disinterested and bored, cleaning his fingernails with a pocket knife, eyes dreary and somewhere else. But he suddenly came out of his reverie. "What the hell does it matter? Who cares if we're found out or not? He's had his chance. If he can't handle it, that just leaves more time for the rest of us."

"It's not that simple, Matt."

"The hell it isn't."

"Hell's bells." Scott giggled again. "That's a hell of a note."

Albert ignored him, instead keeping his attention on Matt, who he knew would be the most difficult one to handle. "I don't think you realize what I'm talking about. If he stumbles, if he makes a mistake and they find out he's not well, then they'll start poking around in here. And sooner or later they'll find the rest of us."

"So who cares? I'm tired of always waiting for a turn anyway," Matt said. He sat up, forearms resting on his knees, eyebrows arched and furrowed, almost an exclamation point. "I'm tired of hiding."

"Hide and seek. Sneak a peek."

"Shut up," Matt warned. He pointed the

pocket knife at the younger boy, glared at him with cold, hard eyes. "Just keep your trap clamped."

"Will you both shut-up and listen? We're all a part of this, you know." Albert steepled his hands against his chin. He knew he was the only level-headed person there. And he wanted to keep things under control, wanted to make sure they each understood the potential problems that might face them all.

"Things are different between here and there. In here, each of us is a whole person. Out there, we're just bits and pieces of the *pretender.* There's nothing we can do to change that. But as long as we can keep it like that—us, a living secret in here, *him* out there, not knowing—then at least we'll be alive and breathing and . . ."

Albert paused for a moment, as much to catch their attention again as to catch his thoughts. " . . . but if someone finds out about *him,*" he said, looking from one to the other and back again, "then they'll think there's something wrong, and they'll start poking around in here until they find the rest of us, and when they do, when they find all of us in here cluttering up his insides, they aren't going to let go of us again until we're all standing at the edge of the light, and *he's* standing center stage. You understand that? He's going to have all the time then. All of it."

"Then we'd be . . ."

"Air pockets. Empty, meaningless air pockets."

"Not me," Matt said. "The hell with that shit. I know who I am."

"And I know who I am," Albert added.

. . . Nicholas had sat in the circle, sat and watched the mouths spouting out words his ears couldn't hear, wouldn't hear. And he had been lost in the flapping until it no longer seemed of interest, until Albert and Matt were carrying on a conversation between themselves, and Scott was grinning too big a grin. Bored then, he went to the painted wall which had been scrubbed and sandpapered and scrubbed again, but was still as alive as ever, and he began drawing between the bits and pieces of conversation which were meaningless buzzings in his ears . . .

"We have to watch him," Albert was saying. "We have to keep an eye on him, make sure he doesn't get into any more trouble."

"Make him a puppet?" Scott asked. "With our hands shoved up his ass, pumping his mouth? Here a smile, there a frown. Today a boy, tomorrow a clown?"

"Don't be stupid," Matt snapped. "We take his place, that's all. Just keep him off the spotlight, keep him in the darkness, sleeping away the hours, the days, the years."

"Rip Van Winkle him!"

Albert sighed and looked away in disgust. "You can't do that," he told them. "People will wonder. They'll hear Matt's language, and they'll wonder. They'll see Scott's laughter, and they'll wonder. And if they wonder just a little too much . . ."

"Then what?" Matt said. He was holding the tip of the pocket knife against his palm, slowly twisting it, watching it absently, as if anticipating the flow of redness. "Then what the hell are we supposed to do?"

"Nothing," Albert said flatly. "We do nothing."

"Nothing doing." Another chuckle.

"That's what we've been doing."

"But we're all aware now," Albert said. "If he begins to get into trouble, we can step in and help out. But only if it looks like he's getting himself into a bind. Step in too much, too soon, and eventually someone's going to notice."

"No more tying tin cans to the old man's cows?" Scott asked.

"No more."

"That old fart," Matt said. "He's got a big mouth."

"Just leave him alone."

"We could pay him a visit?"

"We don't need the trouble."

"Better yet, we could tie tin cans to nosy old Henry Aikens himself," Scott suggested, a grin pressing his dimples into his cheeks. "Tha-tha-that's all, Henry." He laughed.

At the door, still holding the knob in one hand, Kiel was listening.

Through the crack, he was watching.

He'd heard his brother's voice become the voice of others. A boy named Scott who laughed too much. Another, named Matt who laughed not enough. And Albert, who talked at each of them, talked as if he were in control of what was happening, as if Justin weren't there at all. And his brother's voice had been silent.

And he had seen his brother's face become the face of others. A mask of dimples-too-wide, eyes-too-bright, animated at every syllable of every word. A mask too fixed, too stern, long of line, short of smile, dimpleless. And where there were three voices, there was a fourth face. A desolate face, empty, with a lower lip that protruded too far and eyes that sparkled only as his brother added new lines to the painting on the wall.

Kiel had seen and heard them all.

And now that the odd voices and the faces that belonged to somebody else had gone away, he saw his brother again, saw his brother where the others had just been.

And Kiel Reed's fingers trembled at the door knob, unable to let go.

PART TWO
SLIPPAGE

1

Crazy is what came to mind.

Kiel stood at the doorway, his hand frozen to the knob like wet flesh to ice, and all he could think was *crazy*.

Mad-dog crazy was something he'd never seen. But his father had talked about it. A thousand times, his father had sat cold and staring before a warm winter fire, staring empty as if he were going through the flames to seasons long made history, and he would whisper gravel-throated about mad-dog crazy.

"Not a finger-pinch of meat on that damn mutt. All ribs, he was. A scrawny little thing as a pup, not much more all growed up." A sigh would settle over his Pa then, as if he'd suddenly wondered where he had misplaced all his yesterdays. "Don't know what he tangled with. Something fanged and rabid, I suppose. And God, what a

223

change it made." Then the fire's flames would dance in the man's eyes, and his voice would soften sweeter than honey-suckle. "His eyes, you look into his eyes and they wasn't the same. Gray, they were. Cold-granite gray. And before long he was growling and showing his goddamned teeth at sunning lizards. Christ. Then his eyes started leaking yellow and white and colors like you never seen before. And he was slob-bering pocketfuls."

Pa would always stop there, always give the impression that the story had ended. And after a few minutes, when Kiel would be thinking of nothing but how pitiful that poor mutt must have looked, his father's voice would blurt out a last-second epilogue that had all along been the point of the whole damn story. "Had to splatter its brains, you know. Took a shotgun to it. Ain't no place in this world for the devil's madness. No place at all."

No place at all.

But Justin wasn't mad-dog crazy.

He wasn't crazy like a dog breathing up great swallows of air gone stale with rabies.

And he wasn't crazy-drunk. Not like Pa had always been. Stumbling, mumbling drunk to where he couldn't find his way upstairs without Ma helping. Angry loud sometimes, weeping soft others. Always bitter-sweet and contradictions. His brother wasn't crazy like that either.

He was . . .

well, he was . . .

crazy with the devil's madness, that's
what.

Straight-jackets and padded cells? Kiel
wondered. Night long screams, good ears
turned deaf? Eyes gone elsewhere, smiles
painted permanent? The devil's words
jumping out of his mouth as if they were his
own? He wasn't really sick with the devil's
madness, was he? Not that bad, was he?

Not that bad?

He's your brother, Kiel. Your brother.

Of course!

My brother!

When he pushed the door wider, he saw
Justin sitting on the floor, tight against the
wall, dark-eyed and empty-faced, as if he
had just awakened to a strange place. His
brother's eyes followed him into the room.

"Give me a smile," Kiel said, borrowing a
phrase their mother often used.

But Justin was moody, and wasn't
buying any of it.

Kiel sat at the foot of his bed, leaving half
a room between them, plenty of space for
gray, moody thoughts to huff and puff
without bothering anyone. He was waiting
and watching for his brother to peek out
through those few freckles which painted
his nose and say something in a Justin
voice, with a Justin expression.

"I know about the others," Kiel finally

said.

A Justin eyebrow raised, but he didn't seem to understand.

"I was listening at the door."

"So?"

"So. I know about the others."

"What others?"

"I'm your brother, Justin. It's just you and me here. Like it's always been. You go for a swim in Tyler's Pond and I get wet." He grinned, but his brother didn't seem to notice. "I get caught in a hail storm, you feel the cold. Like it's always been."

Helpless is the way Justin looked at him, wide-eyed, slack-jawed and helpless. Because he really didn't know what Kiel was talking about. Their voices—calm and empty at times, excited and rowdy at others—came from *his* throat, from *his* voice box. Their expressions were molded from *his* flesh. And he didn't even know.

"I just want to help."

His brother's eyes began to glisten before he glanced wordlessly away, head shaking because he didn't understand, arms pulling his legs to his chest because it felt safer.

"Please."

"There's nothing wrong," Justin said. "Just leave me alone."

"I know who did the painting on the wall, and it wasn't the ghost of Joseph Little like we thought. It wasn't him at all."

"Who then?"

Kiel felt his own eyes glistening then, felt his throat growing fearfully dry. Whisper a truth in the ear of the devil's madness . . .

. . . but Justin's not really sick with the devil's madness, is he? . . .

and what would he hear? How could he tell Justin that *he* was the one, that *he* painted the mural with CARDEW JAMES MANTOOTH scribbled across the gravestone? And what then? Would the others, Matt—Albert—Scott, come back for him then? Would they want to stand in his place again, pretending to be him, knowing that no one would ever know the difference?

Except Kiel. He'd know the difference. But then Justin might never be Justin again, and there wouldn't be anything he could do about it.

"You don't want to know," he said.

"The ghost of Joseph Little," his brother insisted. "I already know."

"Not him."

"Then who?"

"It was you, Justin. You're the one. It was your hands that scratched and painted and crayoned that thing on the wall. Your eyes gave it that touch of the living, made it breathe life. Do you hear me?"

"I hear."

"Well?"

"It wasn't me."

Kiel slid off the bed, his buttocks resting on the floor, his back braced by the bed frame. An inch closer, maybe two. As if it would make a difference. "I saw you, Justin."

"Liar," he said too weakly.

"Would rather have been blind."

"Sometimes . . ." Justin whispered.

"Yes?"

"Sometimes, I don't remember things. Sometimes I'll close my eyes and when they open again, I'll be somewhere else. And I'm wearing different clothes. And an hour has passed or the sun's gone down, and nothing looks quite the same." His head was lowered, his hair was hanging long on his forehead, and his eyes were shaded from the bedroom light. But Kiel thought he caught a sparkle, like the sparkle of sunlight off a single drop of rain at the rim of a flower petal. A glistening.

"Does that ever happen to you?" Justin asked. "I always thought it must happen that way with everyone. Just blink your eyes and you're somewhere else, like going to sleep at night and waking up in the morning. That's the way it's always been for me . . ."

He filled his lungs with another breath. "Does it, Kiel? Does it ever happen to you?"

"No," Kiel whispered.

"Not ever? Not even on a hot spring day when Tyler's Pond calls you to go swimming, and the teacher's voice floats away like a drifting butterfly, and suddenly you're right there—right there in the water, all cool and soaking wet and not caring about school or books or anything but the coolness? Not even then?"

"Maybe, till the teacher slaps her desk with a ruler."

"You don't understand," his brother cried. "Not just a daydream. Not just a second or two of wishing you were standing waist-deep in cool water instead of sitting in class, sweating hot as a pig over school books with no pictures. Not like that."

"You're really there?"

"Yes."

"Close your eyes and you're really there?"

"Yes."

"But that's wonderful!"

"Is it?" Justin was leaning forward now. His arms were still wrapped about his legs. He had managed to prevent any tears from trickling over his cheeks, but they were still threatening. "And if your eyes open and Pa's standing over you, eyes huge and white with anger, but you don't remember doing anything wrong? And he's yelling at you the same time he's pulling off his belt?"

"You never know?"

"Never."

"Not like a daydream or a wish or having your prayers answered? You just never know? That's the way it is?"

His brother nodded, and buried his head again.

And what happens? Kiel wondered. What happens when Justin's closed his eyes and gone away and can't remember where he's gone? Is that when the others come? Is that when the odd voices speak from his mouth, when the faces of strangers mask his face?

"You don't remember painting the wall?"

A faint shake of head.

"Aunt Faye? Do you remember talking with Aunt Faye?"

"She knows," he said. "She knows I scared Joseph Little to death. She didn't say so, but she knows."

"That's not important now."

"But what if she sends us away? What if she sends you north and me south like you said she would? What then?"

"Don't worry about that now." He crawled, all hands and knees, across the room to sit with his brother. "I know what happens when you go to sleep, when hours pass and you don't know where you've gone. I don't understand it—I'm not sure I can even explain it—but I think I know what happens."

"And?"

With one hand on his brother's knee, the other flip-flapping in the air, Kiel told how he had stood at the door and listened to three voices all coming from Justin's mouth, not a one of them sounding familiar.

And how he had nudged the door just a little wider and found four faces, each belonging to someone else, all sitting right there where his brother's face should have been. And he told how the one with the lower lip sticking out too far had spent time at the wall adding a little crayon here, a little pencil there. And then Kiel sucked up the biggest lungful of air he could fit inside him and blew it all out again.

"The devil's madness," Justin said.

"That's just Pa talking."

"Telling the truth."

"Nonsense." Kiel gave his brother a pat on the knee.

"What am I going to do?"

"Most important, stay out of trouble," he answered. "Albert—he's the one who does all the talking—he's worried about someone finding out about them. So maybe, if you stay away from the cemetery and Trenton Maes and Uncle Wade, maybe then no one will ever think there's anything odd about you, and maybe then they'll stay away and leave you alone."

"But what if they don't? What then?"

Kiel turned his attention away from his brother, focused it instead on where his ankles were crossed and his feet were nervously pumping forward and back, forward and back. "I don't know," he whispered, because there wasn't anything else to say. "I don't know what happens then."

He felt a wiggly finger tickling him then.
And Justin was giggling.

"What are you doing?"

"I knew you were standing at the door,"
his brother said with a chuckle. The
sadness that had dulled his eyes, had made
his face long and drooping, was suddenly
gone. And a deep slice of dimples had taken
its place, puffing his brother's cheeks into
an inflated smile. "All along, I knew it all
along."

"No, you didn't."

"Of course, I did," he said with a voice
too loud. "Saw you and heard you and knew
you were there."

"I don't think so."

"Crack a book . . . crack a smile . . . crack a
back . . . crackerjack," he said with a laugh.
"See? It was just a joke."

"Then tell me who you are."

"Why Justin, of course!"

"Pretending to be someone else?"

"Of course!"

"And who might that be?"

"The name's Scott," he said, and he
presented a hand as if it were the very first
time in their lives they had been intro-
duced.

"And who am I?"

"You're the brother, of course!"

"The brother?"

"My brother! Kiel!"

And was this Justin speaking as Scott?

Or Scott speaking as Justin? Answer that for me, Kiel asked himself. Was this—his brother—a single, playful, faultless actor sitting next to him? Or was it the faultless acting of someone not at all his brother? An artery grown bigger than the heart?

"I want to talk to Justin."

"I *am* Justin."

"The real Justin."

"There is no *real* Justin."

"Scott!"

"Pick a brain . . . let it rain . . . go insane . . . and then what?" The saddest smile Kiel had ever seen fell over his brother's face, and his eyes fell to half-mast, his body filled with a giant breath, then a sigh, and suddenly Scott was somewhere else, Justin was back where he belonged.

Kiel was close to tears. "Are you okay?"

His brother nodded.

"Don't ever leave me like that again," Kiel said, and he pulled his brother to him, held his brother tight within his arms. "You hear me, Justin? Not ever again."

"I promise," Justin answered.

But they both knew it was a promise he couldn't keep.

Faye Richardson woke the next morning at eight-thirty. The gray overcast of the previous day had trekked northward toward Oregon. Her room was washed in a bright lemon yellow, and it was already growing warm. She hadn't slept well, had instead allowed her conscience to shake a finger at her, to scold her for everything that was happening in her life. And now, she felt perhaps even more exhausted than when she had gone to bed.

Her mouth was cotton-ball dry, cotton-ball raw.

She yawned.

An arm stretched, and she reached to touch the emptiness beside her, before realizing for the hundredth time that her husband was elsewhere. Eight years of habit weren't so easily forgotten, she supposed. And she wondered where he was, if he were still asleep or if he had been tossing and turning through a terrible night the way she had. A lick of human nature hoped so, hoped that every moment of his night had been racked with nightmare and stomachache and most of all—regret.

She slipped from beneath the bedsheets, absently wrapping herself in the robe that had waited the night at the foot of her bed. Sleepy-eyed and barefooted, she went to the closet in search of something quick and easy to wear. She had no plans for the day, nothing beyond locking herself in her studio and hoping her work would come and put her mind at ease. If she could make it through the moonrise without obsession taking her, without her thoughts drifting away to what Wade might be doing or saying or thinking, then she'd be okay. Just through moonrise.

When she paused aside the sliding closet door, she caught a glimpse of the emptiness on Wade's side, a glimpse of the lonely blackness that seemed to be there for no other reason than to remind her.

Then someone knocked at the bedroom door and she felt grateful.

"Aunt Faye?"

She tightened the sash of her robe. "Yes?"

"Can I come in?"

May I come in, she thought, remembering back to her father's neverending quest to teach her and her sister proper English. Such a strange, intrusive thought.

"Aunt Faye?"

"Coming." She took a composing breath before opening the door to find Kiel standing there, all dressed and ready for the day. "You're up bright and early."

"City early," he said.

And she realized how silly her comment had been, how her nephew had probably spent his life rising with the first purple-orange glow of the morning sun, out of bed with a yawn and milking cows before the sun was whole on the horizon.

"City early, country late?"

He nodded.

"And where's your brother?"

"Outside," Kiel said. "He already ate a

bowl of cereal."

"And what are *you* doing inside?" Now that she thought about it, Wade would already have been up an hour or two, maybe three. He didn't like sleeping in. He didn't like hanging around the house either. Sunshine and warm breezes were his only justifications for sleep. If only tomorrow would come faster. Like a little kid, he was.

"I need to talk."

Absently, she closed the closet door. "About?"

"Justin."

Wade and Justin, each outside, soaking up the sun, filling themselves with warm rays and high expectations. Just like boys.

"I'm worried about him," Kiel added.

Faye smiled, slid a soft hand through her nephew's medium length hair—not quite so dirty-blond as his uncle's—and drew him to sit at the bed's edge. "He's unhappy living here," she said, dividing her thought between her husband and her nephew.

"No, that's not it," Kiel cried. "He likes it here, we both like it here. Like it a lot."

Wade used to like it here.

"Listen, Aunt Faye. Please listen."

"I'm sorry?"

"I don't think he feels good."

In sickness and in health. Till death do us part. What happened?

"Stomachache? Headache? What's he doing outside playing if he's not feeling well?"

"It's not like that," Kiel said. The next thought caught in his throat before he would let it out, and his sigh quivered as if it had been birthed from an agony too long kept to himself. "You don't understand. There's a crowd inside him, all secret and hiding, looking out through his eyes when no one else is around to look back."

Secretive. Wade's like that. Always hiding behind tired eyes and I-don't-knows. Never allowing even a glimpse of the goings on in his mind. Never a goddamned glimpse.

Out-of-mind crazy, she thought she heard her nephew say. *With the devil's madness.* And it didn't sound right. It didn't sound like something that should come from his still-young mouth. Out-of-mind crazy wasn't something a twelve year old should know anything about.

"What?" she asked. "What did you just say?"

His shoulders slumped, eyes looked away. As if he were ashamed by what he'd said. *Out-of-mind crazy.* "Sometimes, he'll close his eyes and wake up somewhere else, wake up without knowing where he is or how he got there. And while he's away, off somewhere dark and thoughtless, one of the others pretends to be him. One of the others stands in Justin's tennis shoes, speaks strange words through Justin's mouth, watches the world rotate through Justin's eyes. And he never knows," Kiel said. "Justin never knows."

No one ever knows. Not until it's too late. A wife, she never knows, never has a guess if her marriage is working or not, if her husband is happy or if he's out looking, trying to find something that he isn't getting at home, something he's never taken the time to mention to his wife. No one ever knows.

"Aunt Faye?"

"Imagination," she said from faraway.

"I don't think so."

She was patting him on the knee. "Fantasy whispering in a young boy's ear. You can't deny the flight of a good imagination."

"But the others?"

There weren't others, were there? That's not the real reason behind Wade's departure. Not others. No, that couldn't be it.

"What about the others?"

"Don't worry so," she said. "Your brother's fine. It takes time to adjust to new people, new surroundings. He's adjusting, that's all. We all need time to adjust to new things."

And old things suddenly all changed.

She felt her hand being replaced in her own lap. And Kiel touched it gently, as if he understood perfectly what she was trying to tell him. "Breakfast," he was saying. "I think I'll get something to eat."

"Fine," she answered. And as the door

was softly sweeping over the carpet, softly closing her alone again in her bedroom, she added, "Don't worry, Kiel. Everything will turn out all right."

And she wondered again about her husband—where he was, what he was doing, if he were missing her as much as she thought she was missing him.

Things changed so quickly in life.

So very quickly.

On the other side of the bedroom door, Kiel stopped to watch the crack of light grow ever smaller, then disappear completely, leaving him to stand alone in the obscurity of the hallway. And he touched a light hand to the door, as if someone else's hand and not his own, had dared to close him out of his aunt's bedroom when he needed so badly to speak to her.

But she hadn't been listening.

You can't make a person listen.

You can tweak an ear, plead—sob—cry, even shout through cupped hands, but you can't make a person listen. There were other things resting heavy on Aunt Faye's mind. And maybe it was best that way. Maybe she wasn't meant to know.

Out-of-mind crazy with the devil's madness.

Maybe it wasn't Justin at all needing help.

Maybe Justin was the sure-footed one,

the down-to-earth one. The average one
while Ma and Pa and Aunt Faye and Uncle
Wade and even himself, were all just a
touch *out-of-mind crazy* themselves.

Couldn't it be that way?

Couldn't it?

He wished it were.

More than anything in the world, he
wished it were.

*I hate it in here. Maybe it's okay for
Albert or Scott or Nicholas, they don't seem
to care one way or the other. But for me,
when I stand on the spotlight and see the
world through my own eyes, that's the only
time I ever feel alive. I mean really alive.*

*Sometimes, when I'm standing just on
the edge of the spotlight and I'm watching
the pretender, I can't stand not being in his
shoes. He can be such a frigging jerk sometimes. And there's nothing I can do about
it.*

I hate that.

It's like being in a goddam prison.

Like a caged animal.

*Maybe Albert doesn't mind. Maybe Scott
doesn't even mind. But it's driving me frigging crazy, and sooner or later, things are
gonna have to change, because I can't go on
being nobody. I really hate it.*

                              MATT
                              fourteen years old

2

Henry Aikens poured himself a cup of coffee from the old stainless steel pot that had sat twenty-four hours a day on his stove for as long as he could remember. It was the last of the pot, a half-cup at best. So the old man softly shuffled on stiff, morning legs across the wood floor to stand at the sink.

Through the kitchen window, he could see the sun sitting nine o'clock high on the horizon. A handful of cows were milling around the pasture. In two days, not a one had given milk, and there were still a few of the stupid beasts with tin cans attached like ornaments to their tails. Something he'd have to tend to when the time was right and he was feeling up to it.

Water flushed over the rim of the pot.

He turned off the faucet, poured a cup or two down the sink, and wiped his hands against the face of his green work shirt. It was his favorite shirt, with every kind of imaginable stain as evidence. A pair of black suspenders, originally his grandfather's Sunday's best, held up a pair of pants that had grown too big over the years. It was nature's way of punishing him —whittling away at his size, making him live longer than he had ever been meant to live, punishing him for never getting married and settling down like folks were supposed to do. Here a pound, there a pound until nothing was left but a skeleton. And then, maybe then, nature would let him die in peace.

He sat again at the table, sipped from his cup, wondered if he were up to making it all the way to town for an afternoon around the cracker barrel, and thought how a little homemade whiskey would help the coffee go down easier.

It was times like this when he was both tickled and ticked about the cellar. Tickled because it held everything important to him—his elixirs (homemade brews collected over a lifetime of years), photographs of his parents and his three brothers (all long dead and gone) which he kept secret because they hadn't been native Americans, and a family Bible which he feared would crumble in his hands if he ever dared to touch it. Ticked because he no longer found it an easy task to make his way down the dark stairway and grope empty-eyed and senseless for the light string.

But before Henry Aikens had a good chance to imagine his coffee spiked with whiskey, there were knuckles rapping at his door and his train of thought had been derailed.

"What?" he yelled. "What is it?"

After awhile, Kiel had wandered down the hall, out of the obscurity that seemed to crowd around his aunt's bedroom, and he had settled at the dining room table, a table much too big, much too ornate for a single person. In the early hours, when he had first opened his eyes to the day, he'd hoped for a few minutes away from his brother, just enough time to tell Aunt Faye how wrong things were becoming. But now, he wondered if he ever should have let Justin laugh and giggle and smile his way out of sight.

Just in case, he poked his head out the kitchen door to see if his brother might still be around, still playing out front. But the garage, the front lawn, the driveway were vacant and chatterless and lonely in a special sort of way, a way which he found easy to understand.

So he snatched a box of *Super Sugar Crisps* from the cupboards, a bowl and spoon from a drawer, a carton of milk from the refrigerator, and returned to that table that was too big—even with his brother sitting across from him it would have been too big—and too lonely.

And for the first time in his life, he felt brotherless, removed and brotherless and needing more than ever before someone to tell him that everything was going to be all right, that Justin was no more touched by the devil's madness than anyone else. And he wished, when he realized that those were the words his aunt had used, that she had been paying attention and that he could have believed her.

But she hadn't
    . . . and he couldn't.

Matt heard Henry Aikens yelling, heard his calling out, "What is it?" And he almost answered before catching himself. Instead, he kept knocking, kept rattling the old door with a persistence that he knew would anger the old man. Because that's what he wanted more than anything else. He wanted that old shithead so red-faced angry his veins would explode from his forehead if he held his breath for the blink-of-an-eye too long.

Nothing else mattered just then.

Because suddenly the spotlight was all his, and his alone. And not a gift this time, like all the other times when the *pretender* had willingly stepped out—from spotlight to shadows—because his fear was bigger than his courage and he didn't know what else to do with himself. This time, the *pretender* had been forced off the spotlight. This time, Matt had muscled his way on.

He kept pounding at the door.

Henry Aikens kept yelling, "What the hell is it?" And the old man's voice kept growing louder and louder until it was a bullhorn breathing at the other side. "Who is it?"

Matt thought once more, chose not to answer once more.

And the door slowly opened a crack.

"What are you doing here, boy?"

Matt put a hand flat against the door, leaned his weight forward just a bit, just enough to know he could push his way in if the need arose. "Came to visit," he said.

"What for?"

"Because we're neighbors, old man."

"Huh," Aikens grunted. "You're that damn Richardson kid, aren't you? The one that tied cans to my cows. You got your nerve, coming 'round here. You got your nerve. I oughta give you a damn good whipping, is what. Not a chance in damnation your aunt had the guts to take a switch to you."

"She told me I should come and apologize," Matt said.

"What?"

"My aunt—she said I owe you an apology."

"Damn right you do."

The old man wasn't letting an extra inch grow out of that crack. And Matt was doing his best to see that it didn't grow any smaller. "All right if I come in, Mr. Aikens?"

"No need for that, boy."

"I'm sorry about your cows. Honest, I am."

"Just be on your way." Tired hands pushed lightly against the other side. And the crack suddenly threatened to disappear behind the painful squeal of hinges as old as Henry Aikens himself.

"Can't let you do that," Matt said. He put a foot in the crack, put a leg against the belly of the door, a shoulder against a patch of splintering brown paint. And he pushed with an inner strength that the *pretender* had never been able to find within himself.

The door flew open.

Henry Aikens flew back stutter-stepping and tight-roping, caught himself against a rusting crosscut saw that hung on one wall, and came to a standstill. His eyes were wide and white, with fiery red pupils.

Matt stood, black-shadowed, in the doorway. "What now?" he asked himself. "Now that you're here, standing in the man's house, throwing back glares, what are you going to do?"

"Scared, old man?" he asked. "Hand shakin' under that sagging wrap of flesh? Heart stuttering too loud some breaths, too soft others?'' He took a daring step forward, let the door swing shut behind him. Slats of sunshine filtered through unnoticed openings, sectioning the shadowy room into a line of black and white paintings, snapshots altered with the blink of an eye.

"What do you want?" Henry Aikens asked. His back was still pressed against the wall, as if he felt protected if not from the front, then at least from behind.

"You told," Matt said. "You shouldn't have done that."

"I want you out of here."

"But I've just arrived."

"And you've been here too long."

Another step forward. The floorboards creaked beneath his feet. To his right through a half-wall of lattice, he caught a glimpse of the kitchen window where sunlight was slipping in from outside. A lonely, ceramic cup glistened from the kitchen table. The sink sparkled bright and dull from a stack of dirty dishes. A pot of boiling water grumbled on the stove.

"Coffee," the old man said before Matt could ask the question. He was a short man, had always been a short man, even before too many years had begun to press him closer to the ground. And his bones were weedy, brittle things, easily swallowed up beneath the cloth of a shirt sleeve.

"Stunts your growth," Matt said with a

grin.

"What do you want?"

To scare you to death. To see goose flesh gnaw at your arms, to turn you paper white with fear. To see your eyes pop. To scare you so frigging bad that you'd rather cut your tongue out than ever whisper another word to the aunt.

"I want you out of *his* life!" Matt was suddenly trembling with the adrenalin of an anger that had boiled and calmed, boiled and calmed, within the *pretender* for years come and gone most of a lifetime. And he felt it surge, felt it swim through his veins like a taste of hot syrup. And he drank wide-mouthed from the free-flowing emotion, swallowed it with a sense of satisfaction. "I want you out of *his* life, out of *my* life, out of all our lives! There's no room for you and your running to the aunt with your mouth all full of complaints and dying teeth every time one of your frigging cows won't give milk!"

The old man's face changed, grew tight with an anger of its own. "Listen you little bastard—"

"No! You listen!" He slammed a fist into the lattice, ripping one corner away from where it had been nailed to an empty, waist-high planter. "You listen!"

Henry Aikens stepped forward from the wall.

Matt backed toward the kitchen, hands

behind him blindly searching out the way, eyes never leaving the face of the old man. He *was* old; he was weak and old and too spindly to cause any harm. There was nothing there to worry about, nothing there but tired eyes and muscles too old to do much more than a step or two at a time.

But the old man kept coming.

And suddenly, the anger that was boiling hot, boiling in his veins like the water boiling on the stove, turned cold. Cold as fear.

And Matt felt something sharp and painful behind his right eye.

And a thousand tingling dots began to sprinkle inky-black across his vision.

For a moment, Henry Aikens had forgotten that he was a withering old man, unable to get out of bed some mornings and even less able to defend himself against the mad spirit of youth. And much to his surprise, when he had taken that first unthinking step, the Richardson boy had quickly backed away. And the boy's anger had softened just enough to be noticed.

The winds had shifted.

That quickly, the winds had shifted.

Henry blocked the boy's exit from the kitchen, his arms outstretched, fingers clutching the lattice on one side, hand pressed against the wall on the other.

"No way out, now is there?" he grinned.

The boy backed away, backed to the far side of the table, where he gripped the back of a chair with both hands. His face paled then, and seemed to go momentarily numb, frozen somewhere between the anger and the fear. And the boy's eyelids shut down for something longer than a wink.

When they opened again, there was a glimmer of fresh eyes, a sparkle of something strangely unfamiliar, strangely out of place.

When Albert opened his eyes, he found himself standing cat-stalking still in the kitchen of Henry Aikens, and the old man was staring open-mouthed at him. He wasn't surprised; he had watched and listened as Matt dug himself deeper and deeper into the hole. And he had known that sooner or later, Matt would have to be forced off the spotlight and he would be left with the task of trying to get them both back home without any harm done.

"What's the matter, boy?" the old man asked with a grunt. The wonder had gone out of his eyes. "Your mouth ain't clapping so godawful fast all of a sudden."

"I just want to go home," Albert said. "Just let me out of here and I'll be on my way and it'll be the last time you'll ever see me." He took a half-step toward the doorway, then pulled back when the old man refused to budge.

"Thought you wanted to stay and be neighborly?"

"Some other time, thank you."

"Thank you?" The man glanced about, caught a glimpse of the wall phone, and let an ugly grin turn his lips. "All of a sudden it's please, sir . . . you're welcome, sir . . . thank you, sir."

"Please, I just want to go home."

"But we should visit."

"My aunt—she's expecting me."

"Then maybe we should call her?" Too quickly, Henry Aikens tore the phone from its cradle. The receiver swung away from the wall, hit against the floor, bounced back toward heaven, then came to a strangling halt. He held the other end of the cord in his hand.

Albert backed further away, until his buttocks touched against cabinets.

"She ever whip you, boy?"

"Please, Mr. Aikens."

"She ever take a belt to you? Teach you the difference between right and wrong? Teach you not to go bothering other folks, bothering their animals, their property? She ever teach you any of that, boy? 'Cause you need to learn. It's important you learn how to treat other folks with a little respect."

His eyes were dark and glassy.

The phone was swinging from his hand in an ever-widening arch.

"Answer me, boy!" Then suddenly the phone came crashing down against the table. Brown plastic shattered and littered the floor, exposing the phone's metal spine and a hint of wires. Splintered raw wood marked where the plastic had collided with the table.

"No!" Albert screamed, feeling the waves of the explosion rattle through his body, earthquake tempered, hard-shelled and jolting. "She never taught me!"

"Thought not." He reeled in the receiver.

"Can I go, please?"

"Got to teach you, boy. If your aunt never took the time, then somebody's got to teach you."

"Please?"

The old man grinned a brown-toothed, tobacco-stained grin, then pushed a chair away from the table, pushed it to where it was filling up the gap between the table and the wall. "Gotta teach you." He pushed another chair to join the first.

Then Albert felt the familiar pain burn behind his right eye.

And he saw the coming of inky-black dots.

And he already knew who had stepped forward to take the spotlight.

When Matt opened his eyes again, he found himself still trapped in the kitchen, still facing the bitterness of the old man.

And he wondered how long he had been away, thinking it couldn't have been but a few minutes. And he told himself that if Albert had left him alone, had let him stay on the spotlight, then none of this would have happened. The old man wouldn't be standing before him now with the phone swinging like a nightstick from his hand. And one side of the kitchen wouldn't be barricaded with a pile of chairs, making escape all but impossible.

"Never had a boy of my own," the old man was saying. His eyes were staring, but he wasn't seeing.

Matt swept up the chair that was in his hands, a fragile, stick-figured piece of furniture that he hoped would be enough to keep him an arm's length away from further trouble.

"But if I did have a son, I would have taught him respect," Henry Aikens said with a thoughtful sigh. Then he closed the distance between them by another step. "That's the first thing a soul should learn—respect."

"No lessons, Mr. Aikens."

"But there must be lessons. How else will you learn?"

"It's not your place to do the teaching," Matt said, his knuckles showing white from gripping the chair. "I'll do my own learning."

"You need a teacher."

When the old man took another step forward, Matt stuck the chair in his chest, forcing him back again. "I'll stick this thing up your shitty nose. I swear I will." And for emphasis, he took another poke at the man, jabbed, stabbed and carved the chair-legs into ungiving breastplate.

If he could back the old fool out of the kitchen, just a half breath away from the entrance, that's all the frigging room he needed, then he'd scoot himself out of this hellhole before old Henry Aikens turned mad-dog crazy, mad-dog rabid. 'Cause the old man was already foaming at the mouth, already drooling like a goddamned baby. And his eyes were gray agate. And his words were faraway, mechanical jaw-clappings, senseless and out-of-place.

Again, he used the chair as a poker.

And this time the old man came suddenly alive.

"Kids gotta be taught." He slapped away the legs of the chair. And with an afflicted cry he swung the phone high in the air and slammed it plastic-metal-wire into the table again.

Matt retreated a step.

Henry Aikens reeled in the phone and wordlessly let it sail again, this time crashing full-force against the chair, ripping—splintering—tearing away two of the supports. Another shard of plastic exploded from impact, shot across the room, and hit glass behind Matt.

The chair went limp in his hands.

And he suddenly found himself backed into a corner, pressed on one side by a chipped and rust-stained porcelain sink, on the other by the stove.

And he could feel the momentum change as quickly as that. He could see the sleeping madness aroused, the hungry rage fueled. The old man was going to do more than teach him a lesson. And if he didn't find a way out of that corner, out of fury's reach, away from the hot breath that was already gushing sweat, then he was going to be swept up in the old man's fiery grasp and just as sure as there was a hell, the life was going to be squeezed out of him.

"Everybody's gotta learn." Again Henry Aikens brought the phone down against the splintered wood of the chair. Plastic and wood tangled. And when he reeled in the cord, the chair slipped from Matt's grasp, leaving him open and naked and hands-down vulnerable.

The old man kicked aside the broken pieces of wood.

"Nowhere to go, boy." His smile was sadness, a hint of disappointment, a thoughtful resignation. "Just you and me, father and son, teacher and pupil, all alone here."

"Stay away."

There was nowhere to turn, nowhere to

hide, not even another sliver of space he could push himself into. The corner was filled-up with him. And too soon, it would be filled-up with the both of them.

Henry Aikens began to wind the cord tight around his arm, shortening the length of the pendulum, boosting the potential power of future blows, enhancing the accuracy. Then the phone was swinging again, came crashing down again, this time only a heartbeat from the corner where Matt found himself trapped; and it splintered and cracked and chipped against the corner of the stove.

"You see?" The old man seemed morbidly pleased. "There's no escaping respect."

This wasn't the same man. This wasn't the Henry Aikens who had spent a lifetime in Winter Creek Mills, bitching and kicking and screaming about every goddamned change that ever came along. A pain in the ass, yes. But a normal pain in the ass just the same. No, something had gone haywire in this man. Something mad and too many years in hiding had suddenly wiped the sleep from its eyes and was all too ready to do battle with the nearest irritation.

And that was the boy.

And Matt knew full well he wasn't dealing with a man throwing a minor temper tantrum, but something a thousand times worse. He was facing off with a man running on pure instinct, no common sense left, just pure, mindless instinct. And he could stand and do battle and risk losing his life, or he could make a break and pray to Albert and Scott and Nicholas and even the *pretender* himself, that he made it.

The old man grinned bright took another swing.

Matt broke a step, thought he was going to feel the brunt of the receiver against his skull, and pressed himself back against the stove. The flesh of his palm touched unfeeling against the hot grate which supported the pot of boiling water. The phone sliced air next to his ear, then cracked against floorboards.

And suddenly the pain came home.

"Goddammit!"

And he realized where the pain had come from.

Then Henry Aikens raised the phone again.

And running on his own pure instinct— Matt wondered for the flash of a second if it was the same mindless instinct that the old man was thriving on—he snatched the pot of boiling water from the stove.

"Back off!"

The old man froze, then smiled that ugly smile of his, as if *he* were the one holding the boiling water.

"I'll do it," Matt said.

"You've still got to learn."

"Just back off."

"But I'm the teacher."

"Now!" Matt screamed.

Before the echo fell silent off the kitchen walls, the old man took a step forward and Ma Bell's creation came dropping out of nowhere from overhead. Matt fell to his knees. The receiver, all metal and screws and wire now, bounced off the Formica countertop and fell away. Then Matt was back to his feet again, and half the pot of boiling water was sailing through the air.

The hot liquid glazed the old man's chest and right arm.

Henry Aikens screamed, let the phone slip from his hands, and retreated on wobbly legs.

"You burned me." Where the hot water had coated his arms, there were already signs of blistering. He seemed surprised, as if he had always thought himself invincible and was for the first time understanding his own mortality. "Dammit, you burned me."

"I warned you."

"You burned me."

The old man was mumbling. The gray-agate emptiness that had shadowed his eyes had been replaced by something child-like, something little-boyish and confused and frightened. It was more than the shock of the pain, it was the shock of reality bumping against fantasy. His make-believe, this-is-all-a-dream world had suddenly been snatched from his grasp.

And Matt sensed the confusion.

"You're blistering, Mr. Aikens."

And Matt breathed up all the fear he had exhaled, gulped it down, and breathed out a roomful of new-found courage.

"Your arm's already bubbling. It won't be long before the bubbles start popping. That's when the real pain starts. That's when you pray that God Almighty will slap you down with a bolt of stray lightning rather than let you suffer through all that frigging pain."

"Help me." The old man held out his arm.

"I'll help you," Matt said. "But first, you have to help me."

"It's burning."

"Boiling water does that." His mouth was cotton-dry, his upper lip sprinkled with perspiration. But he was in control now. Two moments before, he had only wanted out of the old man's house, out where the sun was shining and the air smelled of something other than tobacco and coffee. But he was back in control now, holding all the marbles, and he was going to play them in his own sweet time.

"How 'bout you give me some room."

Henry Aikens was near tears. He was holding his right arm by the elbow, staring tight-lipped and worried at the lumpy redness which had discolored his forearm. But he must have heard Matt's voice

because he absently backed away until he
was standing next to the wall with the
crosscut saw. On the same wall, in the same
rusting condition, hung a drawknife, a bow
drill, and a scythe. Tools passed down
through his family from one generation to the
next. For a moment, Matt feared the man
might think to steal an antique from the wall
and use it as a weapon, but Henry Aikens
was too preoccupied with his burns.

"Further," Matt said. "Down the
hallway."

"It's getting worse, the burning."

"Hot—hotter—hottest?"

"Yes."

One baby-step at a time, they moved out
of the kitchen sunlight and into the darkness of the hallway. He knew he could run
then, could easily drop the pot and hightail
it out of the dingy hellhole as quick as a
jackrabbit. And he'd be free again. And the
nightmare would be over. But it was *his*
nightmare now. The fear had left him. And
he was curious where the nightmare might
lead if it was left to play itself out.

"What's back here, old man?"

"What?"

"Bedrooms?"

"Yeah."

"And what else?"

"The john." Henry Aikens paused in his
retreat, looked to Matt with eyes made
wide by fear, and held his arm out. "It

needs ice."

"In a bit," Matt said.

"Please?"

"What's the door there at the end?"

The old man turned to peer over his shoulder as if he couldn't recall there ever being a door there before. Then he looked back. "It leads to the cellar."

"And what's down there?"

"Nothing, just junk."

"Keep moving." He wasn't quite sure what to do with the old man now that he had him by the balls. Aikens deserved more than a few blisters on his arm. But he didn't want to do anything that would come back to haunt the *pretender*. There was always a chance, an outside chance, that the old man might say something. But more than likely, he'd keep his mouth zipped tight, too embarrassed to tell anyone about the kid that got the best of him. So what they both needed now was a graceful way out of this mess.

"It's hurting."

"You told me that already."

They came to a standstill at the end of the hall. To Matt's right, there was a door slightly ajar, filling the area with light. He could see the corner of the bathtub where an opaque shower curtain hung dry and spotted. Henry Aikens had his back pressed against the cellar door.

"Open it."

"There's nothing down there."

"Open it."

Left-handed, the old man fumbled and rattled with the doorknob until it turned in his hand and the door swung open to a trail of darkness. A whiff of damp, sun-starved earth rose out of the blindness.

Matt thought for the briefest of breaths he could hear the chatters, the squeal of something playing at the foot of the steps.

"Where's the light?"

"Seven steps down."

"Turn it on."

"But—"

"Turn it on."

He watched the form of the old man, still favoring his right arm, descend an agonizing first step, then another. Each footfall, each hammer of shoe sole to wood, echoed through the unseen chamber, hollow and faraway.

Another step.

A faint indistinguishable chatter.

Hesitation.

"Turn on the light, Henry Aikens."

Another step.

The old man was standing on the fifth step now. All but his calves had been eaten by the shadows of the cellar. And when he took another step, then another, all of him quickly disappeared somewhere beyond the glint of an eye. The echo of footsteps fell still and the quiet was suddenly too quiet.

"The light, old man."

"The light," Henry Aikens repeated. And following shadow-tight on the heels of his last word, the old man screamed through a tongue too thick; and his body howled as it tumbled brittle-bone-to-flesh, flesh-to-wood down the stairway, spilling thud-soft to the earth below.

Then quiet.

"Old man?"

Matt listened and he heard that faraway chatter, not so faraway now.

"Henry Aikens?"

And when the old man wouldn't answer— wouldn't answer because he'd taken a tumble down the stairs, Matt knew that— then there was nothing else to do but follow. He couldn't leave Henry Aikens half-dead, half-alive at the bottom of the stairway, blistered and broken-boned and suffering worse than a man should have to suffer. He couldn't do that. A suffering man should at least be spared the misery. The Pa wouldn't let old man Aikens suffer. He'd just wring the old man's neck as if it belonged to a hen too long on the farm. And Matt would have to do the same.

He followed, footfall for footfall, in the old man's shadow, counting seven steps, exactly seven steps. Then he stood blind and groped one-handed in the darkness for

the light until he touched upon a string
hanging from overhead. When the hundred-
watt bulb came to life, he caught a glimpse
of red eyes, a hundred red eyes, scurrying
out of sight. The pot of water, no longer hot
to the touch, slipped from his hand and
tumbled top over bottom down the
stairway, shattering the silence, clinking
and clanking against wood and pebble and
exposed nail, finally resting in peace next to
the unmoving body of Henry Aikens.

It took a moment for his eyes to adjust to
the brightness, and when they did, he
noticed a sheathed hunting knife hanging
from the wall only a step away. Easier than
wringing a neck, he thought. And he made
the knife his friend, strapping its case to his
belt, carrying the cool metal close to him.

The chattering had stopped.

The red eyes had all scurried away.

But he knew now what they had been.

Rats!

And he didn't want to spend a moment
longer in the damp cellar than was
absolutely necessary.

At the foot of the stairway, he knelt,
watched the old man's chest for a sign of
breath, put an ear to the cold cellar air for a
moan or a groan, and knew that death had
already come to claim Henry Aikens. The
best thing for him to do now was to get the
hell out of the man's house, put as much

distance between himself and this rat-infested cellar as possible. It had been, after all, an accident. A convenient, most-satisfying accident, but an accident just the same. And as long as he was nowhere in the area, there would be no reason for anyone to ever think of it as anything more than an accident.

Matt sheathed the knife, snapped the strap across the handle, and hurried back up the steps, out of the grasp of hell, back to the firmament of the living. At the head of the stairway, he stopped and considered turning off the light again, but rejected the idea, thinking the light string would supply a sound reason for the old man to have reached and lost his balance. Then he closed the cellar door, and leaned back against it, wondering if there was anything his reasoning had overlooked.

I'll give credit to Albert. He's got the brains in the group. But he's gutless. You know what I mean? It takes more than a brain to survive. You've got to know how to take care of yourself. I don't think he could survive without the pretender.

Scott, he couldn't either.

And Nicholas, who knows? He never says anything. So who knows?

But that's not the way it is with me. I guess I'm like the maverick of the group. I don't need any of them, not the way they need each other. And most of all, I don't need the pretender.

MATT
fourteen years old

3

Kiel was sitting on the edge of his bed, staring at the mural of his brother, all wicked and happy atop the gravestone of CARDEW JAMES MANTOOTH. The longer the damned thing was there, the more it bothered him. There were moments, flashes of a second, when he thought he could feel Justin's eyes staring out of the painting, burning a glare into him like Pa would sometimes do when he was looking to stir up a little trouble. And he wanted to rid himself of that feeling.

Aunt Faye had promised they'd resurface the wall, then paint over it. But she wasn't up to doing anything right away. Maybe when Uncle Wade was back home, she had said. Then she smiled that somewhere else half-smile and slipped away.

But Kiel didn't want to wait that long.

If he could just sandpaper his brother's

face down to the sheetrock, then it wouldn't
be so bad. He could live with it then, at
least until Uncle Wade moved back home
again. Then the remainder of the painting
could be put to rest and everything would
feel better. 'Cause no matter how hard he
tried, it wasn't Justin's face that he saw
staring out of that wall. It was the face of
one of the others, the one called Matt. And
that face sent shivers up his spine every
time it turned his way.

Just down to the sheetrock.

His hands were tired, the muscles and
tendons ached, but he grabbed again for the
sandpaper and stood to confront the mural
for the thousandth time. Sooner or later,
sheetrock would have to surface. It
couldn't stay buried forever.

Just down to the sheetrock.

But before he had the chance to shave
away even a whisker of an inch, his aunt
called him. She was still in her robe and
slippers, still hiding in her room. And she
wanted him to answer the door, a knocking
he hadn't heard.

"Please?" she asked.

"Sure."

"Thank you." She slipped back behind
the bedroom door, out of sight, out of mind,
out of touch with anything and everything
except what was hiding in there with her.

It was Trenton Maes at the door, asking
about Justin. He was wearing a blue, netted

half-shirt that showed his baby-fat, and white fatigue shorts. And he seemed oddly uncomfortable, as if he were guilty of something that had just made the front pages, but he wasn't sure if Kiel had read the paper.

"He's not here."

"Where is he?"

"I don't know," Kiel said, ready to close the door at the first opportunity. From day one, he hadn't liked Trenton. And after the trouble at the cemetery, after Justin had come home all white and floured and scared out of his wits, Kiel had hoped that Trenton Maes would simply disappear from their lives. No such luck.

"When will he be back?"

"Doesn't matter," Kiel said. "He doesn't need you hanging around anymore. Just leave him alone."

"What did I do?"

"Just leave him alone, Trenton."

And Kiel closed the door in the boy's face.

It had happened again.

Justin opened his eyes and he was somewhere else.

Not at home, not sitting alone at the breakfast table slurping up the last few spoonfuls of milk from his cereal bowl. That's the way he remembered it. Sunshine pouring in through the sliding glass doors. Kiel still groggy, too grumpy to get out of bed and eat with him. The house creaking like old bones as the earth began to warm.

But now . . .

A million miles away.

He was wearing the same clothes, a pair of cords Aunt Faye had bought in Eureka for him and a solid orange tee-shirt, wordless, pictureless, numberless. The same clothes he had been wearing before he went to sleep and woke up . . .

here.

There were whites and blacks and grays, bands of light and dark which cut hit-or-miss across his field of vision. To his left, through the crack of an opening, he could see the corner of a bathtub staring back at him. Stretching before him was a long, narrow hallway with the promise of something less claustrophobic at the other end. But none of it was familiar, not the too-strong presence of tobacco and coffee or the thick floorboards at foot or the faraway chattering . . .

. . . at his back!

On the other side of the door!

Justin jumped away from the door, stared at it with eyes wider than wide, trying to see through its solidness, trying to catch a glimpse of something he wanted —didn't want—to see. He felt as if he should know what was scurrying alive, lying dead on the other side, but he didn't know, and suddenly he didn't want to know. Whatever it was, whatever breathed out life and death just beyond the peeling paint of the door, it was *his* doing. Just like a day ago, when one of his other selves had risen to the call of a full-mooned night and painted his bedroom wall with a hand that was—wasn't his own and now . . .

. . . he didn't want to know what else that hand had been doing.

Not now, not ever.

He backed slowly away from the cellar door, hearing the chattering, squealing, dying, grow louder and louder inside his head. Then he was turned and running, bouncing shoulders off walls, breathing out his fear and breathing in stale air.

Red eyes

He stumbled and fell palms-first to the floor, picked himself up again, and hit the front door running.

Red eyes and chattering

But it wouldn't open. The damn door wouldn't open.

And something was coming alive in the cellar, coming alive from where it was dead and buried beyond the cellar door. And if he didn't get out of there, it was going to walk up behind him and tap him on the shoulder and then . . .

"Open, dammit!"

He kicked a tennis shoe at the door.

Red eyes and chattering and something dead

"Open!"

Then the workings of the knob fell into place. He gave it a final twist, felt it turn in his hand, and . . .

. . . he was outside, tumbling down a line of steps, tumbling head-over-heels into soft earth and the smell of fresh air.

"Home," he said, not caring if his words carried on the wind to ears that would listen with a snicker. "I want to go home." And he hurried to his feet, looking back over his shoulder at the house that had spit him out, at the house that held a secret dying to get out, and it was Henry Aikens' house. Oh God, it was Henry Aikens' house.

What had he done?

"I'm sorry," Justin said. He had no idea what he was sorry for, but he knew somehow that whatever was still locked inside the old house belonged to him. It was *his* creation, *his* damnation.

"I'm sorry."

Then he was off and running, scooting over the dirt and weed and pasture as quickly as his legs would carry him.

Trenton Maes was hiking along the creek bank when he saw his friend come toppling out of old man Aikens' place, landing on his face. It was a curious sight, the way the kid stared back over his shoulder as if he expected something huge and wicked to follow him out of the shadows. And for that reason, Trenton stopped and watched and elected not to call out.

His friend said something out loud, something that was lost to the breeze, something that carried south instead of north where Trenton was watching. Then, the boy struggled to his feet and was off, kicking up a trail of dust as he went.

Curious.

Here big-bastard-brother Kiel was all worried that Trenton might lead his little brother into trouble and it looked as if the kid was getting into mischief all on his own. Didn't even need any help.

Trenton liked that.

For a while there, as he had stood at the door with Kiel glaring and staring at him as if he had the black plague and was offering free samples, he had the gnawing feeling that the kid had broke down and told everything there was to tell about full-mooned nights, cemeteries, and the passing of Joseph Little. But now, just catching a whiff of the trouble that was swirling in the air, he decided Justin probably had a whole closet-full of secrets and full-mooned cemetery nights that he was trying to keep tucked away out of sight.

What was one more?

No big deal.

No big deal at all.

As the trail of dust was settling again, Trenton wondered what sort of devilment had been raised inside old Henry Aikens' place. He was tempted to check it out for himself. But he had a nose for trouble, and something warned him about this wickedness. Too wicked, is what it was. He could smell it, almost taste it.

Some other time, he promised himself.

Some time when the smell wasn't so strong.

It was ten minutes after the hour of five when Faye placed dinner on the table. Through the sliding glass doors, she could see an evening gust of wind twist and funnel like a small tornado through the backyard. And she wanted to build a metaphor around it, something to explain the way she felt about her recently turbulent marriage. But she let the opportunity pass without a second thought. Hours before, she had promised herself not to dwell on something she had little or no chance of controlling.

"Hungry?" she asked, hoping to arouse a little conversation. The boys had been quiet during most of the afternoon, too quiet. The kind of quiet that makes an aunt playing mother begin to wonder.

Kiel nodded.

Justin was noncommittal.

"If it doesn't get gobbled-up tonight," she said, "it'll be back as leftovers tomorrow. Just thought I'd give you fair warning." She had shed her robe and slippers along with her self-pity in the early afternoon hours after suddenly realizing that she was more than simply a wife now, she was a mother as well. And yes, things were bad. And yes, she missed Wade and wanted him back home where he belonged, back home as husband and father. But that didn't change the fact that she had two children to look after now. Whether or not she was a wife, she was definitely a mother.

Dinner was fresh garden corn, a green salad, and—by Kiel's request—hot dogs. She could still see the suspicion that had peered mistrustingly from behind his dark brown eyes when she had left the decision to him, as if he suspected some sort of a trap. *'Honest? No matter what I choose?'* Odd. And at little moments like that, she thought she could see a sadness in his face, etched by more years than a young life should be able to hold. He was older than his twelve years, wiser, always watching what was going on around him, and . . . sad like a young boy had no right to be. How had he grown to be so sad?

"It's almost gone," Kiel said finally.

"There's plenty more."

"No," he said. "The painting on the wall —I've been working on it all day and it's almost gone. Just a little bit deeper where he scratched in the name of Cardew James Mantooth."

"He?" Faye asked, curious about the ease with which her nephew had assigned someone male to the misdeed. Although, in her own mind, she had always done the same, assuming it was likely the work of one of the boys while sleepwalking. But he had used the word *he* so casually, as if he knew exactly what had happened and who had done it.

A fork slipped from Justin's fingers, rang off his plate like a one o'clock chime. And the two boys exchanged quick, guilty glances.

"You think it was a *he*?"

Kiel forced a swallow. "I guess."

"Have anyone in mind?"

"No."

"Oh." She smiled and nodded, realizing for the first time that Wade had been right, that one of the boys had painted and scatched the mural on their bedroom wall. But the urge to knowingly smile with it came slipping childlike up from inside her. Because she still remembered how it had been when *she* was a child. There was something about an adult; they could look right at you and see inside your head, read your thoughts as if the damn things were flashing across your cerebrum in neon lights. You had to guard yourself, think about brushing your teeth when you were really thinking about the dress that had been splattered with mud on the way home from school. Guilt always seemed to have a way of showing itself. And although she could see it here, she found it more amusing than upsetting.

"Honest," Kiel added.

The voice of guilt.

"How about you?" she asked Justin, playing with their apparent discomfort. "Have any ideas?"

But he was miles away, lost in daydream and fantasy.

"Justin?"

Miles away. Not hearing. Not interested one way or the other. Elbow to the table, arm holding up his head. And he was doodling on his napkin, fashioning the most intricate design from the see-through paper cloth and a ball-point pen.

"Earth to Justin," she said with a grin.

Then Kiel reached and touched his brother on the arm; and his brother's attention was lifted from the drawing on the napkin. His head cocked at an odd, bewildered angle. And there was a long moment when Kiel seemed to see something in his brother's eyes, something that had escaped Faye altogether. Then Kiel snatched the napkin from the table in front of his brother, crumpled it, wadded it, and buried it in his pocket.

"Aunt Faye's talking to you," he said then.

But Justin didn't seem to understand.

With empty eyes, he looked to his brother, and Kiel guided his tired, somewhere-else gaze to Faye. She smiled uncomfortably, not knowing why the moment felt so awkward. Then Justin quickly sat up, straight-shouldered and alive again, picking at his food as if he had suddenly realized how near starvation he was.

"Are you all right?" she asked.

"He gets moody," Kiel said.

"Since when?"

"Since always." Kiel swallowed the last of his hot dog, brushed the crumbs from his hands to his plate, and wiped a sleeve across his mouth. "Can I be excused?"

"That's all you're eating?"

He shrugged.

"Eyes too big for your stomach, huh?"

"I guess."

"You know what that means."

"I don't mind leftovers," he said.

"Okay."

Before he left, he looked to his brother, and there was that strange passing of something between them. Faye knew they were exchanging messages, the way twins might, little telepathic promptings that rise out of knowing someone almost as well as you know yourself. She had never felt that close to her sister, and suddenly found herself regretting it.

Then Justin quickly swallowed down his own hot dog, wiped a sleeve across his face

with the sameness of his brother, and
without using words, raised an eyebrow
that asked if he could be excused to follow
his brother far away from there.

"Of course," Faye said.

And they were up, clearing their places,
piling silverware and glasses on plates, and
tight-roping it all into the kitchen. Wordlessly. With purpose. *To escape her inquisi-
tive eye.* That quickly, they rushed to get
away from whatever it was that had made
them so nervous.

She tried to recall where the conversation
had burped then suddenly spasmed before
growing into this stampede to escape. But
all that came to mind was the wall painting,
the painting with CARDEW JAMES
MANTOOTH etched ominously across the
gravestone, and it seemed now two days
later, not nearly enough to scare them off
that way.

So what was it, then?

What hurried them on their way so all of
a sudden?

"Dessert?" she asked, to keep them
longer.

"Now?"

"In a few minutes."

"Ice cream again?"

"Again."

How typical they could be at times, how
everyday, all-American, childishly typical.
Ice cream again? Even at this moment of

scurrying to get away, they could stop long enough to ask a question of all children. *Again?*

"How about it?" she teased.

Kiel looked to his brother, his brother to him. A shrug of shoulders.

Then she noticed the knife strapped to Justin's belt. As long as a kitchen knife, wide, with a brown and white plastic handle that imitated bone. It looked so out of place hanging from his hip, half-way down his leg, bigger than life, bigger than anything he'd ever have need for. All through dinner, it had been strapped to him, and she had known. Somewhere in the back of her mind, it had registered and she had known, but she had let it slip by, unwilling, as she always seemed to be, to trust the subtlety of her intuition. The same way she might miss a turn on the way to Eureka, think how *different* the scenery looked, but continue on for miles, telling herself every inch of the way that something familiar would be waiting just around the next bend.

She could never seem to trust her instincts.

"What have you got there, Justin?"

Kiel put a hand on his brother's shoulder; they stopped and wondered.

"The knife."

They shared a long pause, eye-to-eye, exchanging non-verbal bits and pieces of an explanation, and they were going to lie. She knew they were going to lie to her. But before it could go any further, the phone rang, they all sighed, and Kiel had pounced on the opportunity to wiggle gracefully out of the situation.

"It's for you." He held the phone out to her.

"Who is it?"

"Sounds like Uncle Wade."

Her legs held her motionless, an awful fear applauded. It was that damned intuition again. She had known he was going to call. All afternoon, she had listened to a faraway whisper. *He'll call. He loves you, Faye. He'll call soon and he'll ask if he can come back home. Because Agnes is a nice old woman and her extra room is clean and well-kept and proper, but it isn't home. This is home. And this is where Wade Richardson belongs.* But she had tried to force it out of mind, afraid that if she listened and she believed and then he *didn't* call—well, she wouldn't be able to handle that. So, she had chalked it all up to wishful thinking. Only now, it was coming true.

"Aunt Faye?"

"You sure?" she asked. "You sure it's your uncle?"

"Want me to ask?"

"No, don't do that." With a laughable touch of self-consciousness, she straightened the cuffs of her plum-colored blouse,

and brushed away invisible ravelings of lint
from her trousers. Kiel and Justin were
watching, a touch of marvel in their eyes, a
touch of laughter on their lips. And she suddenly realized her foolishness.

"Scoot, you two," she said, taking the
phone from Kiel and slipping a hand over
the mouthpiece. "Go on."

Kiel tickled his brother, drew a smile, and
together they tagged, tickled, wrestled, and
frisked their way down the hall, out of
sight.

She sighed, wondering if she had enough
strength to survive all the possibilities that
a phone call from Wade might hold,
knowing there was only one way to find out,
and wishing she had all the answers before
any questions were asked.

"Hello?"

"Faye?"

"Hi," she said. She heard him sigh, felt
the terrible awkwardness of the moment
come shivering up her body, and couldn't
believe the schoolgirl nervousness that had
suddenly intervened. *Faye, this is Wade,
Wade, this is Faye.* As if they were
strangers, touching voices for the very first
time and trying to find some common, non-
threatening thread which they could share
between them without scaring the pants off
one another.

"How have you been?" she asked.

"Getting by."

"Settled in at your new place?"

"As well as can be expected." There was another sigh, the singing of a sad song. And she drew a momentary hope from it. "Look, Faye, I just called to see how you were doing, and . . . to let you know I've been thinking of you."

"Are you coming home?"

"No, not yet."

If you don't want to hear the answer, don't ask the question. She twisted the cord around her index finger. "I knew you were going to call. At least—I hoped you were going to call. It doesn't seem right, being apart like this. You, there. Me, here. Both of us wondering what the other is doing, asking how we managed to get ourselves into this mess, how we're going to get out again and still feel whole. I miss you, Wade."

He was quiet for a godawful long time, thinking slow thoughts through slow breaths, keeping one here, discarding one there, until finally he said, "I think I got a job."

With her finger still twined in the cord of the phone, she wiped a lonely tear which had slipped and trickled from one corner of her eye. "You did?" Her voice was too high, too labored, too atypic; punctuated with a laugh that rose impulsively from disbelief. He was going to step around it. She had placed her feelings before him, pure and honest and painful, and he was going to pretend he hadn't heard, hadn't seen.

"It's not a *for sure* yet, but it looks good."

"That's nice." Her finger touched against a trembling lip. "When—when will you know?"

"Next week at the latest." She had never before noticed how mechanical his voice could sound, robotic, monotonic, so strangely unemotional. Even now, as he told her about the possibility of a job, the one and only thing he had craved (for how many months?) he sounded too-removed.

"Lomax Construction," he was saying. "I did the inspections on their Freshwater Valley Project in '80-'81. Remember?"

"Yes, I think so."

"I guess they appreciated my honesty."

"I guess."

Then another fumbling silence came to be.

"So, how are you doing?" he asked after too long. But it was a question born more of the silence than of a genuine desire to know how she felt. Funny, how easily she could tell, simply by the breath before, the breath after, what was asked out of duty, what was asked out of concern. It had been a matter of duty.

"We're doing fine." Emphasis on the *we're*.

"Any new super graphics on the walls?"

"Wade—"

"I'm sorry. That wasn't called for, it just slipped out."

Too quickly, she thought. Then she said, "Kiel spent the day sanding and scraping that damn wall, and our mural is near history." What was it that she was after? To make her husband proud of his nephew so he'd come back? Or to let Wade know that everything was simply peachy without him—*take your time, no rush in getting back, everything's just fine here.* A healthy shot of vengeance? Both and neither, at the same time, she imagined.

"That's nice," Wade said in a voice too self-controlled.

Faye closed her eyes and held a breath, wishing she could find a way to break through her husband's stoical self-restraint, resenting whatever it was inside her that needed a reaction from him. Sometimes it felt so much like a game. Press a button, see if he frowns or if he smiles. And if he does neither, then press another button and another and another. And all the while, he's busy pressing buttons of his own to see what your reaction is going to be.

"Joseph Little passed away," she heard herself say. And she realized that a concession had been made, that she had quietly agreed to skip over everything too sensitive, too near the exposed root. "He suffered a heart attack."

"I'm sorry."

"Oh," she said then, not wishing to let another prickly moment of silence rise between them. "I almost forgot to ask. I can't find the paint sprayer."

"Leave it," he said. "I'll get over sometime in the next couple of days and paint the boys' wall. It can wait that long, can't it?"

"I wasn't thinking of the boys' room."

"No?"

"I thought I might experiment with some new background techniques for my illustrations. Something not quite so structured."

"And a little faster?"

"And faster," she conceded. "So how about it? Where's the sprayer?"

"I lent it to Aikens a couple of weeks ago."

"You didn't."

"I did."

She sighed, loud and long enough to let her faraway husband know of her cold displeasure. And her cold breath iced the conversation one last fatal time before they each hemmed and hawed, and searched for more superficialities to fill in the remaining dead space. Her finger unwound its way from the phone cord then. Her eyes glanced about the kitchen for a reason to excuse herself from the uncomfortableness—what's left to be said when all is said and done? And when she could find none, she simply said, "I've got to go."

Wade left a number where he could be reached.

In yellow chalk, Faye scratched it across the chalkboard mounted on the wall next to the phone. She scribbled "WADE" above the number, slowly with deliberation. And when she finished, the room fell suddenly too quiet, too alone. And she wondered if she should wait at that very spot for his next call. Nothing else seemed quite as important.

4

Kiel could hear his aunt still on the phone as he closed the bedroom door behind him and watched his brother run a rabbit-dash for the far bed, belly-flopping into the softness, burying his head deep within the pillow.

"Where'd you get the knife?" he asked. He felt the faded, nearly ghostlike presence of the mural peering over his left shoulder, tickling his spine with chills, leaning an ear close to better hear his brother's answer. But Kiel knew better than to expect an answer.

Justin didn't move, didn't raise a vein on his neck, a questioning eyebrow to his forehead. And the pillow seemed to swallow him deeper into its throat.

"You're not Justin, are you?" Kiel sat across from his brother. He wanted to touch a hand to Justin's back, to rub wide, big-brother circles through the light blue tee-shirt, as if that would make them brothers again. Because he couldn't be certain anymore; he couldn't be certain this boy with his head sunk deep into a pillow was really his brother. And he thought if they touched, he might jerk awake from a nightmare and discover he'd never had a brother at all. It might be just like that. So he couldn't bring himself to touch the shirt.

"You're one of the others, aren't you?" he said, knowing it was true, not knowing what to do about it. "Aren't you?"

When his brother wouldn't answer, Kiel gave the mattress a reflexive kick, enough to sink his shoe into the space between the J.C. Penney mattress and box spring, and shove the bed into the wall with a chatter and a bang.

Justin raised his head from the pillow. His eyes were lonely eyes, spiritless and faraway, wanting to be left alone. And something little-boyish looked out from those dark brown eyes, lost and searching, touched with an unknowing, as if Kiel were a stranger.

They're someone else's eyes, Kiel thought. A chill went up his spine.

"Who are you?" he asked, but his brother —or whoever it was—simply cocked a bewildered head as if he didn't understand the question. Or was it that he didn't know the answer? "I know you're not Justin."

Then this stranger—this strange boy

sitting across from him, hiding inside his brother's body—closed his eyes as if sleep had suddenly come to take him. His head bobbed. His features went soft and expressionless. There was a moment that dragged forever, then his eyes opened again and they had changed. That easily, the woodenness had been replaced by a sparkle of new life.

"I am what I am what I am what I am," his brother said then.

"Justin?"

"Wrong! Guess again."

"Then who?"

"I'll give you a hint." The boy sat up on the bed, pulled his knees to his chest, then shared a bigger-than-life grin. His dark eyes shined brighter than Justin's. His expression—wide-eyed and animated—was too extroverted. "Let's see, there's Scott Towels, Scotland Yard, scot-free, and Scotch tape." He shared a giggle that was his alone. "Who am I?"

"I want Justin."

"Scott towel, don't you get it?"

"Where's Justin?"

"He's gone, brother."

"I want him back."

"Quoth the Raven, Nevermore." A playfully wicked smile, tight and pleased, spread across the boy's face. It was the smile of a stranger fitting too comfortably on the face of his brother. And the smile seemed frozen there for a moment before

softly slipping back into Justin's thin
cheeks. "I can't stay," the strange boy
sadly said.

"And Justin?"

"Quoth the Raven, Nevermore."

He didn't understand, Kiel didn't. He
watched as his brother's eyes closed again,
and he knew what was going to happen, he
knew that the one called Scott was going
away and someone new would be taking his
place; but he didn't understand why it was
happening, and he wondered if there was a
chance Justin would never be back. *Quoth
the Raven, Nevermore.*

His brother's head bobbed once, then
twice.

Nevermore?

His father used to change people, used to
smile at you through tobacco-stained teeth
one minute, snarl at you through those
same teeth the next. As if there were more
than just a single person glaring out from
behind those tired old eyes. And thinking
about it, Kiel wondered if that weren't the
way with all people. If there weren't a whole
crowd of people all squashed and stuffed
inside each body like voices in a radio. And
he wondered if that were the way with him,
but it didn't seem like it.

His brother's face softened. His eyes—
darker, friendlier, not as alive, but somehow
more real—opened slowly. The smile was
neither too wide nor too faint.

"Please be Justin."

"Justin's sleeping now," the boy said. He yawned and wiped his eyes with the back of his hands, as if he had just awakened from a heavy slumber.

"Can't you wake him?"

"I could . . ."

"But?"

"But I won't."

"Nevermore?"

"After we've had a chance to talk," the boy said through Justin's mouth. But he wasn't Justin. His eyes sparkled with the dark honesty of his brother's eyes, as if a little piece of Justin were shining through. But he wasn't Justin. The voice was too calm, too detached. The lips too tight.

Kiel watched him, waited for him to say something—anything at all—and when he didn't, asked, "Which one are you?"

"My name's Albert."

"I remember." He nodded. "The one who did all the talking."

"You weren't supposed to be listening." He moved away from the wall, hung his legs over the edge of the bed, found the floor, and stood. There was something older about him, something wise and mature that had always been absent in Justin. "But maybe it's better that you know," he said with a straight face and a voice old for his years.

"I might tell."

"You won't."

"I might." It was odd speaking to Justin

as if he were a stranger, as if they'd just met for the first time. Strangely unsettling, talking to this little brother who wasn't a little brother at all, but someone much more mature, much more in control.

"But if you tell, what will happen to Justin?"

"What will happen to *you*?"

"Nothing will, Kiel." He took a step, then another, away from the bed toward the wall with the mural. But his mind was elsewhere, pondering something that had escaped Kiel's understanding for the moment. "I'll remove myself from the spotlight until it's perfectly safe to step out of the darkness again. A game of hide and seek."

"They'll find you."

"Only if I let them."

"Only then? Only if the game loses its excitement and he decides to treat the world to a quick peek at all the extras living and breathing inside his brother's body? Kiel wondered how much truth there was to the boast, shivered to think it wasn't a boast at all, then let out a bigger sigh than intended.

"What then?" he asked. "What is it you want?"

Albert was standing at the wall now, touching soft fingers to the faint lines of the mural, tracing the opaque shapes and textures which were still fixed there. His back was turned away from Kiel as he spoke in a hushed, faraway voice. "I'm worried," he said. "Worried about Justin, and about you."

"Why?"

"Everything's changed."

"What? What's changed?"

"Everything." His voice trembled and caught, then died away. His head succumbed—chin against chest, oddly humble—to the weight of something Kiel was still trying to decipher. "Nothing's quite the same anymore. All the control—it's slipped away somehow."

Albert turned away from the muraled wall, turned to face Kiel and look him eye-to-eye. His face had gone pale, his eyes shined like dark stones. "It's Matt," he said. "He's doing things on his own. Bad things." His gaze fell to his hands where a fine chalky-white powder of sheetrock had painted his fingers.

"Like what?" Kiel asked. "What kind of things?"

"I can't tell you that."

For the briefest of moments, Kiel thought he had witnessed yet another change of characters. His brother's keeper, Albert, had suddenly seemed hesitant and uncertain, and the cockiness had gone out of his manner. But then just as quickly, with a slap of his palms to shake the dust loose from his hands, Albert seemed to come to life again, stirred from the reverie that had held him.

"Just be careful," he said then, filling his

lungs and letting it all out again.

"Of Matt?"

"Especially Matt."

"You're afraid of him, aren't you?"

"The same as you should be," he said coldly, then he sat on Justin's bed, sat directly across from Kiel. All the life had gone out of his expression. "He's the part of Justin that's strong and unafraid and always angry, the part with the strongest will to survive and an astonishing absence of right and wrong. He has no conscience, no feeling for anyone but himself."

"And?"

"What more do you need to know?"

"Everything."

Albert looked away with another reluctance. "There's only so much room in here," he said. "One spotlight, one person at a time. It's supposed to be shared by each of us. Matt wants it all."

"All to himself?"

"And he's slowly taking it."

"But what about you and Justin and Scott and whoever else? What will happen to all of you? What will happen to my brother?" And suddenly Kiel was worrying if he might never see his brother again. What would happen if Matt or Albert stood on the spotlight from this moment till forever? What then? "I want my brother back," he said then. "I want Justin."

"It may not be so easy next time."

"I want him back!"

"I'll call him," Albert said. "I'll call him and step off the spotlight. But that's all I can do. And for you, it's time to begin looking over your shoulder to see what's following in your shadow. He'll be there, Matt will. Just when you think everything's settled back into place, when you first forget there ever was a Matt, he'll be there."

"My brother, please."

"Yes."

The Albert one slid back on the bed, back to lean against the wall, where he folded his hands in his lap as if in prayer. He said no goodbyes, no gooddays. Simply closed his eyes and swallowed up a lungful of air.

His head bobbed, as if he were walking the edge of sleep.

No Albert this time, please.

No Scott or Matt or whoever.

But my brother.

When the boy opened his eyes, they were his brother's eyes—Justin's eyes—and Kiel felt something heavy go out of him.

"I went away again, didn't I?" Justin said.

Kiel nodded and looked away.

There was nothing else either of them could say.

Wade Richardson was thinking. He was lying on top of his bed, still clothed, hands folded behind his head, just thinking. It was a little past ten o'clock. The room was a

second story extra that sat over The Flat
Rock. A small room, with a single window
that stared at the side of a hill pimpled with
manzanita during the day, moonlit shadows
during the night. A curtainless window,
frozen shut by years of paint and neglect.
Two walls were bare. Two walls had
recently been sheetrocked, but were un-
painted. There was no closet. Wade kept
those few things he had unpacked—a small
Sony radio, a picture of Faye, a travel
Westclok, and a janitor's key ring—on a
small table in the corner.

He felt comfortable there, a little
cramped but more at home than home itself
sometimes felt.

He was thinking about his call to Faye,
wondering if it might have been better
never to have phoned at all. There wasn't
much doubt in his mind that he had
stumbled and possibly taken the marriage
down with him. But she had been so upfront, so goddamned upfront. What did she
want him to say? "I'll be home in an hour?"
He just couldn't do that.

Not yet.

Not quite yet. Maybe after Lomax
Construction came through and he'd
settled into the job. Maybe then he would
feel differently. But he wasn't ready yet,
not so soon after leaving. That would be too
much like giving up and admitting he was
wrong for ever walking out, and he couldn't
do that without feeling as if she had won

and he had lost. A feeling that seemed to be everywhere in their relationship these days.

He had almost made the decision to sack out for the night when Agnes Stearns knocked at the door. "You've got a call downstairs," she said. He was grateful to have her as a friend. If she were only twenty years younger . . .

"You know who it is?" Has to be Faye. He could already imagine the gist of the conversation unfolding betweeen them.

I've been thinking about your call.

Me, too.

It's not sitting right with me.

Me either.

Then silence. Because even though she would want to threaten him with divorce, she wouldn't be able to do it. And even though he would want to promise to hurry back home, *he* wouldn't be able to do it. They were at odds for the time being, each out of sync with the other, and neither with the courage or the strength to do anything about it.

"Haven't the slightest," Agnes said through the door.

"I'll be right down."

He slipped his feet off the edge of the bed, sat upright, and stared beyond the small single window, wondering absently what would happen if he fooled around long enough before answering the call, if she would hang up then and the inevitable silence would burn itself out before he ever made it downstairs. It would probably be her last call. And he would probably feel guilty for too long. Guilt always had a way of hitching a ride on one shoulder or the other, for one thing or another. And if they were ever to talk again, the conversation would be that much more difficult.

Just do it and get it over with.

The phone was a pay phone, stationed at the bottom of the stairs only a few feet away from where Ben Williams was celebrating his seventh beer and amusing himself as well as the others with a tale about a stripper he'd once met in San Francisco. The receiver was still swaying back and forth on its cord when Wade snatched it up. He put a finger to his open ear. "Yeah?"

"Wade Richardson?"

"Yeah." It wasn't Faye, and he felt a rush of relief leave him. "What can I do for you?"

"Stay away," the whisper said.

"Who is this?" He didn't recognize the voice, thought it not low enough to be a man's. Not high enough to be a woman's. For a moment, he wondered if it could be a boy's voice and he thought of Kiel. But that wasn't right either. It just sounded like a boy's voice.

"She doesn't want you back."

Wade felt a tremble go through him then. He told himself it wasn't fear, then realized that's exactly what it was. Someone, some stranger, knew too much about him, knew more than any stranger had a right to know. And the thought of that made him vulnerable in a way he'd never felt before.

"What do you want?" he said too loudly.

"Stay away from Faye."

"Fuck you!" When he slammed the receiver down, he combed a trembling hand through his hair and thought the shaking might never stop. Ben Williams had suddenly turned quiet; the whole place had suddenly turned quiet. And the faces all turned to him, watching him, studying him, trying to imagine what had been said at the other end of the phone.

A half-smile came and went across his face. He mumbled something about a bill collector, then escaped back up the stairway toward his room. By the time Wade reached the top step, Ben Williams was already recounting his tale and the laughter had returned to the Flat Rock Tavern. But Wade's hands were still trembling.

PART THREE
THE NIGHTMARE

"*Your tongue devises mischiefs; like a sharp razor, working deceitfully. You love evil more than good, and lying rather than speaking of righteousness. You love devouring words, O you of deceitful tongue. And you must be punished.*"

His father, half-shadow/half-flesh, took hold of his arm in a vise-like grip that was inescapable, and dragged him deeper into the dark-cornered barn where eyes were blind and great gulps of air went soundless.

And the boy had seen that blackness before, a dream within a dream, a nightmare against a nightmare.

"It's the tongue of the devil speaking from your lips," said his father's voice from everywhere and nowhere. "Devouring words are the devil's words. And if you so speaketh for the devil then you shall wear his mark to separate you from the others."

And he saw a red-hot/white-hot branding iron come dancing out of the darkness, waving a golden tail. 666.

"It's the mark of the devil, my son. So those who cross your path will know you for what you are, a child not of man, not of woman, but of the beast of hell."

And suddenly the hotter-than-fire branding iron was pressed against his inner thigh. And he knew he'd felt that pain a thousand times before. And reflexively he grabbed the iron rod with his hands until the searing pain burned home and he had to pull his hands away.

When he first glanced-then-stared at his palms, they were red and moist and black-charred masses of flesh that seemed detached the way a mirror image seems detached. Then he noticed how the skin had peeled back, all black and worm-like, and he looked from his hands to the face of his father, wanting to ask why? but finding no voice.

He thought he was burning in hell, then.

And the barn began to spin, all flying hay and twirling rafters, until the pain turned unbearable and the dark turned even darker and his dream-eyes closed for just the wink-of-a-second.

When his eyes opened again, he was high above the barn floor, where an outside wind was whispering in his ears. His hands were tied—left hand stretched southward, right hand northward—to a horizontal two-by-four; ankles, waist, and neck tied similarly to a vertical pole that kept him suspended there.

There was still a burning pain in his hands, in his thighs. In the air, there was the smell of charred denim, the taste of burnt flesh. And he remembered seeing the denim of his jeans melting blue and pink and white into his thigh.

But it wasn't the pain that first came to mind.

It wasn't how high he was suspended, how tight the rope felt around his neck and wrists and ankles.

Where is he? Where's Pa?

That's what he thought of first.

"High enough to touch the heavens?" his father said from below. He stepped out of the shadows and into a crack of light that had somehow penetrated from outside. His *face was half-mask, half-monster. Stubbled and bloated. Gray, the way the warm insides of something not-long-dead are sometimes an almost colorless gray. "High enough to smell the sweet breath of the Lord?"*

His father disappeared for a moment, but the sound of his boots against hook and nail and brace, climbing up the barn wall, was louder than the whisper of the outside air. And suddenly that face—sweating beer from its pours, tears from its eyes—was right next to his. And out of his father's mouth flamed words of the Bible and the Lord and the devil, all rambled together and meaningless.

"Behold, I am against your magic, wherewith you hunt the souls to make them fly, and I will tear the charms from your arms, and will let the souls go, even those souls that you hunt to make them fly."

His father fumbled with a black cloth, then clumsily slipped it over his head, until the darkness had become black, the black had become blacker.

"And I shall hide the devil's eyes from seeing, cup the devil's ears from hearing, gag the devil's mouth from speaking."

And then the pain of palm and thigh came burning home again . . .

When he woke up from the nightmare, there was a dying afterimage that tried to stay with him but couldn't. It was bright, the way a flashbulb is bright. But it reminded him of those warm summer nights when he used to stand beneath the mercury lamp in the yard between the barn and the house, catching moths in jars, tossing baseballs at the stars.

Then he rolled over and saw where a rainbow of moonlight was painting the opaque hills and gullies of the wall. How much it still looked like a moonlit cemetery night. How much it still looked ghostly pale.

He rolled away, buried himself beneath the shield of the bedsheets, and tried to go back to sleep.

Justin didn't want to go and said so. It was ten o'clock the next morning. He was wearing a pair of Wrangler jeans and a blue tee-shirt that ran midway down his arms. And he was finishing up a bowl of Rice Krispies, spooning and slurping the last of the milk. Since the night before, when he had awakened and realized he'd been away, Kiel had been watching him with eyes that never looked away. And Justin wondered what his brother was looking for, wondered if something were showing that shouldn't.

"Are you sure?" his aunt was saying. She already had her purse hung from one shoulder, her right hand was on the door-knob. Kiel was standing behind her, ready to follow her out the door. "Henry's not so bad if you don't pay him too much mind."
red eyes

"I don't want to." He still remembered
coming awake and standing in the shadows
of Henry Aikens' hallway. There had been
something at his back, something he didn't
want to think about just now.

red eyes and chattering

"Okay," his aunt said. "We'll be back in a
little while. Make sure you clean up your
breakfast dishes and put things away."

He nodded.

red eyes and chattering and . . .
and what?

His aunt opened the door and disappeared. His brother stood in the doorway
for a thoughtful moment, staring too
closely at him, as if he were trying to see
inside him. "It is you, Justin, isn't it?"

"I'm here."

"Sure you don't want to come along?"

red eyes and chattering and something. . .
   something wrong?

Justin shook his head. *There's something*
bad there, something dark and heavy and
too quiet. And Aunt Faye and Kiel are
going to find it there, hiding in the
shadows, waiting for them. But it's really
waiting for me. "I don't like him. He scares
me."

"What are you going to do here?"

He shrugged. "Just fool around, I
guess."

"Why don't you come?"

"I don't want to."

"He can't do anything with Aunt Faye there."

"I don't care," Justin insisted.

"Okay, be a baby about it."

He watched his brother slip out the door, watched the door slam shut, and listened as the noise echoed up and down the hallway leading to the bedrooms. When the house fell quiet again, he looked back at the stationary door and felt suddenly too alone, the way he had felt that night in the cemetery after Trenton had gone away and left him. A light tremor took hold of his insides.

red eyes
  and chattering
  and . . . and something dead

There was something dead where his aunt and his brother were going. Something dark and heavy and lifeless, stone cold lifeless. Like Joseph Little had been on that moonlit night in the cemetery.

"You shouldn't go," he whispered.

Then he felt something painful stab at him from behind his right eye. A black field splattered his vision. He felt himself being pulled away, and somewhere in the distance he heard the rattle of metal against ceramic as the spoon slipped from his fingers and fell back into his bowl.

Trenton Maes had been killing off another morning on his bike, when he saw Faye Richardson and her nephew hiking off through the pastures in the direction of either the creek or Henry Aikens' place. He sat on his bike, leaning against a tree, with his arms crossed over his chest, watching them disappear from sight, wondering where they were going, speculating on how long they would be gone. Long enough, he supposed.

It was mid-morning, a crisp mid-morning with dew still damp on the gravel road even though the sky was clear and the sun bright. The warmth of the sun settled on Trenton's back, seeping through his long-sleeved jersey as he made the road an obstacle course, weaving and dodging and sliding. He finished with a skid-out that left an ugly patch of loose, wet gravel across the Richardson's carport.

He parked the bike against the corner of the house.

"Hey, Justin!" He warmed his cupped hands, first filling them with warm air from his lungs, then rubbing them together. And when he felt the life come back to them, he pounded an impatient fist against the door, wishing the kid would quit screwing-off and answer. "Justin!"

When the door opened, it opened wide and Justin was standing there, leaning against the jamb, staring out with eyes that seemed angrier than Trenton thought possible. This was the same kid who had freaked out that night in the cemetery? The same kid who had a big brother for a babysitter? He didn't look like the same kid, not altogether he didn't. Something was different.

"Been out to the cemetery?" he asked, trying to hold a grin that wanted to melt under the glare of this kid standing too-indifferent, too-old-for-his-years in the doorway.

"What do you want?"

"I saw your aunt and your brother leave."

"So?"

"So, I thought you might want to do something."

"Like what?"

"I don't know."

"Another good time at the cemetery?"

Trenton grinned and a nervous laugh hiccuped involuntarily from somewhere around his mid-section. He looked away, down the empty street where the sun glistened off dew-covered gravel, and wondered if there was somewhere else that he should be. "Maybe."

"You left *him*," Justin said. "You ran off and left the *pretender* standing alone and naked in the cemetery with a dead man."

"The cemetery's full of dead men." His voice caught in his throat, suddenly too-dry, and he damned himself for letting it happen. Because he realized—without understanding why—that this was more than a casual conversation.

"You shouldn't have left *him*."

"That old man died where he wanted to die."

"I'm not talking about the old man." Justin stood tall in the doorway, taller than seemed natural for his eleven-year-old frame. "I'm talking about the *pretender*. You left *him* by himself."

Trenton coughed his nervousness up with a snicker. "There were only the three of us," he said. "You and me and old Joseph Little. Unless you happened by the ghost of Cardew James Mantooth? Huh? Is that what you saw? The ghost of thirteen-year-old Cardew James?"

The boy remained emotionless, filling up the doorway with a presence that belonged to someone else.

"Your knees were sure knocking that night," Trenton snickered.

"So were yours."

"Yeah, maybe." He shook his head then. "But I don't think either one of us was as scared out of our wits as you were yesterday, tumbling off old man Aikens' front porch. You had the eyes of a rabbit with one foot on the ground and the other in the stew."

"You saw that?"

"I saw it. I don't know what kind of trouble you stirred up inside that old man's house, but you sure as hell were in a hurry to get out of there." Trenton raised an eyebrow then, suddenly feeling back in control, realizing he had something (although he didn't know what) on his younger friend. "What did you do in there? Steal something?" And when Justin's face turned sour, then lifeless again, Trenton knew he'd hit a nerve.

"Something like that," the boy said.

"Really?"

Justin backed away from the door. "Come on in," he said. "I'll tell you all about it."

"Did old man Aikens catch you?" Trenton asked, stepping up to the level of the kitchen floor. "Is that why you went stumbling down the steps? To get away from him?"

"Something like that," the boy said.

And the door closed behind him.

5

The front door was slightly ajar, inviting a shaft of sunlight to slice across the darkness held within. But it wasn't enough for Faye Richardson to see what was inside.

"Henry?" She knocked for the third time.

"Maybe he's not home?" Kiel suggested.

"The door's wide open. He wouldn't leave it open like this." She knocked again, this time against the door instead of the frame. The door swung inward; the darkness slithered back into the corners. "Mr. Aikens?"

"I don't like this."

"Neither do I."

Faye pushed the door until it hit against something, then she took a hesitant step, followed by another and another, until she was standing inside the house. "This isn't funny, Henry."

This was the first time she had ever

pressed a foot against the creaking floorboards inside Henry Aikens' house. And
something inside her hoped it would be the
last. On her right, through a screen of
lattice, she could see where the sun was
slanting across the kitchen, unable to bleach
the murkiness there. Whether it was the
chill of the house or something else, something her senses had noted but her mind
had ignored, she felt a strange uneasiness
take hold of her. Something wasn't right
here. Beyond the fact that Henry Aikens
had left his front door open, something was
terribly wrong here.

"Aunt Faye?" Kiel was standing at her
side, one elbow lightly pressing against her
forearm. He was searching the shadows and
non-shadows, looking suspiciously about as
if he expected something to explode out of
the darkness and take hold of him. "Maybe
we shouldn't be here."

"But something's not right," she whispered.

"We could wait outside?"

When she took another step into the sun-
streaked obscurity, her nephew took the
step with her. "Come on, Henry," she whispered. "Don't do this to us." Her right hand
took hold of the lattice as she turned to face
the kitchen. It was corner-dark and dirty,
too cluttered to make sense with a single
glance, too dusty to sift through without
making the effort.

"What happened?" Kiel asked before she had noticed anything unusual.

Then she saw the broken pieces of wood, and next to them on the floor, what had once been a chair. And she saw the depressions in the tabletop. And she saw the naked makings of the telephone receiver lying in the corner. And she saw the low-burning, yellow-blue flame still alive on the stove. *It shouldn't be burning,* she thought. *Not with the house empty the way it is. Not with no one here to keep an eye on it.* And she moved across the uneven floor to shut-off the gas.

"What happened?" Kiel asked again.

"I don't know."

"Crooks?"

"I don't know."

"Maybe we should call someone?"

Her nephew stood waiting next to the lattice, both hands gripping the woodwork as if he feared being snatched from the face of the earth if he didn't hold on tight enough. Some of the color had gone out of his face, or was it only that the play of light and dark made it seem that way? He appeared younger than his years, wide eyes and long lashes, more innocence sneaking into his features than she had ever noticed before.

"Henry?" She listened, wishing his hoarse old voice would squawk from somewhere nearby, cussing up a whirlwind about the goddam weather or his too-bitchy milkers, anything, just anything, as long as she could hear his voice and know that the chill in his house wasn't as godawful evil as she feared. But his name fell lifelessly from her lips, back to earth, unanswered.

"Aunt Faye?"

"I just want to make sure he's not here, make sure he's not hurt," she said, assuming Kiel was about to again suggest they leave. Across the room, on the other side of the hall, she could see the weathered tools Henry Aikens had collected over the years and now used as wall hangings. Pop art, she thought. Old American like Henry himself.

"We'll just check down the hall, then be out of here."

"Maybe you can borrow a paint sprayer from a neighbor?" It was a question asked of fear. His voice trembled through the words, catching a syllable here, blurting a syllable there.

And Faye suddenly realized, as she looked away from the wall of antiquated implements back to her nephew clasped two-handed to the lattice, how much of her own fear she had spilled over to him. It wasn't enough that her own stomach was knotted and sour, she had unthinkingly managed to pass her apprehensions along to her nephew as well. "It'll only take a minute," she said with a false smile.

The hallway was a maze of intersecting gray and black shadows, shapeless, unchoreographed shadows that closed in around them too quickly. At the far end, a shaft of filtered sunlight fell through the crack of a door and painted a white line across the floor, a white line which seemed to threshold the final hallway door. *Dare you to cross that line.*

Faye had one hand on her nephew's shoulder when they stopped at the first door on the left. "Henry?" Her other hand took hold of the doorknob, twisted slowly, and a click fell into place. But when she tried to swing the door open, it stuck, winter-swollen, stiff and rusty. She pressed a shoulder against raw wood and pushed and felt no give, then pushed harder.

"Maybe it's locked?" Kiel said.

"From the other side?"

She pushed again, then one final time before backing away and wiping the feel of dirt from her hands. "It doesn't want to open."

"Want me to try?"

"No, we'll skip it." Her hands had taken hold of her arms, trying to rub away the goose pimples which had sprouted there, trying at the same time to warm the cold fear that was with her. "Let's get this over with and get out of here."

The next door, near the end of the hall-

way—*dare you to cross that line*—opened
easily and opened into Henry Aikens' bedroom. At the window, there was a white
bedsheet hanging from a curtain rod. It
wasn't enough to keep out the hazy glow of
sunlight. In one corner, Faye could see a
pile of dirty clothing—a pair of overalls,
some once white, now gray socks, and what
appeared to be three identical red plaid
shirts. There was a dresser made of knotty
pine in another corner, a shadeless lamp
sitting on the floor next to the bed, and a
throat-catching odor that rushed to escape
the confines of the room.

Faye coughed, and held a hand to her
mouth.

"Anything?"

"No." Thank God. Because she was
quickly coming to believe that if they did
find something, if they opened a door and
there was something there more than
darkness or musty odors, it would be something better left alone. *Damn you, Henry
Aikens.*

"Should I?" Kiel was holding the knob of
the next door, the door that stood slightly
ajar and invited a shaft of sunlight to paint a
white line across the floor.

She nodded.

Kiel pushed the door open.

They each set free a lungful of air.

It was the bathroom, empty. Peeling,
yellow wallpaper. An opaque shower

curtain. Brown, checkered linoleum. A curtainless window, weatherstained and opened a crack to the southern sun. There was the sharp smell of liniment in the air.

"And then there was one," she said absently. At her feet, shadowy-white across her ankles and toes, fell the threshold of sun. *Dare you to cross that line.* She reached, took hold of the last doorknob, felt the rough texture of metal against skin, and couldn't make her fingers obey her.

"Wait," Kiel said. "Don't you hear it?"

"Hear what?"

He pursed his lips, pressed an index finger over them.

And it was there, at the other side of the door, a crying—squealing—chattering noise. High-pitched multiples. *Scurrying,* she imagined. *There's something scurrying only a door's thickness away.*

"What is it, Aunt Faye?"

"I don't know." Her fingers wouldn't let loose of the knob.

"We could skip this one," Kiel said. "We've checked everywhere else. There's nothing here. We could borrow a sprayer from someone else."

We could, she thought. But the doorknob turned in her hand until it clicked and they both felt a damp breath leak through the narrow opening.

And the narrow opening grew to be a wide opening.

And a naked, overhead light bulb burned too bright in their eyes.

"The cellar," Faye said.

They each took a step forward, came to stand at the threshold of the doorway, and stopped there. Faye shaded her eyes from the light. At the foot of the stairway, she could see something moving, a hundred somethings, all scurrying out of the light into shadows. Red-eyed. Chattering. And there was something else, man-sized and too-still, sprawled face-down there at the bottom.

And she knew it was the body of Henry Aikens.

And she saw a hundred places where sharp teeth had whittled and gnawed and chewed at the old man's flesh. Red places. Red pools. Too many red pools.

And she screamed.

Matt finished washing his hands, wiped them on a towel, tossed the towel into the corner of the bathroom, and wandered back into the bedroom. At that very moment, he thought he'd never before felt quite as alive. Free of the darkness that guarded the spotlight. Free to come and go, almost at will now. Free the way the *pretender* had always been free.

He glanced back at the closet door, all dark and quiet, thought how thin that hollow half-inch piece of wood really was, and realized something would have to be done sooner than later. The boy would have to be moved before the *brother* came nosing around and found little Trenton Maes, eyes all white and extended, mouth all stuffed and speechless. Because all hell would break loose if Trenton was discovered in their closet.

All hell.

He'd known from day one that Trenton Maes was a jerk-off. Big mouthed and bragging, trying to make his empty brain sound smarter than it really was. All pretend and make believe. And the *pretender* should have known better than to trust such an asshole. This whole mess could have been skipped right over if the *pretender* had half the brains of an avocado.

Matt tapped a closed fist against the wall, smiled to himself. Aunt Faye would probably have heart failure if she knew what was hiding in the space between her bedroom wall and their closet door. And the *brother*, he'd crap his pants.

All kinds of hell.

Matt shared a laugh with himself, tapped the knuckle of another closed fist against the wall, listened to hear if an odd knuckle-tap would sound back at him, and when it didn't, he made his way down the hallway toward the kitchen.

The front door was open, lighting up the

entrance and the hallway with dust-sprinkled sunlight. And the kitchen window was open, slowly ridding the house of its coffee and tobacco stench, slowly replacing the smell of death with fresh air. Faye was leaning against the kitchen wall. Through the door, in the distance, she could see Henry Aikens' pasture, Henry Aikens' grazing cows. She hugged herself tighter, trying to hold down the chill that was snaking up her body.

Kiel was sitting at the table, occupying one of the wobbly, stick chairs. Head in hands. It had taken him a good ten minutes to piece together the telephone, plug it back into the base, and dial 911. Another twenty minutes had come and gone—not quickly enough—while they had waited for the sheriff to arrive.

"Tired?" Faye touched a hand to his shoulder.

He nodded.

She sighed. She had tried to take the stairway a step at a time, tried to check the body of Henry Aikens just in case there was still a breath of life there. But the sixth step had held her, made her look closer at the lump that had lost all semblance of humanness, and the sight had sent her hurrying out of the cellar, back down the hallway to join with her nephew again. That sight came back to her now. And she thought she might cry.

"Can't we go home?"

"In a little while, Kiel."

"I'm worried about Justin."

"He'll be all right." She squeezed her nephew's shoulder, silently wishing there were some way she could have protected him, kept him from the sight. All for a damn sprayer. And now his nights would be haunted recollections and nightmares. All for a goddamn sprayer she could have easily borrowed elsewhere.

Then the breath of silence that had suddenly grown between them was interrupted. The footfalls of Sheriff John Hague echoed hollowly down the hallway as he climbed the last few steps from the cellar. He stopped at the threshold. The echo died. Then the rhythmic tempo of his amble kicked up again.

He came to a standstill next to the lattice, filling up the kitchen doorway. "It's a mess down there."

Faye looked faraway to the pasture where a half dozen milkers were milling around as if today was the same as the day before it. Then she glanced again at her nephew.

"How did you happen by?" the sheriff asked. He was a heavy-faced man, with hanging jowls and a missing smile. Fifty-four years old, always with a stick of *Double Mint* in his mouth. He enjoyed snapping his gum as he spoke, as if it were meant to punctuate his questions.

"Came to borrow back our paint
sprayer."

"And the boy?" He nodded toward Kiel.

"Oh, I'm sorry. This is my nephew."

"He come with you?"

"Yes." The word was a soft whisper.

The huge man pulled a stick of chewing
gum from his jacket pocket, unwrapped it
with fingers that looked too big for the job,
let the paper wrapper and tin foil flutter
floorward, and added the gum to what was
surely three sticks already being mangled
and mashed by his mouth of straight teeth.
Faye wondered if it was the man's nervousness doing the chewing.

"Looks like he fell down the stairs," John
Hague said. "Looks like he was reaching for
the light string, lost his balance and went
tumbling head over heels all the way to the
bottom."

Where he became a rat feast

But the man didn't mention a word about
rats.

Faye shook her head. "Things weren't
right."

"What?"

"When we arrived," she said. "The front
door was open. And—"

"Did you fool with anything?"

Kiel glanced up at her, with that same
look he sometimes shared with his brother,
almost as if he were trying to tell her to be
careful now, not to say anything that would
get them in trouble.

She tapped his shoulder, gave it a reassuring squeeze. "I shut off one of the burners on the stove."

"There was a burner on?"

"Yes."

"But nothing cooking?"

"No."

"You fool around with anything else?"

"The kitchen was a mess, John. Three of the chairs were piled together between the wall and the table, right here. The fourth chair was just as you see it, a pile of broken sticks. And the phone was lying in the corner, as naked as it is now. Kiel had to piece it back together so we could call out."

"Okay," he said then. "Why don't you and the boy walk through it with me. Just exactly like you did when you first got here. Step by step, so I can get an idea of what you might have fooled with and just what the hell you really saw."

"John . . ." What she couldn't seem to say out loud, she tried to express facially. *Is it really necessary? The boy, he's tired and I don't want him to have to see what's in the cellar again. I don't want him to ever have to see such a horrible sight again.*

"It'll only take a minute," the man answered.

Kiel looked at her, his face expressionless, but his eyes trying to connect, trying to find a reason to be excused. And she wished she were able to pat him on the behind and send him scampering on his way back home, as far away from the sight in the cellar as possible. But she knew that wasn't realistic under the circumstances.

"I covered the body with a sheet of plastic," the sheriff said then. "Please," he motioned them to join him. "It'll only take a minute."

From the front porch, they slowly began to retrace each and every step they had taken through Henry Aikens' house, questioned continually about why they had done this or that, how come they hadn't thought to do something else.

What prompted you to enter the house when no one answered the door?

The door was open.

So you just walked in?

I could feel something was wrong.

So you just walked in?

Yes.

In the kitchen, she retraced her steps to the stove, remembering the puddle of water on the floor and the bits of brown plastic everywhere underfoot and the strange shadowy pockets of non-light.

I kept calling his name.

And when he didn't answer, what made you continue on?

The feeling.

That something was wrong?

Yes.

What did you expect to find?

I don't know.

They left the kitchen and shuffled down the hallway to the first door on the left, and stood there. "I couldn't get it open," Faye said. "We left it and moved on." The sheriff turned the knob in his thick hand, pressed his huge frame against the door, and the noise of something cracking sounded before the door finally gave way. The room was curtained the same as the bedroom had been, with a white bedsheet over the window. There were wall-to-wall stacks of boxes, mostly cardboard boxes, occasionally wood crates, all cobwebbed and dust-layered. Not a footprint in the dust, as if the room had been sealed for what must have been a long time.

The sheriff seemed unimpressed.

And on down the hallway they continued.

They checked the bedroom again, and the bathroom again, assuring the man that they had never taken a step into either. And suddenly they were standing at the threshold, knowing too well what was only a few horrible steps away.

Was the light on?

Yes.

Faye could see the covered body at the foot of the stairs and through that thin layer of blackness, she could still imagine a thousand pools of red.

And then?

I sent Kiel back to the kitchen to call you.

The man turned to the boy, told him to go on back to the kitchen and wait there, but he left only after sharing a glance with Faye, something that asked if it was really okay for him to be gone.

Did you check Henry Aikens to see if he was alive?

I wanted to.

But did you?

I took a step down, then another and another.

And?

Until the sixth step.

And she found herself standing on that same sixth step again, unable now to look down into the light and dark patterns of the cellar. She found herself staring absently at the wall, trying to erase what she knew was lying beneath the black plastic. And she was seeing something else, something she had never noticed before, right there on the wall. She was seeing the dustless outline where there had recently been something else. It was the outline of a sheathed knife.

And you didn't touch anything?

No, nothing.

And did you notice anything missing?

No, nothing.

And did you notice anything unusual, anything that's missing now?

No, nothing. Except . . .

Except?

The rats.

John Hague had made a couple of phone calls into Eureka. One to arrange for a corner. Another to the police department for some sort of equipment he didn't otherwise have access to. It was all background chatter to Faye, distant and mindless and unimportant, because she had something else on her mind as she sat at the kitchen table with her nephew.

Too many things were beginning to make sense.

She thought now, how easy she had found it to overlook things which were so obvious, how she had worked not to see things that were perfectly clear. And where once she had refused to see the connection between the death of Joseph Little and the mural on her nephew's wall, now she thought she couldn't ignore it any longer. And if she thought about it, she knew a search of the cemetery would turn up a missing shirt and a missing pair of socks, all brand new and fitted for Justin.

But he's my baby.

And she knew if she were to take the knife from her nephew's belt and hold it against the dustless shadow on Henry Aikens' cellar wall, the knife would match that shadow all too perfectly.

My sister's baby.

And she felt herself still trying to deny it, still trying to believe it was all no more than coincidence. But . . . it wasn't, was it?

My nephew.

All powdered white and breathless one night. Sleepwalk painting another. Too quiet sometimes, too noisy others. With dark brown eyes that kept everything a secret. And too many years stuffed inside his eleven-year-old body.

It was Justin.

"Aunt Faye?" Kiel touched her arm, then nodded toward the sheriff.

"I was just saying, you could be on your way, Mrs. Richardson."

"Oh." To where? Back home again? "Thank you." But she didn't move. She couldn't move. Even as Kiel took hold of her arm and gently tugged, she found herself firmly in place.

"John," she asked then. "How did Joseph Little die?"

"Coronary."

"That's all?"

"He was in his seventies. That's all he needed."

"In the cemetery?" she asked absently.

"He was always in the cemetery."

"Yes, I guess he was."

"Always waiting for the second coming."

"What?"

"The second coming. Never heard the story? That's why he spent his nights out there. He was waiting for the ghost of some hundred-year-old kid to pop out of the grave and talk to him." The sheriff laughed. "Crazy old coot."

"Yeah, crazy." She nodded slightly. "And the name of the ghost?"

"You got me."

"Mantooth? Could it have been Mantooth?"

"Sounds like the name Weatherbee mentioned."

"Aunt Faye, let's go." Kiel tugged again at her arm, pulling her to her feet, pulling her from her thoughts. "Please."

"Okay, okay." She smiled weakly. "If that's all?"

"For the time being," John Hague said. "I may need to catch you again in a day or so. Depends on what the coroner has to say."

Outside, on the porch, Faye came to a standstill. She looked away to the pasture with Henry Aikens' cows. "I want you to do me a favor, Kiel."

"Sure."

"I want you to gather up Henry's cows and see if they need milking. Then herd them into the barn for the rest of the day. Will you do that for me?"

"Are you going home?"

"I'll make us something hot for lunch."

"Okay."

As he took two steps at a time down the stairway and scampered off toward the pasture, Faye wondered how much alike him and his brother really were. And she wondered how much of this Kiel already knew about, if he knew it all and had simply kept a clamped mouth to protect Justin. And she wondered if she would be able to do the same thing.

6

It was twelve noon. The place was empty except for Ben Williams, who was working on his first beer of the day while knocking a few pool balls around. The echo of ball hitting ball was enough to put a little life into the otherwise dark and dreary noon atmosphere.

Wade was sitting at the bar, drinking a Coke with a twist of lemon. He had spent a nervous morning, pacing too often, sometimes laughing too loud, wondering every now and then who had called him the night before, wondering more often if Lomax Construction would soon be calling with a job offer.

Agnes Stearns was behind the bar, cleaning glasses, restocking her liquor supply, generally busying herself with the same routine of business that occupied every mid-day hour of every day of her life.

From anyone else, Wade would have expected to hear a complaint of boredom, a wishful thought of something better out of life. But The Flat Rock was all that Agnes had ever wanted, all that she had ever needed to keep her happy.

Wade kept watching the phone, waiting for it to ring.

"It won't, you know," Agnes said.

"Huh?"

"The phone, it won't ring as long as you're watching it. Same as a pot of water waiting to boil. You've got to busy yourself with something else. Take your mind and put it somewhere else altogether. Then sure enough, before you know it, that call will come along."

Wade smiled. "You think so, huh?"

"Sure of it."

"And what if it never rings?"

"Then you saved yourself a lot of watching time that otherwise would have been wasted, now didn't you?"

He tipped his empty glass at her.

She refilled it. "Off the hard stuff?"

"Can't very well receive a job offer when I'm blitzed out of my mind." He grinned, but it was a mixture of something sad and something off-the-cuff. "Me and the fire water weren't getting along too well anyway."

"For the best, huh?"

"Something like that."

The front door opened then, and a man stepped into the shaft of sunlight which had suddenly spilled into the darkness. He smiled comfortably. A stranger. Then the door closed behind him, the sunlight crept back into the corners, and The Flat Rock became a world unto itself again. The stranger looked about and headed for the phone.

Wade watched as the man dialed the number of a mistress or an auto club mechanic or an out-of-town friend, and he sighed, feeling as if his own private phone had been taken from him. Against the glass in his hand, his fingers tapped out a nervous Morse code, something to hurry the stranger on his way. There were expected calls still expected.

"Sorry about that call last night," Agnes said.

"Huh?"

"I take it the news wasn't good."

"Oh, that. No, nothing like that at all. It was just a prank." He had for the most part been able to put aside that call, attribute it to nothing more than some kid playing with the telephone. After all, Winter Creek Mills was a small town with a word-of-mouth network as good as the best of them. It couldn't be a secret anymore. Everyone in town must know that he had moved out. And some dumb kid had probably overheard his parents flapping their jaws about it, thought he'd have a little fun, and there you go—a nice, safe phone call to see what kind of reaction he can stir up in old man Richardson.

"It wasn't important," he said.

Agnes tilted her head, a little body language there, saying, *Oh sure it wasn't important, that's why you screamed loud enough to close the whole place down for a full goddamned minute.* But she didn't say anything. And Wade turned back to watch the stranger mumble some final words into the phone before hanging up and hurrying out the door again.

Wade stayed with his watching.

Agnes went back to her washing.

And in the back room, Ben Williams could still be heard knocking pool balls around.

It was the longest walk of her life, less than a quarter of a mile in measured footsteps, an agonizing forever in anxiousness. The glare of the noon sun went barely noticed. The places in the path that were too rocky or too muddy went unfelt, except for something far at the back of her mind which wondered if her nephew had noticed such things when he had come sneaking his way over this same path, heading not home but the other way, heading toward Henry Aikens' place. Did he walk this path with purpose? Or was it something that had simply happened? Unplanned. Unimagined. An act of fatal fate?

Trenton's bike was leaning against the corner of the house when she arrived there. And there was a skid mark in the damp gravel that was her carport. The mark of Trenton Maes himself. And she hoped, almost prayed, that it might have been that little hellion from the other side of town who had caused the trouble at the cemetery, who had visited Henry Aikens and walked away with a souvenir knife presented later to her nephew like a shiny, well-earned trophy. She prayed it had happened like that, and she prayed that Justin was no more than an innocent bystander caught up in the curiosity of it all. But then that same intuition she never seemed able to trust—yet always seemed to be right there, whispering things in her ear that were truer than true—told her it was more than a mistake of innocence that had involved her nephew, and she should know better than to believe otherwise.

And for the first time ever, she knew she had to trust that inner voice.

The kitchen was exactly the same as she had left it. Justin's breakfast dishes were still sitting on the dining room table, next to a box of cereal and a carton of milk that had surely soured by this time.

"Justin?" She stood at the doorway,

almost as if she feared taking another step into her own house, as if she expected the unexpected, expected something not quite Justin to step out of the darkest corner looking just like her nephew, breathing out a breath too hot, grinning an ugly amusement, laughing at her for not having seen through the mask of innocence long before.

but he'd just a child

"Justin?"

The dining room curtains were wide-open to the mid-day sun, revealing a strange montage of finger prints, palm prints, and rain stains. Outside, above the line of the fence, she could see a hawk set its wings and glide majestically above the terrain, in search. We're both in search, she thought.

"Hi." He was standing at the corner of the hallway.

"Hi."

"Where's Kiel?"

Faye forced herself away from the kitchen door, forced herself to smile and relax. "He stayed behind for a few minutes."

"To ride the milkers?" He smiled.

"No." Deliberately, she went to the table and busied herself clearing away the dishes. Her nephew came to stand next to her, took the box of Rice Krispies in hand and silently closed the flaps. "So what have you been doing all morning?"

"Just kicking around."

His eyes were so goddamned honest, dark

and innocent and honest. And when she looked into them, she found it impossible to see anything malevolent there. This was a boy, not a monster. This was her nephew, raised with the smell of fresh cut hay at his backside, too young to know anything beyond the sweet taste of laughter, the wide eyes of wonder.

She ran a hand through his straight blond hair. "We need to talk."

"I didn't do it."

"What's that?"

"Whatever you're mad at me about, I didn't do it."

"I'm not mad at you, Justin." She took him by the hand, seated him in a chair that looked much too big for his little-boy body, and she sat next to him. His eyes kept dancing about, catching brief moments of contact with her own, then suddenly flitting away before anything could be made of it. "I want you to tell me about the knife."

"What about it?"

"Where'd you get it?"

"I found it."

"Where?"

"Well . . ." He hesitated, looked toward the floor in thought, then said, "I didn't really find it. Trenton Maes gave it to me. For protection."

Of course! Trenton Maes, the hellion himself!

"He *gave* it to you?"

The boy nodded.

"Was it his knife, his to give?"

"No."

His lips were pushing at the edge of a pout, and she could feel something vulnerable and fragile in him that caused a wave of guilt to sweep through her. On one side she held her guilt, on the other her intuition. And they seemed too much at odds, too different to belong to the same person.

This is my nephew, with the face of a child.

And he carries the scythe of the Reaper.

"Whose knife is it?"

"I promised not to tell."

"No games, Justin." In her right hand, she took hold of his little-boy chin, turned his eyes to face her. "I have to know where the knife came from."

He swallowed, tried to look away again.

"Justin?"

"It belongs to Mr. Aikens."

Yes! Yes!

"And Trenton gave it to you?"

The boy nodded, then tore his chin away from her hand, as if he were ashamed that he had confessed, ashamed that so easily he had given away something that was supposed to have been a secret. And he couldn't, wouldn't, look at her again. But it didn't matter. It didn't matter because suddenly every terrible fear her intuition had so hastily planted in her mind could now be put aside, disregarded, attributed to nothing more than a mad flight of imagination.

Yes! It was Trenton Maes who was the spark of the devil.

Trenton Maes who needed watching!

"I knew it," she said. "I knew it couldn't be you."

And for a breath, the room fell quiet. Somewhere outside, zig-zagging its way down Four Wheel Drive, the sound of a distant engine coughed and heaved. Then a high-pitched hum grew loud from the background, the hum of something always running, never noticed. The refrigerator. And over the hum, something louder, not as pleasant, not as everyday in its noise. Something odd.

"What is that?" she asked.

The boy kept his eyes away, said nothing.

"Hear it?" Something muffled is what she thought. Not faraway, but nearby. Not the sound of the house settling. Not the sound of water dripping from a washerless faucet. But still, a sound that seemed reluctant to fade back into the background of things. Something so strangely odd.

"Justin," she said. "Where's Trenton?"

The boy shrugged.

She took his chin in hand again. "His bike is outside, leaning against the corner of the house. He came to visit, didn't he?"

The boy kept his gaze focused on the floor, quietly resisting an answer.

"Didn't he, Justin?"

"Yes."

"Then where is he?"

It came again, the sound. Something hollow and thunderous and echoing. Louder this time. And Faye rose from her chair, looking toward the bedrooms, looking to where she felt certain the noise had orignated. Then it came again. And again. And she thought she could feel the floor trembling beneath the weight of her body as she pursued the disturbance down the hall until she was standing face-to-door at her nephew's bedroom.

Justin had wordlessly followed her. He stood at her side.

She looked down at him, hoping he would say something that would explain away the noise, looking into his eyes for just a glimmer of the innocence she had always believed resided there. But he glanced away again. And she knew—without knowing— that she had come to stand before another too-fragile cellar door, a too-thin piece of wood, separating her from something better left unseen.

"What did you do with Trenton?" she asked.

"Nothing," he whispered back.

"He's here, though. On the other side of this door. Isn't he?"

Silently, he shook his head.

And she opened the door.

And the noise that was shouting too loud

for her to come and see, grew louder still. And it was the noise of Trenton Maes, all wrist and ankle tied, mouth stuffed with a sock, and he was spilling out of the bedroom closet, hammering his heels against the floor. His face was tear-stained. His wrists damp with perspiration. His long-sleeved jersey nearly on backwards where he had tried to wiggle free from his bonds.

Faye pulled the sock from his mouth. He swallowed a huge lungful of air, had trouble taking in another breath, then finally began to breathe normally. His eyes were shadowed in white. He peered over her shoulder, peered at Justin standing in the doorway.

"He's crazy," Trenton said through a breath.

Faye glanced back at her nephew. He was leaning against the doorjamb, watching, mouth clamped tight, hands nervously tinkering with the doorknob. What was there about his expression? Something detached. As if he were removed from what was happening right there in front of him, as if he were somewhere else in mind and body.

"I saw him," Trenton said. "I saw him come spilling out of Henry Aikens' place, all scared out of his hide and looking back over his shoulder like he'd done something worse than worse inside that old man's house."

Faye ripped the masking tape that hand-cuffed the boy's wrists.

"He said he'd cut out my tongue if I told anyone, but I'm telling you, Mrs. Richardson. I'm telling you so you'll know what he said. 'Cause a threat ain't worth spit when everybody knows." Trenton had turned himself about, was leaning against the wall now, and staring at Justin with watchful eyes. "He's crazy."

She freed the tape from his ankles and he back-crawled up the wall until he was standing tall. "One minute he's all smiles and kidding, another minute and he's looking out through blood-red eyes that would just as soon kill you as not." Trenton rubbed his sticky wrists. "He changes people, like there's more than just one of him."

Like there's a whole crowd of people inside him.

She had heard that somewhere before. She remembered hearing it. And it was a phrase that bothered her. "What are you trying to say?"

There's a crowd inside him, all secret and hiding, looking out through his eyes when no one else is around to look back.

"Like he's someone else?" Faye asked, her mind thinking other thoughts.

"Yes, just like that. Not Justin at all, but someone else."

"I think I understand." She had knelt to remove the bindings from the boy and now she rose to her feet again, one hand against the wall to help her keep her balance. There was something she felt she should say, facing her nephew just then, but it escaped her and where her lips had opened to speak, they quickly closed again. All of it made sense, yet none of it made sense. And she wondered if she would ever really understand the churnings that went on behind her nephew's eyes.

"Can I go now?" Trenton asked.

She nodded numbly.

Still rubbing his wrists where the tape had served as handcuffs, he pushed away from the wall, bent and twisted around Faye so he wouldn't touch her. At the door, he stopped for a moment, stopped and looked at Justin until he couldn't look any longer, then he brushed by the boy and disappeared down the hallway.

Justin's gaze fell.

Faye sucked in more air than she thought her lungs could hold, before blowing it all out again.

And suddenly they were two.

There was a light breeze swimming through the grass of Henry Aikens' pasture. In the distance, Kiel could see the gentle sway of the trees which lined Winter Creek. At his back, the old man's house still loomed, still waited with its black-plastic body and its gum-chewing sheriff. He was relieved to be gone from there. But without knowing exactly why, he wished his aunt hadn't left him behind to tend the dairy cows.

He used a reedy cottonwood branch to herd the milkers toward the barn, slapping branch against grass, branch against hide, prodding them this way then that, one lonely step at a time. There were seventeen black and whites altogether. Not a one with a full udder, which wasn't surprising since they were near as old as Henry Aikens himself and probably hadn't given milk in years. And he wondered why the old man had kept them around, why he had always complained about his cows drying up when he'd known all along they were past their milk-giving days anyway.

Strange Henry Aikens.

Dead.

Buried in his cellar.

Beneath a black-plastic shroud.

A chill tickled its way up Kiel's spine. He wondered if he would awake the next morning, sit up in bed, and there on the wall, etched and scratched and crayoned over the phantom CARDEW JAMES MANTOOTH he would discover another mural. This time the face-down, rat-nibbled body of Henry Aikens lying at the bottom of a cellar stairway.

It wouldn't surprise him.

He still remembered standing at the bedroom door, watching and listening and holding his breath while the Matt-one occupied his brother's body and flapped his brother's jaws about old man Aikens, about teaching the old man a lesson. And that's what it had come to, hadn't it? Henry Aikens wasn't lying dead at the foot of the stairs all because his arms were too short and the light string too far out of reach. Not because of anything so ordinary. He was dead because he had come face-to-face with someone he thought was Justin, someone who was pretending to be Justin.

And that's why Justin had stayed behind this morning. He had somehow known what was lying dead in Henry Aikens' cellar. He had somehow sensed what one or two or all of the others had done there.

It is you, Justin, isn't it?

I'm here.

Or maybe it hadn't been Justin at all, looking over his bowl of cereal and pouting and swearing that old man Aikens scared the devil out of him. Maybe it had been someone else altogether. Maybe it had been Matt himself, knowing better than anyone else in the world what would be waiting to greet them if they stepped into the darkness of that old man's house.

Just be careful.

Of Matt?

Especially of Matt.

You're afraid of him, aren't you?

The same as you should be.

Albert had tried to warn him, had told him to keep a watchful eye on the one called

Matt. *There's only so much room in here,* he had said. *One spotlight, one person at a time. And Matt wants it all.*

Kiel herded the last straggler through the gate and into a small holding pen which enclosed the north entrance to the barn. At foot, the ground was a solid mixture of dirt, manure and sawdust. Smells like home, he thought. Feels like home. And he stopped cold in his tracks, remembering what hadn't been so long ago, remembering the yard and the way the dying sun painted shades of orange on the bedroom wall and the way the mercury lamps came alive at night, lighting up the outside darkness as bright as the parking lot of the big shopping center in Jefferson.

And he thought again of that night when he had stood at the bedroom window and stared transfixed at the yellows and blues of barn-high flames. The light of the mercury lamps had disappeared in the wash of the fire that night. And so had his Ma and Pa, all black-charcoaled ash. Hushed and put to rest. Eyes closed and sleeping. Forever sleeping.

The same as the ghost of Cardew James Mantooth.

The same as Joseph Little.

The same as old Henry Aikens.

They had all been hushed and put to rest, forever sleeping. And as he thought of that, he could still feel the heat of the flame as it had fanned across the yard and brushed

against his face. And through blinding
yellow-orange-reds, he had looked down
upon the barn, had taken note of the two-
by-four holding the barn doors shut, had
listened to the sound of living things dying,
and had done nothing. Someone had locked
them in the barn and set fire to their coffin.
And he had done nothing. Through the
bedroom window he had watched and felt
numb and done nothing.

He had wanted it that way, wanted them
dead.

And he had always known—without
having to tell himself—that it had been
Justin's hands that had dropped that two-
by-four across the barn doors. Justin's
hands that had dropped a match in the
knee-high grass that was dryer than crisp
autumn leaves.

Justin's hands.

The same hands that had sat his brother
atop the marker of CARDEW JAMES
MANTOOTH and let him scare all the life
out of a man older than old, simply because
the man had waited too many years to see
something. The same hands that had done
something to make old Henry Aikens go
stumbling head over heels down those
damn cellar steps of his.

Justin's hands.

His brother's hands.

The realization jarred him, shook him
awake from the madness of what had been
and brought him back to that very moment,

standing shoe-top deep in the muck that was Henry Aikens' barn. She was alone with Justin, his aunt was. Alone and not knowing any better than to think he was her nephew. But he might be Albert or Matt or any one of a crowd of people, and she'd never know. Not until it was too late, she'd never know.

Kiel slapped the hide of the last milker, and hurried to get the barn door closed again. The breeze had left and gone elsewhere. Now the air was still, and the trees lining the creek were quiet where once they had been whispering and giggling and ever so softly making themselves known. It was an eerie stillness. And he stood a moment, trying to recognize it, before finally tearing himself away and taking flight for home.

She should know, his aunt should.

She should know that Justin wasn't always himself.

And Kiel prayed it wasn't too late to tell her.

7

Wade was still stuck tight to a bar stool, popping peanuts and washing them down with a mouthful of soda. In the mirror behind the line of liquor bottles, his reflection was watching him, sizing him up the way it might size up a stranger. And he had the hollowness about the eyes, the weakness about the spine, of a man broken by life. Unemployed and alone and passing mindlessly through hours which became days, days which became weeks. And in a way, he felt as broken as the reflection told him he must be.

Agnes Stearns was at the other end of the bar, serving up a scotch and water to a salesman on his way to Redding. He was a three-piece, gray-suited gentleman, particular in his attire. And there was a hollowness about his eyes that Wade thought he recognized. As if somewhere on

351

the road, the salesman had given away control of his life and was now resigned to an endless number of white-striped miles, town to town, always a day's drive further from where he really wanted to be. And where might that be? Home?

Wade looked back to the peanuts on the counter, spun one between finger and thumb, and watched it struggle to find its center of balance before scooting helter-skelter away from him.

"Why don't you just call again?" Agnes said. She was standing next to him and he clamped a quick palm over the peanut, as if he could hide his foolishness. At the other end of the bar, the abandoned salesman was staring glassy-eyed at his reflection in the mirror, face-to-face and still all alone. "It couldn't be any worse than spinning peanuts to pass the time. Besides, one call couldn't hurt."

"And say what?"

"I can't be telling you that." She untied the back of her bleached-white apron, shook it out as if she were trying to rid herself of something unseen, then wrapped the sash around her and tied it again. "What is it you want to say?"

"I'm not sure."

"Makes it harder that way, doesn't it?"

"I guess." He looked again to the salesman, saw a bit of himself sitting there, and without turning back to Agnes, added, "Maybe she won't want to talk to me?"

"And maybe prohibition will return."
Agnes followed his gaze down the bar to the
gray-suited salesman. "You can't spend
your life hiding behind *maybes* and *what ifs*
and *if onlys*. Sooner or later you got to take
a chance, you gotta be willing to hang
yourself out there and let what happens
happen. If you don't, young man, you're
gonna end up spending too many hours in
some out-of-the-way hole in the wall like
this place. Which is just as dandy as a strip
tease if you happen to own the place, but
hell on earth if you're there 'cause there's
nowhere else to be."

He tipped his empty glass at her. "Is the
lecture extra?"

"Should be." She refilled the glass with
another Coke. "Oughta be getting seventy-
five bucks an hour and sitting behind an
oak-top desk big enough for a little pro-
creation," she said. "But for you, Wade
Richardson, it's on the house."

He smiled. "Free wisdom, huh?"

"If you prefer, I could charge."

"No thank you."

She touched a hand to his shirt sleeve.
"So what do you say? Have you got the
guts to hang yourself out there a little?"

"I don't think so." He popped a fistful of
peanuts into his mouth, chewed not long
enough, and washed it all down with
another gulp of soda. "You know, making
the call isn't the hassle. It's coming up
against that goddamned silence. I say

something wrong. She sighs. Then there's this gap in the conversation while I try to figure out how to undo whatever it was I did; and she just watches me squirm, doesn't say a goddamned word. Just like she's enjoying every second of it.''

Agnes smiled. "She knows how to handle you, doesn't she?''

"She knows how to make me feel guilty.''

"Same thing.''

"Yeah, I suppose.''

The salesman raised his glass and asked for a refill. Agnes obliged him with a double this time. On her way back down the bar, she stopped at the cash register, rang up NO SALE, and pilfered a dime out of the tray. She slapped the dime, heads-up, IN GOD WE TRUST, on the counter top in front of Wade. In 1967 it had been mint-fresh. The shine had gone out of it since then, and the ridges had worn away.

"What's that for?''

"Your phone call.''

"Don't give up, do you?''

"Not often.'' She pushed the coin at him. "The phone's right there, same place as always. Just waiting for your company.''

He took up the dime, gave it a spin between finger and thumb, and watched it dance across the black counter top until Agnes reclaimed it. She pressed it into his right palm then, and folded his fingers over its cool metal. "You better do it before you forget the number.''

"I've got the number memorized," Wade said. And still clutching coin in hand, he stood and backed slowly away from the bar. "I'm holding you responsible if this thing blows up in my face."

"And giving me credit if it doesn't?"

The carport door slammed and the shudder of Trenton's escape went through the house. Faye leaned back against the wall, hands tucked behind her, clasped, holding a bit of her together. There was a fear grumbling inside, something stirred and restless by the face of her eleven-year-old nephew, all madness and murder and secrecy behind those innocent eyes. She looked at the strands of masking tape in her hands, the tangled heap of wrappings at her feet, and couldn't understand where things had gone wrong.

"What now?" her nephew asked.

"You pushed him down the stairs, didn't you?"

"He fell." The boy was shaking his head. "He reached to turn the light on and something happened in the darkness. All of a sudden he wasn't there anymore, and Matt could hear him smacking his head and his elbows and his knees against the wood stairs, rolling over and over all the way down. It was an accident, that's all. Just an accident."

"Matt?" She let the wrappings slip from her fingers, and thought to push away from the wall, lean closer to her nephew, and pounce upon his subtle slip of tongue. *Someone else was there? Oh God, yes! It must have been the doings of someone else.* "You said Matt could hear him falling."

"No, I didn't mean that. It was me. I was the one who heard Henry Aikens banging his head all the way down the stairs."

"But you said *Matt.*"

"No."

"Who's Matt?"

He was shaking his head, eyes wider than she had ever seen them before, lips parted enough to sip from the stale air and nothing more. Then he suddenly said, *"You don't want to know, Mrs. Richardson."* His body slowly slid down the brace of the doorjamb until he was sitting on the floor. A single tear ran over his cheek. *"It was an accident, that's all. Just an accident."*

"Matt was there, wasn't he?"

"Yes."

"And so were you, weren't you?"

"We were all there."

"Everyone?"

There's a crowd inside him.

He nodded, and wiped away the tear stain. *"Except Justin. He stayed away because he didn't want to know. He's afraid of knowing."*

"But you aren't?" she asked. There was a tremor in her voice, so slight she thought perhaps it wasn't noticeable, perhaps it didn't give away the uneasiness which had constricted her stomach. This was madness. She was speaking to madness.

"I can't be afraid of knowing," he said. *"I have to know. I have to keep an eye on all of them. They don't know what they're doing most of the time. Someone has to watch over them."*

"And that's you?"

He nodded again, almost absently. In his hands there was a gleaming, the play of light off metal as he spun something in his fingers. It was the knife, Henry Aikens' knife, the same knife that had sparked the conversation, that had sparked the madness. And while something instinctual within her wanted to photograph the irony of the light-reflecting metal held too-big in the little boy's hands, the sight made the madness all too real.

"What's your name?" she asked.

"Albert."

"Albert." Her breaths were an exaggeration, difficult, weighted, something she had apparently lost control over. She spoke too softly, and slower than she wanted. Sounding patronizing when she wished she could sound understanding. "And there's Matt. And who else is there? Who else was standing at the top of Henry Aikens' stairway."

"I told you, we all were."

"You and Matt and who else?"

"Scott and Nicholas." He kept turning

the knife in his hands, concentrating on something there that wouldn't let go of him. *"But Nicholas, he didn't hear the fall. He didn't hear the flesh and bone hit against wood. Not like the rest of us."*

"Why's that, Albert?"

"Because he's deaf."

The room felt incredibly cramped. Crowded? Too many people, all stuffed and packed into too small a space? And she wondered if that was the way it felt inside her nephew, too full, too busy with the workings of more minds than a single body could cope with. And didn't it hurt? Didn't the crowd press against the inside of his brain, bursting to get out?

"There were so many things he didn't want to hear," Albert said. *"He just quit listening one day. Just put his hands over his ears and blocked everything out. All the bad stuff. Everything."*

"Sometimes I wish I could do that," she whispered.

"Then you couldn't listen to the rain splash against the roof."

"I know."

"Why would you want that?"

"Just sometimes," she said. "When everything seems too noisy."

"He has other talents."

"Nicholas?"

"Yes." His feet were flat against the floor, knees bent, elbows resting there.

And suddenly he bent forward, put his head
between his knees, staring at the floor,
balancing the knife between fingers like the
weight of a pendulum, letting it swing back
and forth, slowly, deliberately. *"He's the
one who etched the mural of Cardew James
Mantooth into your wall. He likes to draw.
He likes to play around with odd shapes,
uncommon things."*

"He's talented."

Albert nodded without looking up from
his hiding, then said, *"You never answered
my question."*

"I've forgotten."

"What happens now?"

Faye closed her eyes for a moment,
knowing the all-too-real answer to his
question, yet resisting the impulse to blurt
it out. Albert or Matt or Nicholas, it didn't
matter; he was still her nephew. And even
with the contradiction of his little-boy
hands dangling the weight of a big knife in
its fingers, even with the contradiction of
his little-boy voice and the still fresh bodies
of Joseph Little and Henry Aikens, she
couldn't bring herself to see beyond the
youth trapped in a world too old for his own
comprehension. And what could she tell
him? What could possibly be said that
would bring sense to such a senseless situation?

He looked up from his lap. *"It could be
our secret,"* he said. *"You don't have to tell*

anyone, do you?"

She was staring into his dark eyes, those same eyes that had always before seemed to reflect something uncorrupted. But now there was a sadness there, as if they held all the sorrows of the world. And she found herself absently shaking her head in answer to his question.

"You know what they'll do, don't you? The doctors?"

"They'll help you, Albert."

"No they won't. Just like you, they won't understand. They'll poke around inside his head, looking for all of us and trying to figure out just how many of us there are, and why in the hell we all happen to be living inside him. And when they think they've got it all figured out, they'll kill us. One by one, they'll kill us off until he's the only one left." Albert lolled his head back, rested it against the doorjamb, and sighed. *"That's what they'll do, Mrs. Richardson. That's how they'll help, by killing us."*

"No," she said in a whisper. "It doesn't have to be like that."

"Yes, it does."

She thought she might cry, promised herself she wouldn't, and turned away from the boy to look out the window. Outside, it was just another late spring day. The sun was out. The morning dew that hadn't evaporated, had been soaked up by the ground. There were the sounds of bluejays squawking from somewhere unseen, and the sense that everything was business as usual. Everything that is, beyond the four walls of the bedroom.

"I don't know what to say."

"Because you know I'm right."

She was shaking her head again. "No one wants to hurt you, Albert."

"They'll send us away. You know that, don't you?"

"Only until you're better."

"Until he's better, you mean." Albert brought the knife up from where it had been hiding behind his legs. He ran a finger over the sharpness there, as if he were checking to see if it was as sharp as it appeared. But he seemed absent in the motion, even as he did it. *"They aren't going to make me better, they're going to make him better."*

"But . . ." She thought to point out that he was a part of Justin, a part of her nephew, and by helping one, the doctors would be helping the others as well. But the thought caught in her throat as she recognized the meaninglessness of the words. He was right, Albert was. The doctors would poke around inside Justin and when they found all the others, they would try to kill them.

He was right.

Then from faraway, the phone rang.

She tensed.

Albert peered down the hall, as if he were watching the phone on the kitchen wall, watching it with the hope that the ringing was a mistake.

"The phone," she said.

"*You don't have to answer it,*" he stated, as if it were a question.

"It could be important."

"*You won't tell?*"

She swallowed and shook her head.

The phone rang a third time.

"I better get it." She pushed away from the security of the wall, for the first time daring to move out of that somehow comforting position. And as she tried to appear relaxed, taking an easy, self-confident step at a time, she kept an eye on the boy, watching him for the slightest sign of hesitation, the slightest sign of unwillingness. But he seemed not to mind at all.

The phone rang again.

Albert's knees dropped, no longer blocking the doorway where he sat, letting her step over him and start down the hall. "*Promise you won't tell?*" he asked after her.

"I won't."

It was the sixth ring when she grabbed up the receiver, praying that whoever was at the other end hadn't given up. "Who is it?" she said.

There was a pause, then, "That's a fine way to greet your husband."

"Wade." She had her back to the wall, was looking down the hallway, watching her nephew wipe the knife across his jeans as if he were cleaning something from the metal. He seemed uninterested in the call, seemed satisfied that she would say nothing. "Listen to me, Wade."

"You sound terrible. Is everything all right?"

She turned away from the hall, hoping to hide her mouth, muffle her words, as she spoke. "You've got to listen to me, Wade. No questions."

"What is it?"

"It's Justin. He—he needs help, Wade." She rubbed the goose bumps which had grown on her arm, hoping to make them go away again, hoping the chill that was with them would also disappear. "I'm scared."

"Just calm down and take it easy."

"I need you over here, Wade."

"Is Justin all right? Is he hurt?"

"You aren't listening to me. He's a little bit crazy. I mean—"

It was an eleven-year-old hand that reached around her, snatching the cord and pulling until the connector popped free and the line went dead. She sucked up a lungful of air, held it. In her hand, the receiver dangled, her last touch with sanity suddenly severed, leaving her alone again. Too alone.

And Justin—Albert—Matt—whoever, was standing there behind her.

"*You promised,*" he said in a voice that

didn't belong to Albert, didn't belong to Justin. *"You promised and then you did the exact fucking thing Albert asked you not to do."*

The receiver slipped from her grasp and fell to the floor with the clatter of plastic against linoleum, bounced once then twice, until the sound was too faraway for her to pay notice. It was his face that she suddenly could no longer ignore. The darker-than-dark eyes. The high eyebrows. Her nephew's face all changed and belonging to someone else.

And she held back a scream by stuffing a trembling hand into her mouth.

Wade called out her name once, then again, tapping a finger to the cradle of the phone, trying to bring the disconnection back to life again. When he finally realized it was useless, he hung up the receiver and leaned against the wall.

"What happened?" Agnes asked.

"I'm not sure."

"She hang up on you?"

"No." He shook his head, wondering if that's what had happened, knowing that it hadn't been like that at all. "No, we were disconnected."

"Then call her up again."

He was thinking, trying to recount everything she had said in their short conversation, trying to make sense out of the confusion. *It's Justin. He needs help*. She sounded so damned frightened. *He's a little bit crazy*. She had said that, hadn't she? He's a little bit crazy?

"Wade?"

A little bit crazy.

"No, I think I better go over there."

He started up the stairs to get his jacket, changed his mind half-way, and was on his way out the door again when Agnes called after him. "Anything wrong?"

"I hope not," he said without turning back. "God, I hope not."

The boy was holding the knife—as if it weren't as big as it appeared—in his hand, twisting it in such a way that the light coming in through the sliding glass doors reflected off the polished metal. Glimmering. Shimmering. The sparkle of a diamond, the coldness of steel.

"*Albert's a fool,*" the boy said. "*He'll believe anyone.*"

"I just wanted to help."

"*You promised.*"

"I know," she said.

"*You lied.*" His eyes were darker than their brown, almost an obsidian black, glassy and alive, hollow and faraway, all at the same time. His face was shadowed in a grim expression, a sadness that had etched as deep into his flesh as the sadness that had lined the face of Joseph Little. Too many years of living and dying had left their mark there.

"Where's Albert?" she whispered.

"He had to go away. But I'm here."

"It's Matt, isn't it? The one who watched Henry Aikens tumble down the stairs?"

He smiled or grinned or somehow twisted his face in such a way that she sensed his satisfaction at being recognized without an introduction. There was something egocentric there, something pleased at finally being called by his real name. Not Justin or Albert, but Matt. And it was not Albert or her nephew who held the knife chest-high as a warning. It was this one who called himself Matt, taking pleasure from the fear that Faye knew she was exhibiting.

"You know now," Matt said then. He was still an arm's length away, breathing heavy breaths, anxious breaths. It was a moment of realization for him, a moment of uncertainty. *"You know every fucking thing there is to know. All of it."*

"Maybe it's better that way."

"No, it's worse. It can't be better." The knife was twisting in his hands, as if his muscles were caught in a spasm, first tight, then loose.

"I can get help for you, Matt."

"Shut up!" He pushed her and she hit her arm and shoulder against the wall. *"Albert already warned me about that. I know what would happen. I know they'd try to make*

me go away, try to squeeze me into the brain of the pretender. " He was shaking his head, as if in a daze. "*No, I can't let them do that.*"

Faye was pressed against the wall, her fear holding her there, keeping her a safe distance from the knife that was fitting too comfortably into the hand of her nephew. The house was unearthly quiet, as if it had stopped breathing, stopped to listen and watch and see what would happen next. And the noise of her nephew's anxious breaths seemed louder than life, louder than the noise of her own frantic breaths even as she tried to bring them under control.

"Albert?"

"*I'm Matt!*"

"Can't I speak with Albert? Please?"

"*I told you, he's gone.*"

"Okay," she said with a shaky voice. "Okay, I understand. Albert's gone away. It's just you and me now." With her back still against the wall, she slowly began to inch her way around the phone, toward the dining room where there was sunlight and warmth and room to stretch muscles that had grown tight. "We can work something out, Matt. I know we can."

"*No we can't,*" he said in a daze. "*There's nothing that will make it all better again.*" He glanced outside, through the sliding glass doors which lined the wall at the far side of the dining room, as if he wished to be gone from where he was standing, off running through the tall grass fields and shallow ponds that had been the playgrounds for Albert or Nicholas or Scott, but had always somehow escaped him.

She slipped away from him then, slid back against the wall away from him until she was standing in the dining room with a chair held between her and the knife and the boy, who suddenly came alive again.

"It'll never be the same again," he said, as if he were sharing only a small portion of the conversation that must have been rolling through his mind, here a word, there a sentence, sometimes making sense, more often not. *"Now that you know, it can't ever be the same."*

"I know," she whispered, almost without thinking. She had put more distance between her and the knife, and stood at the far side of the dining room table as she spoke. "Some things can never be the same again."

"You know?" He watched her as he moved to stand at the other side of the table, his eyes staring cold and empty as if they saw not her but someone else, someone hated. *"I had to, you know. The Pa would have killed him sooner or later. He would have taken a strap to him one time too many, all hot breath and fiery eyes, and he would have killed the pretender. I couldn't let that happen, could I? I would have died with him."*

For a moment, she caught herself and tried to understand what the boy was saying. What was he trying to tell her? "I don't understand."

"*The fire*," he said. "*I had to burn the barn down.*"

And all of a sudden she understood too well. "You killed them?"

"*Don't you see? I had to.*"

"My sister? You killed my sister?"

He took a step sideways, then another, one hand gliding along the waxy wood surface of the table, the other still holding the knife. Slowly inching around the corner, always a step closer. "*The mother, well, she was just there. In the way. There wasn't anything I could do about her. She was never further than an arm's length from the old man, always close at his side where he could keep an eye on her, sometimes a hand on her. She was just there.*"

Faye mirrored his movements, taking a cautious step at a time until they were standing catty-corner from one another. Both hands were touching the table top, guiding her steps as she kept an intent eye on the boy, somehow fearing that a break in eye contact would unleash whatever restraint was still holding him back. And somewhere in the back of her mind, she realized that the china cabinet was coming up on her left. And she remembered the gun, the .22 she had begged Wade to sell when they had first been married. It was

still there, still at the bottom shelf of the
cabinet where she had left it only a few
nights before, still waiting.

"She was just there. In the way."

"The same as me, Matt?" She took
another sliding step toward the cabinet,
wanting desperately to glance in that direction, yet somehow holding herself back.
"I'm in the way now, aren't I?"

"Yes."

"You're going to have to do something
about that, aren't you?" Keep him talking.
Keep him moving clockwise. Keep his mind
busy with thoughts that blind him to your
own.

"Another accident," he said. His face lit
up with the thought. And he followed her
movement another step around the table.
"Another fire. There could be another fire."

"I don't have to say anything, Matt. It
could still be our secret, between you and
me. No one else would have to know." And
she was there, standing only the length of
her body away from where the gun waited.
She couldn't resist any longer, and let her
eyes tear away from his, glance at the china
cabinet, then back again. His gaze followed
hers, and when he looked away from the
cabinet, back to her face again, there was a
moment of puzzlement that furrowed his
brow.

And she thought he had to know what
she was going to do.

And she thought if she waited another second it would be too late.

And suddenly she was there, sprawled over the thick, golden carpet, toe to outstretched arms, hands fumbling with the cabinet door.

And it wouldn't open!

She could hear herself somewhere in the distance, whimpering like a wounded puppy, breathing out all the fear that she had kept too long inside. Her finger first picked at the corner of the door, trying to pry it open with nails that had never been long enough. Then she caught hold of the handle and gave it a tug and it fell open effortlessly, and there was the gun, staring back at her, a finger's length away. She crawled to her knees, felt the cold metal touch her, felt her finger wrap so very comfortably around the trigger, and she knew she was going to make it.

She knew she was going to make it!

Then suddenly the door slammed against her arm, a shot of pain made her scream, and the cold smooth metal of the gun fell from her grasp. The boy was standing over her, gazing down with angry eyes, the knife poised near her face as if it were meant to remind her of its presence.

"I'll break your arm in half if you make me." His knee was pressing against the door, keeping pressure there, pinching imitation walnut against the flesh of upper

arm. He added a little body weight. She moaned. *"Hurt?"*

"Yes."

"I could let go."

The pressure eased. She took in a huge breath, flexed the fingers that had for a moment lost their circulation, and tried not to think of the pain that was throbbing from elbow to shoulder. Then the pressure came again.

"Please," she cried.

"But you still have the gun."

She shook her head, feeling the warm trickle of a tear suddenly slide down the crease between her nose and cheek, and fall into her open mouth, salty and bitter. She had lost all sense of where the gun lay, surely somewhere within reach, but her hand no longer held the strength to grab it up. She shook her head again. "I dropped it."

"Did you?" He wouldn't release the pressure of his leg against the door, didn't seem the slightest bit interested in doing so. But he pulled the knife away from where it had threatened her face. He stood tall again, looking down on her, almost father to daughter in stance and stature. *"You wouldn't lie to me, would you?"*

"Please?"

He let up on the pressure, just a little, enough to see what she would do, but not so much that he couldn't quickly take back any advantage he might have given away. *"Better?"*

She nodded.

"Take it out, then."

She glanced up from the floor to read his face, to make sure she had heard him correctly, to make sure he wasn't going to change his mind with her arm half-in, half-out of the mouth of the cabinet, and suddenly crush it with all his weight.

"Go on," he said. *"Slowly."*

With the return of circulation to her arm, the throbbing came sharply home, swollen and pulsing, as she began to withdraw that part of herself that was still held in the grasp of the cabinet jaws. And he kept the pressure firm, closing off the slack as she worked her way toward the forearm.

"Slowly."

"I know," she answered, with more irritation than she had intended. It was such an absurd position she had caught herself in, floor-bound with one arm free, one arm trapped. Absurd. And painful. And frightening. Everything had been taken from her, dignity, control, adulthood. Everything. And this boy—nephew—madman was threatening to take the one last thing still held in balance—her life.

When her wrist had reached the crack between door and cabinet, he applied the pressure again, pinching off her movement. *"Hold it,"* he said, and he leaned forward to

peer into the light of the crack, making sure
the gun wasn't still holding on by a finger.
"No gun. You were telling the truth."

The pressure fell away.

The cabinet door opened wide.

And Faye suddenly had her arm back
again.

"Move away," he said then. And rubbing
her upper arm, trying to soothe the pain
and bring back some of the life that had
been choked off, she knelt and crawled
away. *"Right there's fine."* She sat back,
resting against the table supports, and
watched as the boy reached into the cabinet
and brought out the .22 pistol.

"This is crazy, Matt. Things are getting
way out of hand."

He tossed the knife away.

She watched it skid across the kitchen
linoleum, hit against a distant cabinet on
the other side of the refrigerator, and come
to a rest there. Out of reach. Faraway. And
now he had a gun instead of a knife as he
stood over her, grinning not her nephew's
grin but someone else's. She thought just
then, that if she survived, if she lived
through whatever it was that fate had in
mind next, that she would never—ever forget the hideous darkness that had come
alive on the boy's face at that instant. As
if he had suddenly realized the extent of the
power he held in his hand. Something long
awaited, just arrived.

"What are you going to do?" she asked.

He shrugged. *"Kid around a little."* He pointed the gun at the far wall, then slowly swung it around until it was aimed at her face. Eye-to-eye, he sighted down the barrel, grinning wider than his cheeks could hold, and he pulled the hammer back until it clicked with the crispness of a snapped twig on a dry summer day. Then he whispered, *Bang,* bringing the word up from somewhere at the back of his throat, coarse and lingering.

She shivered, looked away.

"Scary?"

It's a game, she thought. A war of nerves. And she looked back at the boy, back at the eye that was peering down the sights of the gun. Her fears were still there, still pressing against her abdomen, cramping her stomach muscles, sending chills up and down her body. But she forced them back, forced her lips tight, forced her hands still, and faced him as if they were each on equal ground.

For a moment, he seemed surprised. He lowered the gun an inch or two, looked above the line of the sight, and smiled something wicked in his admiration for her courage. But the moment was short before he impulsively pointed the .22 at a spot just to her right and fired. A small slug exploded into the carpet there, digging through the golden brown fibers, the backing, the pad, and tunneling into the sub-floor.

She screamed, first holding her hands over her ears, eyes shut tight, mouth wide. Then without thinking, she rolled away from where the bullet had burrowed itself into the floor, rolled toward her left, behind a dining room chair. And she was suddenly on her feet, no longer screaming, but still feeling the effects of the explosion shuddering through her. Both hands clamped to the back of the chair, planted there as much for the little bit of protection as for the stability.

He laughed, aimed the gun again, fired another shot. A splinter erupted from the table top at her right.

"No!"

She heard herself scream, but the sound came from faraway. She was going to die. The next shot, the shot after, he would take aim not at the floor or the table, but at her. And his eleven-year-old finger would squeeze the trigger. And there would be a deafening explosion. And she would feel something sharp and murderous invade her body. And she would die.

He added his left hand to the grip of the gun then, steadying his arm. And he raised his aim from where it had centered on the table top, until she was staring down the barrel again. For the final time, she thought. For the very last time of her life.

And she watched his finger nervously tighten against the trigger.

And she knew she was going to die.

And she turned away from the boy—madman. Thinking nothing but escape, she turned away and bolted for the sunlight.

Another shot fired, spider-webbing the sliding glass door at a place above her head. In that instant, out of the corner of her eye, she saw the shattering of the glass; and she realized too late that between her and escape there remained the matter of the sliding door. And she was stepping into a shower of splintering glass. Slashed, slit, sectioned by a thousand brittle, transparent shards. And there was the dark color of red splashing from nowhere seen, painting chips of glass, splattering bright out-of-place circles over the cement patio at foot. And as she was falling in a timeless warp of motion, seeing the vivid color raining from somewhere nearby, feeling something painful that was already growing distant, she thought of the bright red pools at the bottom step of Henry Aikens' cellar. And she wondered if it was her own blood that was so thoroughly painting her world red.

There was a scream, louder than any cry he'd ever heard before in his young life. And when he opened his eyes, Justin found himself standing in his aunt's dining room,

a gun held loosely in his right hand. There
was a sharp powdery scent still in the air,
and a cool breeze catching the delicate
curtains next to the sliding glass door and
waving them flag-like at the dining room.

He first thought how odd it was that
someone would leave the door open.

Then he noticed the glass, a hundred-
thousand, see-through fragments, scattered everywhere. Pieces of what had once
been the sliding door. That's why the
breeze was blowing outside-in. Not because
someone had left the door open, but
because the glass had fallen out.

scattered everywhere

Around the ragged edges of the hole,
where the window putty was still holding
on to a few resisting shards of glass, there
was a splash of color that caught his eye.
And suddenly he could see where someone
had splashed and splattered red paint over
some of the glass and the door frame and. . .

. . . and his curious eyes followed the redness

. . . he saw something else, something a
million times worse than the breakage.

Aunt Faye was lying there, on the
ground, half-in/half-out of the doorway. She
was lying as still as a held breath, not
moving an involuntary muscle. And there
was red weeping from places on her arms
and hands, forehead and face.

scattered everywhere

More than any other time in his life
(except one)

Justin wanted to scream his insides out just then. But he found himself benumbed, unable to make a sound rise from his vocal cords, unable to make his legs kick into action and spirit him away from there. He was set in place there, as set

as that other time?

as if his arms and wrists, neck and waist, were strapped inflexible

as they once were?

to . . .

to what? What had kept them immovable?

squealing . . .

They had been tied! His arms and wrists, neck and waist, had all been tied to the cross his father had erected in the barn. And his head was almost touching the roof, and his feet were dangling higher-than-high off the ground. And . . .

chattering . . .

and then his father was slipping a black hood over his head. And there was a breath of alcohol, a spattering of the bible, and . . .

multiples . . .

and everything light became dark, and everything warm became cold, and everything once familiar became strange.

"Sightless, and you'll see no evil, boy. Deaf, and the devil's whispered words will go unheard. An hour, a day, a week, a

*month. However long it takes, boy. You're
staying strapped to this cross til the
laughter of the devil's gone out of you. You
hear me, boy? However long it takes."*

The barn door closed, and the air turned
midnight cold, and it seemed like forever
that he was alone there, hanging above the
ground the way his father told him Jesus
had done. And . . .

squealing . . .
and he was being cleansed. That's what
his father told him. He was being cleansed.
And . . .

chattering . . .
and that must have been why it hurt
sometimes. Because the devil's madness
was being all squeezed out of him. That's
why it hurt. He was being cleansed. That's
why it hurt. It was . . .

multiples . . .
his soul being made ready for heaven
instead of hell.

That's why it hurt.

No!

Wasn't it?

No!

It wasn't that at all.

It was . . .

squealing and chattering and multiples. . .
the rats!

They came scurrying along the rafters,
chattering back and forth in armies, close
enough to hear, far enough to go unseen

Until he could feel them touch a damp nose against his arm. Until he could smell their rodent breaths. Until he could hear them next to his ears . . .

multiples . . .

and their foot pads and claws were running up and down his arms, and they were slipping beneath the hood and coming face-to-face with him, warm fur and whiskers, and

chattering . . .

and then the nibble of a finger . . .

and he screamed!

and a nibble of the arm . . .

and he screamed louder!

And that's the way Aunt Faye was looking, here a nibble, there a nibble, a thousand tiny nibbles on her arm and face and legs. The rats! Just as if the rats had come back again . . .

. . . and again

. . . and again

Justin closed his eyes, and a tear slid over his cheeks.

I hate you, Pa!

I hate you, I hate you, I hate you, hate you, hate you!

8

He had run and walked and jogged through
the pastures and empty fields between
Henry Aikens' and home. And now that
Kiel had reached the driveway, he was
forced to stop and catch his breath. Hands
on bent knees, he filled and emptied his
lungs with several great heaves before
taking a step down the drive, then another
and another. Nearby he could see a scar
where someone had dragged a bald tire over
the damp carport gravel. He couldn't remember it being there earlier in the day,
thought it odd, and wondered if Trenton
Maes had been by. Then he heard the first
shot, a single pop, muffled by the walls of
the house but still sounding too much like
an explosion from a gun.

It was a race made of nightmare, a
solitary step at a time, agonizingly slow, as
if his pockets were full of wet sand, heavy

and dragging. *Too slow,* he kept thinking. *Something's happening inside the house, something too terrible to imagine, and Lord Jesus, my legs are all Silly Putty and rubber. Too damn slow.*

As his fingers wrapped snugly around the kitchen doorknob, a twist away from where it was all happening, another shot exploded. He winced, almost fell away, then pulled the door wide as the third shot was fired. And he saw it all. He saw his brother —or was it one of the others? Albert or Matt or Scott or Nicholas?—take aim with both arms stiff, elbows locked, and suddenly pull the trigger. He saw the shattering of glass, his aunt's mouth open wide to scream with nothing sounding out, and then an explosion of red. So much red. And for what seemed like forever, he could hear the haunting chime of glass, hailing sky-to-earth all around his aunt's body.

Too late.

Too damn late.

His brother's arms fell to his side.

The last tinkling of glass came to rest.

And Kiel quietly closed the kitchen door behind him.

There was an easy breeze which carried through the hole in the sliding glass door and mussed his brother's straight, blond hair. But Justin was frozen still, eyes fixed to where his aunt's body had merged with a thunderstorm of knifelike glass shards.

The gun was hanging by a finger as Kiel softly took it from him.

"I killed her," Justin whispered without looking up.

"It wasn't you."

"Yes, it was."

Kiel settled an arm over his brother's shoulder and gently pulled him away. "You shouldn't be staring. It'll just make everything worse." At the far end of the table, he pulled a chair out and sat Justin there, sat him so he was looking away from the red ugliness, down the hallway that led to their bedrooms.

"They'll send me away now, won't they? Like you said they would."

"Don't think like that." Kiel hopped up on the table, sat directly behind his brother, ran a hand lovingly through his brother's hair.

"But I killed her."

"Not you. One of the others."

Justin shook his head. "It's all the same."

"No," Kiel whispered, afraid to speak louder. "It's not the same." The gun was lying on the table, behind Justin, a finger's length away from where Kiel had set it down. "I tried to tell her," Kiel said then. "I thought she could help."

"Aunt Faye?"

He nodded. "I thought because she was an adult, she might understand."

"She didn't, did she?"

"I don't think I said it right, in a way that made sense to her."

"I don't want to go away."

Kiel sighed, and in the breath he caught the fragrance of the house, that pleasant odor that was more Aunt Faye than Uncle Wade. And suddenly he thought how strange this place was, how faraway it was from *home*, from the farm that had smelled not like Aunt Faye's perfume but something more like him and his brother, something more like a home should smell.

Justin glanced over his shoulder at Kiel. "We could run away?"

"To where?"

"Home again," the boy said. "We could go home again. Just you and me, like it was after the barn burned down. And this time we won't let anyone know that we're there, and we can stay as long as we want. Forever. Just you and me. We could, couldn't we?"

Kiel smiled, ran his hand again through his brother's hair. "Sounds nice."

"Couldn't we?"

"Would you like that?"

"More than anything." Justin settled deeper into the chair, crossed his legs at his ankles, suddenly becoming more comfortable, as if just the thought of being away from there, of being back home again, made him feel better. "And maybe then . . ." Again, he peered over his shoulder.

"What?"

"Well then maybe the others would leave me alone. Maybe they would go away, and then when I open my eyes I'll always know where I am, always know what I've done and what I haven't."

"You think it could be like that?" Kiel was going to cry. The tears were beginning to crowd into his eyes, gathering there, ready to spill out if he even gave a thought to what his brother was saying. And still he couldn't help thinking about home, about that comfortable family smell, about those six months when his brother and he had survived on their own there. Those had been the best six months of his life. And he wanted them back, he wanted to go back there and try to make it happen all over again. But it would never be the same. Justin would never be the same. He would always be Albert and Matt and Scott and Nicholas and whoever else, all pretending to be his brother.

"Don't you want to go home?"

"Just you and me? The way it was?"

Justin turned around. "Can we?"

"If I don't say yes, you're gonna keep hounding me, day-in, day-out, aren't you? You'll always be asking why not and how come, won't you?"

"Till you change your mind."

Kiel grinned, but it was forced and twisted and made more of sadness than anything else. "You do all the packing."

"I will."

"And no changing your mind tomorrow or a week from now."

"I won't."

"And no complaining about chores."

"I promise."

Then he looked away from his brother's hopeful gaze, unable to meet those dark eyes that he had always known and had never been dishonest with. "I never liked it here all that much," he said. "Not like home."

"I'll pack." Justin was all smiles and white teeth and half-way down the hall before Kiel could say another word. "Just the stuff we brought, right? Nothing new, nothing that Aunt Faye bought for us, right?"

"Sure. Just the old stuff." He watched his brother disappear into the darkness that was the hall, heard him throw open their bedroom closet and begin rummaging through the contents. And his finger took up the .22 that was still there on the table with him. The metal was still warm from firing and there was the smell of gun powder still detectable.

Maybe they would go away, and then when I open my eyes I'll always know where I am, always know what I've done and what I haven't.

"It won't ever be like that," Kiel softly whispered. "It'll be a day of Matt, two o Albert. Sometimes Scott, sometimes th quiet one. Always a mystery, because I' just never know for sure. And neithe would you."

His eyes were filling with tears again a

he slid off the table top and went to stand where the corner of the hallway and dining room came together. He leaned against the wall there, wiped a hand across his face, and closed his eyes. In the background, he could still hear his brother making noise, packing this and that for a promised trip that was never going to happen.

And Kiel waited with gun in trembling hand, hidden almost naturally out of sight behind his back.

There was a part of him that wanted his brother to hurry back down the hall, all packed and thinking warm thoughts, so it would finally all be over with. And another part of him prayed that Justin would forever be busy packing, like one of those eternal nightmares, only this time the dream would be a blessing because then Kiel wouldn't have to do what needed to be done.

"How's that for fast?" Justin said, holding a suitcase in each hand. He was suddenly standing right next to Kiel, staring dark-eyed right into his face. "Are you okay?"

"Fine." Kiel stood straight against the wall, practiced a smile, and sighed. In his hand, he felt his fingers, sweaty and trembling, tighten around the gun. He rested his head against the wall.

Justin placed the suitcases on the floor. "So let's go."

"In a minute," Kiel said.

"What is it? What's the matter?"

"I guess I'm just a little scared," he said, feeling the weight of the gun in his hands and wishing it would go away. The way nightmares go away when the sun comes up and the darkness disappears.

but the darkness is here to stay this time, isn't it?

Justin was looking at him, studying his face as if he could read the glint of his eyes, the turn of his mouth. "Scared of what?" he asked, and Kiel thought it sounded like Albert's voice asking the question. Or was it Scott's? Or Matt's?

you'll never know

"Scared of what I have to do," he said, the words choking in his throat. *I love you, Justin.*

"I thought you wanted to go back home?"

I do

Then Kiel pulled the gun from behind his back, pressed it against his brother's head, and fired once, then twice, then heard the hammer click and click again. And when he opened his eyes again, Justin was lying face-down on the floor, motionless.

The gun disappeared from his hand then, fell to the carpet somewhere. And Kiel first knelt, then sat on the floor where he had shot his brother, taking Justin and pulling his lifeless body into his lap. There was a puddle of red that kept growing, kept getting on everything, and he tried to wipe it away, tried to stop it from flowing out of his brother's head and into his lap. But it wouldn't stop.

And Kiel began crying.

When Wade arrived home, he found himself standing hesitant outside the carport door, his heart beating heavy in his chest. Something was terribly wrong on the other side of that door, he could feel it. And it took all his nerve to turn the knob and peer in on the horror.

The tangy smell of gun powder rushed through the crack to meet him.

He stepped up into the kitchen, stopped there, and saw his nephews on the floor near the hallway. Kiel was holding Justin's head in his lap. Both of the boys were splattered with blood.

"My God," he whispered.

When he knelt at Kiel's side, he could see the boy was in shock—glassy-eyed and absently rocking his brother, mumbling words and phrases which were senseless to a deaf ear . . .

. . . *the devil's madness never lets a soul go, does it?*

. . . *that's what happened in the barn, the devil came and made him mad.*

. . . *I think Pa was the devil.*

Wade saw where Justin had been shot in the head, and he saw the lifelessness there.

"Where's your aunt, Kiel?" he asked, not expecting an answer. He touched a hand to the boy's forehead, wiped the damp hair that was pressed against skin. "Is she here? Is she in the house and all right?"

There was no answer, no understanding of the question.

He stood then, and noticed for the first time, where the breeze was easily making itself at home, where the sliding glass door had lost most of its glass. And the sight drew him around the dining room table, not in haste but slow-footed, as he both sensed and feared what might be found there.

She was lying in a glittering collage of shattered glass, a thousand different shapes and sizes, some still pure, some soiled with a sticky red, some imbedded in cold flesh.

He stepped lightly over the broken glass, as if he feared causing more damage, until he stood next to his wife's face-down body, and he knelt there. "I would have come back," he said, touching a hand to her hair, brushing it away from her shoulders. Then he sat in the glass, next to her. "I never stopped loving you."

It was a long time before he was able to move from there.

AFTER

Kiel was alone in his room. Outside the door, there was a deputy—tall and thin, with a pockmarked face—who was there to make sure he didn't wander off. Down the hall, there was a houseful of people coming and going, shouting questions one way, obscenities the other, snatching up evidence—broken pieces of glass, the knife, the gun, the slugs—and leaving behind cigarette butts and gum wrappers. Sheriff John Hague was out back giving orders and snapping his Double Mint. The coroner from Eureka was with him, had followed him right on over after finishing up with Henry Aikens. Wade was sitting in the dining room, answering questions with uncharacteristic whispers, eyes all watery and shining back the sunlight.

But none of that mattered.

Nothing mattered anymore.

His back was against the wall, his legs
were crossed, his feet—still wearing the
Nikes his aunt had bought just a few days
before—were tucked under him. And
staring back at him, from the opposite wall,
was the faint, ghost-like self-portrait of his
brother sitting atop the gravestone of one
CARDEW JAMES MANTOOTH. It was
little more than a colorless etching now, not
a painting but a sculpture. And it was odd,
when he looked closely at the eyes that
were molded from the sheetrock—the same
eyes that had once sent chills through him
—that it wasn't his brother staring back; it
was himself. A mirror put to a mirror.

He unfolded his legs, let his weight roll
off the bed that had been Justin's, and felt
drawn across the room. When he first
touched fingers to the etching, it felt cold.
But as his fingers traced the fine lines and
crosshatches brailled there, as they walked
over the part that was his brother's face,
the surface grew warm, then warmer. And
he felt something numb and tingling creep
up his arm, fingertip to knuckles, knuckles
to wrist, as if those parts of him were being
put to sleep. The sensation frightened him,
intrigued him.

He pulled his hand away, looked closer.

And there was something coming alive
there.

The life color was coming back to his
brother's eyes, staining the pale sheetrock
dark and alive and full of that glimmer that

was Justin. And the face turned fleshy, the hair stringy. And the wicked smile that was the etching, grew wider, pushing deeper into cheeks that were suddenly three-dimensional, grinning with teeth white and shiny and not at all formed of sheetrock. And the face that was his brother's turned toward him, swelled, then surged, thin-skinned and elastic-like.

"Justin?" Kiel absently retreated a step, then another.

Who else?

"That's you?"

In the flesh.

"But . . ."

You can't get rid of me that easily. We're brothers, aren't we? Practically twins, aren't we? Whisper a word in my ear and you'll hear it, won't you? Nick my palm with a pocket knife and you'll feel it, won't you? We're brothers, Kiel. There's no changing that. Not ever.

He backed away until his legs bumped against the corner of a bed, and he sat there, automatically, thinking not of where he was but of this fantasy-come-to-life that was happening right there in front of him, right there on the bedroom wall. "What I did," he said. "I had to. You know that, don't you?"

You did right, Kiel.

"Did I?"

Things were crazier than crazy, all Matt and Albert and Scott and Nicholas, and

*hardly an hour or a day left over for me. It
was getting too crowded in here, Kiel. Too
many minds and only one brain. You did
right.*

"I'm glad."

*Me too. They're gone now, all of them.
It's just me now, you and me. Like we
talked about before.*

"The two of us?"

We're brothers, aren't we?

"Yeah."

There was a knock at the door then, a
short double-knock before the door opened
and a woman peered in. She smiled, slipped
through the crack, and closed the door
behind her. Her hair was long, strands
spilling over her shoulders, thin and
straight and reddish-brown. She had a pale
face with a spattering of freckles and blue
eyes that were cold in contrast.

"Hi, my name is Kara." She extended a
hand which he ignored, then she sat on the
bed next to him. "I'm from the Eureka
Police Department, Juvenile Division. I'm
here to help you, Kiel. I just want to ask
you a few questions so I can understand
exactly what happened today. And then
we'll see if we can get you out of this room
and away from here."

Don't believe a word she says, brother.

Kiel looked to the mural on the wall
where his brother was still sitting, lifelike
and real and talking to him as if no one else

were in the room. And he wanted to shush his brother, tell him to shut up or else the woman might hear him and then everything would be spoiled.

She's blind, Kiel. Deaf and blind. She can't hear me or see me, doesn't even know I still exist. I'm just a body to her, something dead and stuffed into a black plastic bag.

Kiel moved away from her then, to Justin's bed where he pushed himself into a corner and felt a little safer. He wasn't going to answer any questions. There wasn't anything needing explanation. What happened, happened. It was then, and this was now. And he just wanted to be left alone, just him and his brother. The way things used to be.

"I'd like to understand what happened here today," she said.

Remember that day when you came back from the pastures, brother? And there was a roomful of people, all asking questions about why you and me were living alone, about why we had buried Ma and Pa without telling anyone? They made us come here after that, took us away from where we belonged. She's going to do the same thing, Kiel. She'll take us away and put us somewhere we don't belong.

Kiel shook his head. "I don't want that."

"What?" she asked.

"I want to go home again."

She moved around the bed, sat across from him, looking as if she wanted to sweep up his hand and hold it in her own. "You can't go home again, Kiel. I'm sorry, but it just isn't possible."

Lies, brother.

"Now, how about telling me about today?"

Remember that summer day we went to play in Tyler's Thistle? Remember the two bullfrogs we found and the frog jumping contest? You let me win that day, gave me the biggest frog, taught me how to scare 'em into jumping a frog-leg mile. I won't ever forget that, Kiel.

"Me either."

"Kiel?" She finally took his hand in her own, and peered into his eyes as if she were looking for someone else in there. Then she pressed the back of a hand against his forehead. "Are you feeling all right?"

We could still go back there, Kiel. Back to those summer days, without Ma and Pa there to keep an arm on us. It would all be ours. Just you and me. Better than ever.

"Just you and me."

He felt the woman shiver, felt the shiver run up through her hands and into his own. Then she pulled away from him, stood over him, and there was puzzlement on her face, puzzlement and something else. He thought it might be fright, and he wondered why she would be afraid of him.

"I'll be right back, Kiel," she said then. "Right back."

And she hurried out of the room.

And the mural—etching—lifelike Justin smiled cheek-to-cheek dimples.

Just you and me, brother.

"Just you and me."

Make the Most of Your Leisure Time
with
LEISURE BOOKS

Please send me the following titles:

Quantity	Book Number	Price
_____	_____	_____
_____	_____	_____
_____	_____	_____
_____	_____	_____
_____	_____	_____

If out of stock on any of the above titles, please send me the alternate title(s) listed below:

_____	_____	_____
_____	_____	_____
_____	_____	_____
_____	_____	_____

Postage & Handling _____

Total Enclosed ___$_____

☐ Please send me a free catalog.

NAME _____
(please print)

ADDRESS _____

CITY _____ STATE _____ ZIP_____

Please include $1.00 shipping and handling for the first book ordered and 25¢ for each book thereafter in the same order. All orders are shipped within approximately 4 weeks via postal service book rate. PAYMENT MUST ACCOMPANY ALL ORDERS.*

*Canadian orders must be paid in US dollars payable through a New York banking facility.

Mail coupon to: **Dorchester Publishing Co., Inc.**
6 East 39 Street, Suite 900
New York, NY 10016
Att: ORDER DEPT.